DARK DADDIES OF NEW YORK

submitting to DADDY

J.L. QUICK

This novel is recommended for adult (18+) readers.

As a contemporary, dark romance work of fiction, this novel is not intended to be a portrayal of a healthy relationship or a 'how to guide' for the kink and lifestyle elements depicted within. For those interested in exploring aspects of kink and/or dominant-submissive relationships explored in the following chapters, please do so responsibly and with appropriate reference materials.

This novel may contain scenes and descriptive adult content that might be triggering for some readers. To see what you can expect, please use the QR code below.

TWELVE WEEKS AND ONE DAY AGO

"Where the fuck have you been?" Enzo shouts, the second I push the front door open. His shoes slap against the hardwood floor as he angrily storms toward me from the kitchen. "The meeting is in twenty fucking minutes. We were supposed to leave five minutes ag—"

Eavan's shrill scream slices through the air, interrupting him. "Put me down, Cian!" She writhes on my shoulder, her fists pounding against my back and her feet flailing, as Enzo steps into the front hall.

She kicks, and her foot slams against my balls so hard that my knees buckle and nearly give out beneath me. Gritting my teeth, I snarl, "For fuck's sake! Would you fucking stop? I'm not going to hurt you." Eavan is fucking relentless, trying desperately to remove herself from my shoulder as I shove past Enzo and carry her into the apartment. She fights me with every step, her fists slamming on my back, and her legs struggling against my firm hold—ensuring she doesn't get the opportunity to kick me in the groin again.

"What the actual fuck?" Nikolai huffs the second I step into the kitchen. "We're bringing women here now? Or *anyone* for that fucking matter?"

I know I shouldn't have. This place is our secret, and we don't share it with anyone. But I had to. Outside of Enzo and Nikolai—my brothers, not from blood—Eavan is the only person I have left in this world who I care about. She's my little sister, and it's my job as her big brother to protect her. And after tonight, when these men become my family, she's going to need all the protection the three of us can give her.

"If she's for later, Cian, I'm gonna pass." Nikolai disapprovingly shakes his head as I walk past him. "I like my women feisty as fuck, but I also like them willing."

Nikolia's words hit a nerve, and I see fucking red—I feel it creeping up my neck and spreading over my face as I spin on my heel to fist the front of his crisp, white shirt. My nostrils flare from angered breaths as my gaze flits between him and Enzo. "Even if she were fucking willing, I'd fucking end you for trying to put your *manky* cocks anywhere near her. Either of you." It's not a threat. It's a promise. Releasing my hold of him, I mutter, "She's my little sister."

"I'm sorry? Your fucking what?" Enzo exclaims with a mixture of anger and curiosity. Matching my brisk steps as I cross the open space to the adjoining living room, he huffs, "We're about to... And you brought your fucking sister here?"

"We're late. We can talk about this later," I gruff, dropping Eavan to the couch. Her messy red hair still tousled over her face, she clambers to her feet. I press my hand to her shoulder and lightly shove her back into the cushions I dropped her on. Staring down at her, I gruffly demand, "Stay. We'll be back in a few hours."

I don't give her a chance to complain or argue. She grumbles as the three of us leave her behind, briskly walking to the elevator. Waiting for the cab to arrive, I anxiously glance over my shoulder at the door to the apartment. *This is for the best... her best.* We step into the cab when it arrives, and Nikolai grouses, "Really? Your fucking sister?"

"Later," Enzo grunts, not even remotely trying to mask his displeasure with my sudden, undiscussed change to our previously well-defined plan. He shakes his head. "We don't need the fucking distraction. Not tonight." *Knowing she wasn't safe would've been a far bigger distraction.*

Our heavy footsteps slap against the concrete and echo through the parking garage as we make our way toward Enzo's G-Class. He turns over the engine, and I meet his narrow eyes in the rearview mirror. *This upset him more than I expected it would.* Letting out a heavy sigh, I grumble, "I know I fucked up. I had no cho—"

"Fucking later!" Enzo shouts, pulling into traffic. "We have twenty minutes until the biggest meeting of our family's lives. Your sister isn't what any of us need to be thinking about." Fighting my need to explain myself, I listen intently as we verify tonight's plan.

By the time we reach the meatpacking district of Chelsea, the SUV falls silent. Enzo makes a sharp left toward the abandoned warehouse, and my eyes roam over the four very out-of-place cars parked before the meeting spot. My father's Bentayga, a black Tahoe, a Rolls Royce Ghost, and a BMW Z4 —the latter likely belonging to the other people attending tonight's meeting.

"They're all here," Enzo mutters, almost underneath his breath. I'm as surprised as he is that everyone actually showed up to this meeting. Irish, Bratva, and Italian sitting down at one table—a meeting like this is practically unheard of. The three of them coming together to discuss a joint business venture—like tonight—is even more ludicrous. Apparently, to the three of them—*especially my father*—money matters more than anything.

Enzo, Nikolai, and I have talked for what seems like forever about how great it would be to merge our families. We would be practically unstoppable with how strong and powerful we'd be if we were all working together. On the surface, tonight seems like everything we've wanted—but I can't take it like that. As if their decision to delve into the deplorable world of human trafficking isn't bad enough, there isn't a part of me that is okay with the cost we're paying to forge this deal—my sister.

"This is her role," my father spat when I shared how much I was against this deal. "She'll be a good little wife for whoever I promise her to." *Translation: A good little whore.* With the family he's promising her to, she'd be lucky to only be subjected to the bastard she's being married off to. And that isn't something I'm willing to make her endure.

The three of us pause at the front door to the warehouse, our gazes meeting.

Both their faces are stoic, but there's faint hesitation hiding behind their eyes. I'm sure they can see the same tinge in mine.

"My brothers," I exhale with a slight nod. Nikolai and Enzo echo my sentiment, and Enzo pulls open the door.

It creaks loudly on the hinges, alerting our fathers to our arrival. The three of them—Tazio Roseti, Rian O'Brien, and Rurik Romanov—are seated around a dimly lit table with the fourth in their business plan—an Armenian who is going to supply the women from overseas—and all their eyes lift to us into the dark space. The four of them rise from their seats as we approach, but I'm unable to pull my eyes from my father and the Armenian—both clearly displaced by the lack of Eavan on my arm. The Armenian leans toward my father and grumbles, "I thought you were bringing your daughter."

"Where is your fucking sister?" my father grouses as I approach him, only furthering the rage coursing through my veins.

I shake my head, mostly in displeasure. The deafening bang of Enzo's gunshot reverberates off the metal walls and through the massive space. By the time my father's gaze snaps from Tazio Roseti to me, my gun is aimed at his chest. Without hesitation, I pull the trigger and pump three rounds into my father, muttering, "She's your fucking daughter."

Tazio Rosetti falls at my feet, his hand clutched firmly to his bleeding abdomen, desperately trying to pull the gun tucked in the waistband of his pants. I turn my aim to him from my father and put another round into his chest. Finalizing the plan—each of us putting a bullet into each man—I squeeze a slug into Rurik, the light in his eyes immediately dimming.

Rounding the table, I step over the men who have ruled this city toward the Armenian, clinging to life in a puddle of blood on the concrete floor. "You don't deserve to live. And your family sure as fuck doesn't deserve my sister." His gaze is fixed on mine, silently pleading for his life, and I empty the rest of my clip into him. The echo of my final gunshot fades, and the warehouse grows quiet.

"To my brothers." Nikolai's toast cuts through the silence that has filled the room. I turn to find him raising a bottle of vodka from the table into the air. He takes a swig and passes it to me.

Taking the bottle from him, I swallow back a couple of gulps. It burns the back of my throat, and I choke, "Ugh... fucking vodka... To my brothers."

"To my brothers..." Enzo repeats, taking the bottle when I pass it to him. He throws back a shot and shouts, "The Kings of New York City."

Tonight is just beginning.

CHAPTER 2
madison

ONE WEEK AGO

My lungs burn as I take the final few stairs, grateful to finally reach the landing, and that this is my last box. *Note to self: My next apartment will **not** be a walk-up.* Skillfully, I juggle the box with one hand and the wall and I manage to slip my keys into the door and open it.

After hooking my arm tighter around the last cardboard box, I step inside and nudge the apartment door shut with my hip. The knob catches the pocket of my hooded sweatshirt and nearly yanks me off-balance. I recover—*barely*—and stagger into the middle of the studio apartment. My phone is wedged between my cheek and shoulder, and I'm trying not to drop it

—or the box—as I listen to my mother ramble on about my move and her hesitations for the umpteenth time.

"Yes, Mom," I grumble, still catching my breath after the three flights of stairs. "I brought the pepper spray. And the flashlight. And even the emergency whistle."

"Mock me all you want, sweetheart." Mom sighs. "But those things are important. New York City isn't like Lolita." *And thank God for that.* My aspirations far exceed that tiny town in Virginia and the even tinier dating pool of eligible bachelors— a handful of boys I've known since I was six.

I lower the box to the floor with a grunt, wiping my dirty hands across the tops of my jeans. "I'm not laughing. I packed everything you told me to. Plus extras. I'm prepared for everything from a creepy guy on the street to the zombie apocalypse."

"That's not funny." *We never did share a sense of humor.*

"It's a little funny," I playfully insist with a chuckle. "Seriously, Mom. The emergency kit you gave me is already under the sink and I easily have a year's worth of birth control. I'm officially a responsible adult."

She lets out a heavy huff, and there's a pause on the other end. For a second, all I can hear is the traffic humming outside my window and the noisy neighbor upstairs.

"Well," she exhales, her voice suddenly softer, "you still could've waited until Saturday. You didn't have to drive all the way to New York today by yourself."

"I wanted to." I look out the window, resting my hands on my hips. *I needed to.* "It felt right, doing it on my own. New city, new job, new life."

I smile, stretching the kink out of my neck and stepping around a box. The apartment isn't big—just one open room, maybe five hundred square feet on paper—though it feels smaller with the skyscrapers of boxes piled along the walls and in the middle of the floor. But what it lacks in space, it makes up for in personality.

The building is a converted factory, full of character and charm —and a slightly suspicious smell near the stairwell. A tall and narrow floor-to-ceiling window throws long shadows across the brick walls from the exposed beams. The pipes that run along the ceiling hum and groan—apparently whenever anyone in the building uses the water. It's not much, but it's mine.

"Well, I just... You're in a huge city, Maddie. Alone. And this job you got..." Mom trails off.

I move to the tiny kitchenette and wish I had thought to order groceries for delivery. Sitting on the chipped laminate counter are the only consumables I have—a sad-looking box of flavorless, crunchy granola bars and a half-empty bottle of iced tea from the last gas station I stopped at.

"I know," I mumble, unscrewing the cap and taking a sip. "But it's not scary. I promise. It's just... new."

"Have you met your neighbors yet?" she asks suddenly.

I shake my head, then remember she can't see me. "No, not yet. I think someone else is moving in upstairs." *Or so I hope, considering I've been listening to furniture dragging across the floor since I got here.* "And I heard a dog bark earlier. That's a good sign, right?"

"Hmmm." *She* doesn't have to say it, but that's her version of 'not exactly.'

Leaning on the counter, I stare across the small apartment, cataloging all the work I still have to do. There are a few IKEA boxes in the corner—deliveries made before I arrived that the super kindly moved inside. They contain my bed frame, a bookshelf, a desk, and a chair—all of which will probably take me hours to assemble. Which means the mattress currently leaning against the wall will probably be on the floor tonight.

"I know you can take care of yourself, Madison. You always could."

"I can," I reply, heading toward the window and sitting cross-legged on the floor—the creaky hardwood cool beneath me. "I've lived on my own for a little over six years."

"That's different. That was all campus housing. This is... well, not."

I grumble, reaching my limit with her overprotectiveness. "I've got locks on the doors. Several of them. I can read the subway map. I'll be perfectly fine, Mom. I promise."

She sighs—half amused, half worried. "I know. You're your father's daughter."

Her words unintentionally gut me. I look down at the floorboards and trace a small crack with my fingertip. Silence stretches between us, and I swallow down the ache creeping up my throat at the mention of Dad.

I miss him...

"Yeah," I respond quietly. "I am."

"He'd be so proud of you, sweetheart."

I still feel him sometimes...

I wish I could to tell him about the new place. But she's right. I know he would be beyond proud of what I have accomplished these last few years—especially the past few months. Graduating, making this move to the city, and starting the life I know I was meant to live. I close my eyes, trying to hold the tears at bay. "Thanks, Mom."

"You're going to do amazing," Mom muses, like she's reading my thoughts. "Just promise me you'll call often."

"I will," is all I say, and I mean it.

"Don't be afraid to ask for help if you need it. There's no shame in that."

"I know. But I think I've got this. I've got a ton of unpacking to do," I inform her. "Plus, unless I'm eating granola, I also need to get to a grocery store at some point tonight."

"All right, Maddie. I'll let you go," she begrudgingly agrees. "You need to settle in. Just... don't forget to eat something tonight. And lock your door."

"I love you, too, Mom." I shake my head, hang up, and place my cell phone on the window ledge. Resting against it, I listen to the city below through the slightly cracked window—sirens wailing in the distance, honking horns, and a group of men laughing loudly on the sidewalk directly below me. The chaotic, noisy patchwork is somehow comforting.

As much as I should actually unpack, my stomach won't stop growling. I'm also exhausted from the drive and lugging boxes upstairs. I turn to the mattress, give it a firm tug, and let it flop to the floor. Grabbing my phone, I forgo sheets—*I have no idea where that box is, anyway*—and lay down on it.

My stomach grumbles again, and I decide to listen to Mom's advice. *At least about dinner.*

CURRENT DAY

The smell of garlic and seared meat still hangs in the air, mixing well with the warmth of good whiskey and laughter— even if most of the laughter is at my expense. Apparently, my complete inability to cook anything besides scrambled eggs and shit that comes from a can is quite humorous. *At least to everyone else.*

The evening is light and fun—an unusual combination for the four of us. For the first time in months, we aren't looking over our shoulders. Tonight's family dinner feels almost normal, and I can't stop wondering when the other shoe is going to drop. It's been quiet. *Too quiet.*

A sharp, unexpected rap against the front door cuts through the laughter in the room like a blade, and I can practically hear the figurative shoe clattering against the hardwood floor. Gunnar's voice follows a moment later, calm, but alert. "Hey, sorry to interrupt. I ran into a guy in the lobby looking to speak with Cillian," he apologizes, stepping into the kitchen. My fork pauses mid-air. "I frisked him in the elevator."

My brow furrows. "I wasn't expecting anyone." Hell, no one knows I'm even here except the people in this room and a few trusted others. I push my chair back to stand, but Enzo beats me to it, waving me off. "Eat," he insists, already walking away. "I'll take care of it."

I listen as the door opens, Enzo inviting the already searched stranger into our home. His footsteps carry down the front hall and into the kitchen. His entry is preceded by his uncertain voice. "I was looking for Mr. O'Brien." *That gets my full attention—no one refers to me as Mr. O'Brien.*

The uninvited guest steps into the kitchen, and I immediately size him up. He's wearing a suit that looks like it came from a gas station clearance rack. His haircut is courtesy of either a ten-dollar discount store or a blind barber. But his true tell is the way he walks—definitely a *Fed.* He looks out of his element in our kitchen, and I assume he's not the kind of Fed that kicks in doors—more like the kind that shuffles papers behind a desk.

His eyes land on Nikolai first, blowing wide. "Mr. Romanov." *That surprise isn't fake.*

Nikolai doesn't even blink. "And you are?"

The guy flashes his badge like it means something. "Special Agent Frankford. With RICO." *There it is.* The room falls silent, all of us surprised by his disclosure. Even Eavan freezes, her hand hovering above her glass. I set my fork down slowly and deliberately, unable to refrain from glaring at the man who had the audacity to saunter into my home.

Frankford looks around the room, as though he still can't believe the dinner party he walked in on. "You'll have to excuse me." His voice is steady, but disbelieving. "I clearly wasn't expecting to find the heads of three rival families laughing and sharing dinner. Bonding over the untimely passings of your fathers?" *Cheap fucking shot—but well fucking calculated.*

His narrow eyes barely containing his disdain, Enzo asks, "What do you want?"

"Truth be told, I had a few questions about Rian O'Brien," Agent Frankford answers without hesitation.

"Rian O'Brien?" Enzo asks with a scoff. "Is that the reason you're standing in my apartment, Agent Frankford?"

He condescendingly raises a brow and smiles. "Among others."

"You want to tell us why you're really here? Because I don't think you showed up to compliment the risotto," Nikolai jests as he stands, unable to take even this moment seriously.

"You're right," Frankford retorts with a dry chuckle. "I didn't come for the food. Though the company... Now, that's interesting."

He paces nervously for a moment, easing further into the room "Your fathers bled this city for decades, carving it into pieces like a pie none of them wanted to share," he shares, as though suddenly fueled with brazenness. "And now—suddenly—it's quiet. Almost like someone turned down the volume."

"You got a problem with peace, Agent?" I ask.

"What I have a problem with is the unknown. O'Brien, Romanov, Roseti—each of you inherited an empire built on violence. Now you're having dinner together? It doesn't make sense, unless you figured out that together, you're untouchable."

None of us responds. Why would we? There's nothing we can say that won't be twisted and dissected later in some sterile office.

He steps further in. Suddenly confident—*maybe too confident* —his gaze flitting around the island at each of us. "Here's what I think," he shares. "I think you're planning something big. Bigger than territory, bigger than protection, rackets or drugs. I think you've already started it."

"And what would that be?" Nikolai asks quietly.

Frankford grins like a man who thinks he's clever. "I was hoping you'd tell me."

That's when I know exactly what this is. He has nothing. He's bluffing. Poking the edges, waiting for someone to twitch. This visit might be official, but it's a fishing trip. The man is armed with nothing more than suspicions and theories. He isn't here with evidence. If he was, we wouldn't be having this conversation with drinks in our hands. Our hands would be in cuffs as we were served warrants and Miranda Rights.

I lean back in my chair and cross my arms over my chest. "You came all the way up here, flashed your badge, threw around some nonsensical conspiracies... but you still haven't asked a real question."

Frankford tilts his head, studying me, his eyes narrowing

slightly. He opens his mouth but I push back from the counter and gruff, "Are we done here?"

There's a pause. The tension tightens like a noose. But then he nods—slowly. "For now." He walks to the door with a faux stiff posture, like he's trying not to show how rattled he is. Gunnar escorts him out, shutting the door a little harder than he needs to.

I let out a heavy exhale, glancing down at my half-finished plate—my appetite suddenly gone.

Nikolai leans forward, resting his forearms on the island, his fingers laced together like he's praying—or planning a murder. "We underestimated how fast they'd move."

"No," Enzo says, quieter. "We didn't."

"He doesn't have proof," Eavan cuts in. "He's grasping."

"You're probably right." Enzo rises, reassuringly placing his hands on Eaven's shoulders. "He's looking for the weak link. He wants to know which one of us will break ranks first."

Nikolai scoffs. "He's going to be waiting a long fucking time."

ONE DAY LATER

The plan for tonight was to order a pizza and unpack a few more boxes. Then maybe light a candle, take a long bubble bath—after giving the tub one last thorough scrubbing—and call it a day. I hadn't considered going out. Yet, here I am, walking down the street toward The Corner Pub—an aptly named bar at the end of my block.

Stepping inside, the place smells like old wood, citrus-scented cleaner, and fried food—the latter of which is only causing my stomach to continue to growl. Edison bulbs hang low over both the tables and the bar, their warm amber glow reflecting off the heavily polished mahogany. The place has a worn charm, teetering between a hipster and dive bar.

I slide onto a stool at the end of the bar, far from the rowdy frat boys at the other end. The heavily tattooed bartender nods at me. "What'll it be?"

"Tennessee Mule," I respond, glancing around the bar. "And do you have a food menu?"

He places a postcard-sized menu before me with a slight grunt, already turning to make my drink. A moment later, he slides a small copper mug across the bar toward me—my nostrils immediately flooded with the zesty spice of the ginger beer. I take a sip, and the ginger and whiskey bite at the back of my throat as I swallow. "Anything else?" the bartender asks.

"Yes... Uh..." I quickly glance over the menu again, trying to make up my mind. "The loaded fries with a side of ranch." He gives a nod and takes my menu before disappearing to the computer at the other end of the bar.

My gaze flits around the room, watching the other patrons as I listen to the soft hum of the mellow, jazzy music playing through the sound system. I swirl the ice in my near-empty glass and take the final sip as the bartender slides the plate of fries before me—my mouth immediately watering at the sight and scent. The cheese melts over the fries in a glorious mess of bacon, jalapeños, and whatever zesty blend of seasoning they use here. Dunking a cheese-covered fry into the tiny cup of ranch dressing, I quickly thank the bartender before shoving it into my mouth. *Fuck... that's good.* I take another bite, moaning under my breath, before washing it down with the last watery sip of my Tennessee Mule.

My eyes catch the reflection in the mirror, and I immediately find myself drawn to a party of four behind me. They are tucked into a booth in the corner, slightly shadowed by dimmer lighting. Two remarkably handsome men flank the ends of the booth. On the right, a blond man with striking cheekbones and eyes like pale ice. Clean-cut, buttoned-up, but with a glint in his expression that says he knows exactly how good-looking he is. The kind of man who could flash a smile and talk his way out of a felony.

Sitting opposite him, is a man with sleek dark hair, olive-toned skin, and a smirk that looks permanent. He lounges—like he doesn't have a care in the world—with his arm draped over a gorgeous redhead.

Once my eyes land on the man in the center of the group, it's near impossible to drag them away. Even sitting, it's obvious that he's tall. His broad shoulders push at the seams of the soft gray T-shirt clinging to his frame, barely containing the muscles beneath it. His hair is mussed—purposefully—every strand falling from his modern pompadour appears to have been meticulously placed to create the perfect messy style. His beard is neat, copper red and golden—like his hair—under the glow of the bar lights. It is full, well-kept, and trimmed to a sharp edge along his jawline. He is gorgeous—rugged and yet refined, like he could snap someone's neck and then charm the hell out of your mom at family dinner the same evening.

Together, they are captivating; beautiful people who ooze power and confidence. They're too polished for this borderline dive bar. But they fit somehow—like they could make any place their own just by walking into it.

I should look away—I know I should. But I don't. Can't. My eyes are locked on the red-haired man in the center of the group, like I've forgotten how to blink. His presence is a gravity all its own, pulling my attention to him. He glances toward the bar, and through the mirror, our eyes meet, and my heart skips a beat—stuttering in my chest. His gaze is calm and curious. His eyes not wavering from my stare at our reflections, the corner of his mouth quirks into an almost smile.

My stomach flips hard, and I panic, quickly looking away as embarrassment paints my cheeks a bright shade of crimson. I take a sudden, unnecessary interest in my fries, pretending they're the most fascinating thing I've ever seen. Curiosity gets the best of me, and I glance from my plate to the mirror to find his attention still completely focused on me. He leans forward slightly, one elbow on the table and his fingers turning a glass tumbler in slow, deliberate circles, his smile broadening slightly.

His stare not leaving mine, he nudges the blond man to move out of his way. Even if I weren't watching him, I swear I would hear the scrape of his sliding from the booth and the unmistakable thud of his boots on hardwood over the sounds of the bar. I sip my mule—forgetting it is empty—then stir the ice like that'll cool the heat in my chest. *It doesn't.*

As I watch in the mirror, he walks through the bar like he owns the place, the small crowd parting to let him pass. My skin prickles with nervous goosebumps, and I fight the urge to smooth my hair or adjust my top—anything to attempt to calm myself before he reaches me.

He slides onto the empty stool beside me, and his intoxicating scent floods my nostrils. *And fuck does he smell good.* It's leather with a hint of something sweet and spicy, like a spiced rum. It's addictive. So addictive that I fight the urge to lean closer and inhale him deeply.

"It's not every night you find a breathtaking woman sitting alone at the end of the bar," he overtly flirts, his voice low and smooth.

I turn slowly, trying to stow my expression and keep my overwhelming interest unreadable. But with him this close— and my gaze flitting between his sharp jaw and the bulging muscles—it's out of the question. Taking a measured breath, I retort, "I'm sure you say that to all the women you pick up in bars."

His grin morphs into a smirk. "Only the ones who make loaded fries look like an orgasmic experience." Unable to hold it back, I laugh—just a little. *Damn it!* The bartender approaches, clearly familiar with him, and waits without a word. "Whatever she's having, put it on my tab."

"I'm good, actually." I slide my empty mug toward the bartender, even though I did actually want another. I don't need him buying me drinks. I don't need him turning this into anything.

"You sure?" he asks, watching me with those piercing hazel eyes. "You don't strike me as the kind of woman who drinks one watered-down cocktail and runs home."

He's been watching me... Even before I was watching him.

"You don't know what kind of woman I am," I retort, my tone sharper than I intend.

He leans in, that assured smile still playing at the edge of his mouth. "Not yet." God, he's dangerous. Not just in the way he looks or the quiet confidence he wears, but in the way he *talks*, like every word leaving his mouth is the foreplay to him undressing me.

"I'm Cillian King," he provides the unnecessary introduction. I might be new in town, but the King brothers—as they've renamed themselves—are notorious. Even if he weren't my new boss, I'm quite certain I would know his name.

"Madison"—I hesitate for a moment, debating whether or not to provide him with my full name—"Madison Roark."

"You live nearby?" he asks.

I grab another fry instead of responding, dipping it in the ranch to stall for time. *Oh, this is a bad idea...* "I do."

"You always come here on your own?"

"This is my first time. I actually just moved into the neighborhood."

"Well, it's already my lucky night."

I roll my eyes and shake my head, but I'm smiling. *Shit—I'm actually smiling.*

He watches me for a moment, long enough for it to border on indecent, but his gaze doesn't drop below my face—he's not ogling me. He's reading me, like he's trying to figure out how I work and what I'm thinking. I'm a puzzle he's decided he wants to solve.

"You here with someone?"

"No."

"Meeting someone?"

"Nope."

He arches an inquisitive brow. "Live with someone?" he asks, his tone now matching his curiosity.

Every savvy girl knows you don't tell strange men you live alone. Yet, against my better judgment, I answer, "No."

He tilts his head. "Then you've got no excuse not to let me take you home."

I laugh. It slips out before I can stop it, and when I look at him, he has a full smile spread across his gorgeous face. He's certain he's getting what he wants. "You really think that works?" I snark, matching his raised eyebrow. "Dropping your name and a few compliments with strange women in bars and just... walking out with them?"

He casually shrugs, and his body language answers my question. *Of course it fucking does! Fucking look at him.* "It's not about what I think. It's about knowing what you want." His eyes flicker with a dark heat, and my pulse thuds low in my throat. A flash of heat rolls down my spine and settles low enough in my belly that I unintentionally clench my thighs together to quell it. *Apparently, my body agrees with his assessment of what I want.*

I should say no. Firmly. Getting personal with Cillian King is a bad idea. *A horrible one.* I reach into my pocket and pull out two twenties before tucking them half under my plate to cover my bill and a tip for the bartender. After slipping from my stool, I inadvertently brush against his arm and static tingles across my skin. He turns on his stool to follow after me, and I plant my hand firmly against his chest, indicating for him to keep his seat.

The change in his demeanor is immediate—his easy, confident smile falters slightly, replaced with something more calculating. He's clearly not a man used to hearing no. "I'm not the kind of girl who takes strange men home," I whisper the lie, holding his golden gaze. "Good night, Mr. King."

"Cillian," he corrects too quickly as I slide my hand from his firm chest.

"I'm pretty certain you'll be seeing *plenty* of me soon enough."

He grips my wrist lightly before I can slip away. "I don't come to this part of town very often. What makes you so sure?"

"Just a hunch."

I pause at the door, glancing over my shoulder just in time to see him watching me with that same unreadable expression—part curiosity, part hunger, and something else I can't quite put my finger on.

By the time I get back to my apartment, the sky is growing dark, and I've missed my window for a relaxing night in. The echo of our interaction at the bar is looping in my head like a record I can't turn off. I toe off my sneakers and peel off my jean shorts as I walk toward the kitchen, too wired to sleep. My body is buzzing, every nerve still lit up from the heat of Cillian's stare.

After opening the fridge, I grab a cold bottle of water and press it to the side of my neck. My skin is flushed, overheated, even though the apartment is cool. I take a few sips and lean against the counter. *Why hell are you thinking about him, Maddie? Cillian Fucking King.* I knew what kind of man he was before he even opened his mouth, but sitting inches from him, I suddenly didn't care. I sat there and flirted with him, liking that he looked at me like he needed to have me.

I didn't move to the city to get tangled up in men like him. I pad across the room to the mattress and flop onto it before staring at the ceiling. My mind not once deviating from thoughts of Cillian King—his voice, that smile, those sparkling eyes. And fuck... The way he looked at me like I was a challenge—a game he's very interested in playing.

I swipe open my phone, click on the notes app, and type:

Don't fall for Cillian King.

I stare at it for a second. Then, add to it.

Especially if he's going to keep looking at you like you're already his favorite sin.

In a couple of nights, he's going to see me again—up close, in heels, and under stage lights—at the opening night of King's Temptation. I have no idea how he's going to react when he finds out he's my boss. What I do know is that I'm not as ready for this as I thought. And worse? I still want it anyway.

Madison walks out the door with only a short pause to glance over her shoulder.

I'm left standing at the bar like an idiot—one hand still holding my drink, and the other twitching anxiously at my side. For a moment, I merely stare after her—with a befuddlement plastered across my face—watching the door close and wondering what the fuck just happened.

That never happens.

Women don't turn me down.

It sounds arrogant and cocky as hell as it runs through my thoughts, but it's true. I'm not delusional. I know who I am, what I look like, and what my name carries—now more than ever. I don't chase after women, because I don't have to. I meet a cute girl, chat with her for a bit, share my interests, and the rest usually falls into place. But Madison Roark? She smiled, shot me down with a few words, and walked out of this bar like she owns the whole fucking city. *My fucking city.*

I set my glass on the bar roughly and shake my head.

Madison Roark...

She wasn't just pretty. She was fucking stunning. Dark brown hair, long and loose, cascading down her back like it had a mind of its own. Brown eyes, but not the soft and warm kind, hers are dark and deep. Her perfect skin had soaked in summer —golden and smooth—framed by that oversized tank top that hung off one shoulder like it didn't belong to her. Her shorts —cut off, frayed, and unforgivably short—made it impossible not to notice her legs. Long. Strong. Toned from more than just countless hours of walking on the treadmill at the local gym. She was petite, but not the slightest bit delicate. Nothing about her struck me as a woman who needed a man to take care of her.

And that face...

There aren't words for a face like Madison's. It's the kind you don't forget—high cheekbones, expressive brows, and pouty pink lips I can think of several uses for. Beautiful. *Devastatingly beautiful.*

It's what drew me to her from across the bar. A gorgeous woman to spend the night with. And then she opened her mouth. *Absolute fire.* She was quick, sharp, and didn't hesitate in the slightest to call me out on my bullshit. From her confidence, I can only surmise that she's very used to being underestimated. Nothing about me intimidated her.

From our short interaction, I'm certain she's a feisty little brat. I don't enjoy brats... Normally.

The more I replay our conversation, the more irritated I get—not because she walked away, but because she left me wanting more. She didn't outright reject me. Not really. With those parting words—*"I'm pretty certain you'll be seeing* plenty *of me soon enough"*—it was more like she was baiting me as she walked out the door and disappeared into the night. And fuck, did it ever work.

Those words... I don't know if they were supposed to be a warning, a promise, or if she was just fucking with me. But the way she said it... stuck. They burrowed deep, and I need to know what she meant—almost as much as I need to know more about her.

I don't realize how long I've been standing at the bar, staring at the door, until the bartender gives me a curious look. I shake my head, mutter something about closing my tab later, and make my way back to the booth.

Enzo's the first to notice my expression. His eyes flick up as I approach, reading my face the way he reads everyone—sharp, fast, accurate. His brow arches, and a faint smirk tugs at the corners of his mouth, but he stays silent.

Nikolai leans back in the booth, grinning like the devil himself. "Oh no. You struck out, didn't you?" I slide into the booth, ignoring him as he scoots closer to Eavan to make room for me. Without reacting to his comment, I pick up his half-finished drink and take a long sip. "Wait—*seriously*?" he adds, leaning forward and plopping his elbows on the table with intrigue. "That wasn't just a flirtatious chat? You made a move, and she shot you down?"

"She left," I answer flatly.

Enzo raises a brow. "Was she with someone?"

"No."

"I know this is going to come as a shock to the three of you," Eavan snarks, "but not every woman in the city is going to spread her legs simply because you're a King."

"You sure about that?" Enzo smirks. "Because it worked with you, princess."

Eavan lightly smacks his arm as I swallow my semi-feigned disgust. "I was really hoping after the two of you moved into your own place that I wouldn't have to hear about your sex life anymore."

"I've heard more than enough about their sex life for three lifetimes. I want to know more about the mystery woman at the bar." Nikolai pulls the conversation back. "What's her name?"

"Roark... Madison Roark," I answer. "Why?"

"I need to know the name of the woman who gave Cillian King the boot," Nik laughs. "Next time I see her, I need to buy her a drink."

"She didn't *boot* me," I huff, irritation prickling me. "She just went home."

"Without *you*," he emphasizes. "That's new."

"She said I'd be seeing plenty more of her," I add, not quite sure who I'm trying to convince.

Eavan frowns slightly. "What does that mean?"

"That's what I'm trying to figure out."

"Could be a threat," Enzo laments with a shrug. "Or maybe she knows someone we know. Maybe she works with one of the organizations we deal with?"

I shake my head. "She said she was new in town. And if she was... like us... There's no way I wouldn't have noticed her before tonight. Yet, she was certain I'd be seeing her again."

Nikolai chuckles. "You sound obsessed."

"I'm curious," I correct, but the word sounds too soft for what's crawling under my skin. "She didn't act impressed. Didn't flirt. She didn't *try*. That's what's sticking with me."

"You're used to being wanted." Eavan sips her drink. "She didn't give you that. Now your ego is bruised, and you need to fix it."

"My ego isn't bruised."

"Sure," she exhales dryly.

I lean back in the booth, one hand tapping against the side of my glass. "It's not about rejection. It's the way she handled it. Like she wasn't just brushing me off, it was more that she had plans. Like walking away from me was step one toward something bigger."

"Bigger how?" Enzo asks.

"If I knew, I'd be following her," I mutter. "But she left me standing there. Barely gave me a second glance."

"You going to let that go?" Nikolai half-smirks.

"No." I look up slowly. "No, I'm not."

He laughs. "I knew it. Ob-sess-ed," he emphasizes every syllable with such cockiness, I have to fight the urge to slug him.

"If she was bluffing," I mumble, "if that was her way of blowing me off, fine. But if she meant it? If we're really going to cross paths again—"

"You want to be ready," Enzo finishes.

I nod. "Exactly." *Just... ready for what?*

There's a short pause before Nikolai raises his glass. "To Madison Roark, the first woman to leave Cillian King with his cock in his hand."

Eavan clinks her glass against his with a giggle. "May there be many more."

"Really?" I huff.

"What?" Eavan shrugs with a sassy glint in her eyes. "The three of you could stand to be humbled once in a while."

Shaking my head, I mutter under my breath, "Such a fucking brat."

"*My* fucking brat," Enzo whispers against her neck, just loud enough that I overhear him.

The three of them toast to my striking out, razzing me as my attention drifts back to her. The curve of her smile, the glimmer in her eyes, and—*fuck*—the way the gentle sway of her hips drew my eyes with every step toward the door.

Madison Roark might have walked away from me tonight, but she was right—I'll be seeing her again. I'll make sure of it.

The powerful roar of my Aston Martin's engine fades as we pull up to the building. When I park at the valet, neon lights flicker across the windshield, pulsing in pinks and reds. The marquee glows above us, *King's Temptation,* in a gold script that's impossible to miss. Confident, I step out into the warm night air and I straighten the cuffs on my black button-up. I stare up at the building we've poured months—and a disgusting amount of money—into. This club was ours before the city was, and it's finally opening night.

Enzo is standing on the sidewalk beside me, fixing his tie like we're heading into a gala instead of a strip club. "This is going to make us kings." His voice is smooth and rich as a pleased smirk tugs at the corner of his lips.

"We already are," Nikolai scoffs, flicking a cigarette into the gutter as he joins us. "But this? This is a fucking throne."

He's not wrong.

King's Temptation isn't just a strip club—it's a statement. Three stories of opulence dressed in sin. Black marble floors and gold-veined columns. Crystal chandeliers that hang like upside-down ice sculptures. Velvet booths that wrap around low-lit tables, designed to make the rich feel even richer. Every inch of it is curated to perfection—luxury that whispers power instead of shouting it, because the men we're catering to know how to read a room. We built this place for the elite—the kind of men who want to be worshipped behind closed doors. And behind those doors, they can spend ten grand without batting an eye while we clean our dirty cash under the disguise of champagne receipts and lap-dance tallies.

I step through the front doors, greeted by a wall of perfume, desire, and money. It's intoxicating, exactly how it's supposed to be.

Girls in stilettos and designer lingerie prowl through the crowd like a pride of lionesses on a hunt, weaving between men in bespoke suits and the equally as powerful women some of them have on their arms. The lighting is low, red and gold shining from hidden strips, making everyone glow like they belong on a magazine cover. The bass throbs through the floors. Champagne bubbles sparkle in glasses. And everywhere I look, people are watching us, waiting for a sign from the Kings that it's okay to indulge.

Enzo heads to our reserved VIP booth overlooking the main stage. Nikolai peels off to check the bar and security feeds, like the obsessed bastard he is—always watching for cracks before they form. I take my time crossing the club, pausing to mingle with a few familiar faces—city councilmen, a judge I'm definitely not supposed to be on a first-name basis with, and a few CEOs whose real names we'll keep off the books. *Everyone wants a piece of this place already.*

I stop at the bar to grab a Tullamore Dew on the rocks and then join Enzo in our booth. It's the best seat in the house; angled perfectly toward the stage, high enough to see everything, yet private enough to watch without being approached. On nights we aren't here, the cost of bottle service for others to reserve this spot will practically cover our costs for a month.

The crowd is warm and generous. Drinks are flowing and money is flying at the talent. Dancer after dancer takes to the stage—each one beautiful, talented, and fluid—but none of them truly holding my attention. Not really. I spend more time talking with my brothers than I do checking out the girls on stage—until the DJ's voice slinks from the speakers, his tone so devilish that I can practically see his Cheshire grin. "Gentlemen—and the lovely ladies joining us tonight—you're about to meet your new obsession. Please welcome to the stage... *Raven.*"

The bass drops, and the lights shift as the opening notes of *Wild Side* thrum throughout the club—dark, smooth, and dripping with temptation. A silhouette slinks toward the pole with a slow, deliberate stride, and I forget how to breathe. She knows *exactly* what she's doing. Framed in red light, my eyes rake over every sinful curve of her body, long legs and ample hips that curve into her trim waist. I can't take my fucking eyes off her.

She's dressed in black lace—barely. Thigh-highs. Panties held together with a thin chain that dangles along her hips when she twists. It's not the outfit that gets me, though, it's the way she moves. Controlled. Sensual. Powerful. She sways in perfect rhythm with the music, like she owns it—like she's the one *scoring* it. She exudes the confidence of a woman who knows every man in the room would set himself on fire for a chance to touch her. And the way she's drawn the attention of every man, she has earned that right.

I lean forward, elbows on my knees, completely spellbound. *Fuck...* She hasn't even turned around yet.

"Jesus Christ," Enzo mutters beside me. My pulse is thudding in my ears so loudly I barely hear him. "I think half the men in here just forgot how to speak."

I don't respond. *I can't.*

Raven climbs the pole like it is second nature to her, swinging upside down with a strength and grace that makes my chest tighten. When she spins, her dark mane fans out around her like smoke. She slides down slowly, arching her back and ass, and the room fucking reacts—collective gasps and a hundred dropped jaws.

Gliding around the pole, she turns, and the world shifts beneath me when I finally see her face.

Madison Roark.

Her eyes are closed, and her makeup is much heavier, but there's no mistaking her. It's the woman from the bar. The feisty little firecracker I tried to take home two nights ago. The one who told me I'd be seeing plenty of her.

God damn.

I practically swallow my tongue as she tosses her barely-there lace bra to the stage floor. *She wasn't kidding... This is a **lot** more of her.* I sit back, stunned, heart hammering, and my cock growing hard enough to uncomfortably tent the front of my pants. She dances like she's been doing it forever—flawless, magnetic, every inch of her body telling a story I can't stop watching. Her golden skin gleams under the lights. She owns that fucking stage, and every person in the room knows it.

"Wipe your chin, Cian," Nik teases, shoving a napkin at me with a smirk. "You're making a mess."

I ignore him, because now I'm watching with new eyes. She's no longer just the woman with a challenging smile and a fire in her eyes who caught my interest a couple of nights ago.

The way the bastards in this club are staring at her—like they're one more gyration from worshipping at her feet—makes something ugly rise in my throat. They can't have her, because she's going to be *mine*. I drain my bourbon in one go, trying futilely to swallow it.

Her hips roll one last time as she works the pole, slow and smooth, until the song ends. She grabs her bra and struts offstage with confidence, the crowd surging toward her. Wall Street guys waving wads of cash and shouting offers at her as more of the crowd rise to their feet—all of them reaching for her like she's an auction lot.

My chair scrapes the floor as I abruptly stand. Fueled with adrenaline and desire, I cross the room without thinking. Shoving my way through the crowd, my eyes are locked on her as she smiles and takes a bill from an older man in a well-tailored suit. They can try to buy her all they want, but she won't belong to any of them.

A man reaches for her, and I shove him away before he can put his hands on her. I grab her wrist—not hard, just firm—and pull her into me. A startled gasp flies over her lips when she crashes against me. She looks up, and her eyes blow wide when she sees my face—a smile already playing at my lips. "Sorry, fellas," I announce, loud enough to be heard over the surrounding commotion. "Raven has already been requested in the VIP suite." A few men grumble, and one loudly protests. I shoot a look that immediately silences him, and he backs off without another word.

Her skin is soft, and her wrist is warm in my hand as I drag her away from the crowd. She doesn't try to pull from my hold—not once. Madison is still staring at me as I walk us across the club and steer her to the open staircase leading to the VIP rooms. Not a word passes between us as I guide her up the stairs. We approach the room at the end of the hall, and the assigned personal host—who doubles as security—opens the door for us. Leading Madison into the room, I dismiss him as I usher her inside.

The VIP suites exude the same opulence as downstairs. Plush leather couches surround a sleek, mirrored stage bathed in soft, golden light. Music plays from the hidden speakers—much softer than the booming songs playing in the main room. Cinnamon and vanilla lightly scent the air—aromas that my research has found encourage spending. The recently dismissed personal host was our final detail for these luxurious rooms. The discreet service offering top-shelf bottle service and premium cigars, ensuring guests are afforded uninterrupted indulgence in their personal performances.

Shutting the door behind us, I finally let her go. She turns to face me, crossing her arms over her bare chest. Her cheeks are flushed, but her dark eyes are as sharp as glass. Huffing softly, she tightens her arms folded across her chest as she studies me in the low golden light of the VIP suite. Her expression is hard to read—half amused, half assessing—still guarded and sharp.

"Well..." she remarks coolly. "What do you want?"

I tilt my head, letting the silence sit between us for a moment before stepping forward, close enough to catch the faint scent of her perfume. It's warm and sweet with a hint of spice—orange and cinnamon, maybe. "I want to be the man who gets Raven's first private dance."

That earns me a quirk of her brow. Her lips twitch, barely breaking into a smile for a nanosecond. "First dances are expensive."

I lean back in the middle of the leather couch and casually spread my arms along the top. "Did I ask for a discount?"

She holds my gaze for a second longer, not saying a word as she steps toward me—her hips swaying gently with the slow, sensual beat of the music softly filling the room. She slides into my lap with the same self-assurance she had on stage. Raven isn't only confident, she is in complete control.

Her touches are careful but deliberate, and she moves against me with the throbbing rhythm of the bass. She doesn't merely grind on my lap—she *performs*. Every movement has a purpose and lingers just long enough to leave me begging for more. Resting against my chest, she rolls her body against mine. With her head on my shoulder, I gravelly whisper, "When you said I'd be seeing plenty of you, this isn't quite what I had in mind."

She pushes from my chest and swirls her hips over my lap as she glances at me over her shoulder with a devilish glint in her eyes. *Fuck...* "Isn't it?" she husks seductively, grinding her ass firmly against my hardening cock. "Because it sure feels exactly like what you had in mind."

A deep chuckle rises from low in my throat. "You like being a brat, don't you?"

"I like being paid," she emphasizes with a sweet but wicked edge. Her movements become more playful, and her smirks more daring. This is no longer just a performance, and we both know it—this is flirtatious. The song ends, and she rises from me. "Time's up, Mr. King."

Breaking all the rules, I wrap my hands around her waist and drag her back into my lap. "We're not done yet, firecracker."

"It's your dollar." She shifts her weight, climbing from me just enough to turn and straddle my thighs. Tracing a finger over the buttons of my shirt, she asks, "You always this bossy?"

"Only when I'm truly interested," I reply. "Which isn't often."

Her lashes flutter slightly, but she ignores my confession.

By the third song, her fingers are laced in my hair. She's riding my lap so seductively, I can't help but imagine her sliding over my cock. Chewing at her lower lip as she continues to teasingly circle her hips—barely brushing against my rock-hard cock. "Is that how you like it, Daddy?" That one fucking word nearly causes me to lose all of my resolve, and I fist the top of the leather couch to keep from putting my hands on her again. When she sees my reaction, she smirks—clearly pleased with herself.

"You're enjoying this way too much," I gruff.

"You're paying for it," she playfully shoots back. Her face brushes against mine, and her lips dust the shell of my ear. "I'm just giving you what you want," she whispers, her warm breath blowing against my skin.

My voice, low and firm, I disclose, "I want you."

The music winds down, and she slowly pulls away. Standing before me, she redresses with assuredness, well aware of how much power she holds in here. I reach into my pocket and pull out a folded stack of bills, more than enough to cover my dances and a generous tip, and offer it to her. She takes it without hesitation, grinning wide. "Tempting, but I have a firm rule."

I rise from the couch, closing the distance between us. Towering over her, I ask, "Which is?"

With the bills still in her hand, she lightly fists the front of my shirt to lift herself onto her toes. Leaning in, she softly exhales against my jaw, "Sorry, Daddy... but I don't sleep with clients." She pulls back slowly, revealing a devilish grin. Her eyes not once leaving mine, she lowers herself onto her heels and walks toward the door. Her hand on the knob, she adds, "Or my boss."

Before I can say a word, she turns and steps out into the hallway, swaying like she knows I'm watching every step. Which I am. Madison Roark is nothing like I expected—she's so much more. *And earning her is going to be fucking fun.*

He's watching me.

I feel it before I even step back onto the main floor again. His heavy stare cuts through the lights, tracking my every step like I'm the only woman in the room. I don't have to look at the owners' booth to know he's there. I've seen him watching since my first set tonight—his tall frame, golden eyes, the subtle way his jaw clenched when I laughed too long with someone else.

Cillian fucking King.

I didn't plan to end up in his lap tonight. But when he pulled me through the crowd with *that* look—the one that said I was already his—I let him. I danced. I teased. I leaned in close enough to smell the bourbon on his exhales and feel the desire in his heated breaths on my skin.

And then I walked away.

Because I had to.

I'm not about to ruin my life just to be another name he forgets by the morning.

Still, I haven't been able to shake the warmth of his hands gripping my waist and yanking me back onto his lap. Or the way he grew—*impressively*—hard beneath me as I danced for him. And God help me, I liked it.

It's been hours since the VIP suite, and I have some finance guy's face practically buried in my tits as I ride his lap. But all I can think about is Cillian. I can feel him watching—his eyes burning through the crowd as I pretend to be interested in the man asking if I do "private parties." Keeping my perfectly rehearsed smile in place, I laugh flirtatiously. I lean in and whisper the answer he wants to hear—something that sounds like a maybe, but definitely isn't.

Mr. Finance slips a couple of hundreds and his business card a little too deep into my thong as I slide from his lap. I only make it a few feet before one of his friends requests the same attention. I wink at him and climb onto his lap. He rather overtly solicits me—with quite a striking amount of money —for an Eiffel Tower with his friend. Much like the raging erection beneath me, I try to ignore it. I focus on the job, making money, keeping boundaries, and staying professional.

My gaze wanders behind the man I'm dancing for, where I find Cillian's heated stare on me. Still watching, his jaw is tight and only emphasizing his disapproving scowl. His eyes on me are impossible to ignore. Not pulling my stare from him, I ride the sleaze like I'm trying to earn a thousand-dollar tip.

It's fine... I try to tell myself this is good. If he's this interested in watching me, it means he wants something. *Me.* The more he wants me—and the less I give him—the more power I have to get what I want out of this job. So, I'll flirt and tease, and keep him on the hook until I'm ready to play my card.

I spend the night keeping my distance from Cillian as I make the rounds—dances, drinks, and polite smiles as I am subjected to deplorable conversations and wandering hands. All the while, the heat of his eyes never leaves my body. And even worse? Part of me doesn't want it to.

When I slip behind the velvet curtain that separates the performers from the customers, I'm pleased to find the dressing room finally quiet. Most of the girls are packing up—stuffing wads of cash into their purses and throwing on hoodies and sweats—or already halfway out the door. Some are still buzzing from the night, riding the high that comes with easy money. Others look straight-up exhausted.

I drop into the chair at my station. Being careful of my lash extensions, I start ridding myself of Raven—the glitter on my cheeks, the red lipstick I reapplied more times than I can count, and the thick black liner that makes my eyes look sharper. Bit by bit, she disappears beneath the makeup remover and the soft scratch of the cotton rounds, until what's left in the mirror is just me. Madison Roark. A very tired, wired, and deeply unsettled Madison Roark. Less than a week in this city, and I don't recognize myself already. Not fully, anyway.

After throwing on joggers and an oversized hoodie, I shove the last of my cash and essentials into my duffel bag. Most of the girls have already gone, and the building is relatively quiet when I slip out the back.

Stepping into the alley, the city feels still, uncomfortably so. Still feeling eyes on me, I anxiously glance over my shoulder as I hastily make my way toward the subway station down the block. I make it just in time to hop into a car before the train pulls away from the station. Keeping my hooded head down, I pretend to be enthralled in the music playing softly on my AirPods.

There are only a few others in the car with me—a sleeping couple, a man muttering to himself, and a girl scrolling on her phone. Not one of them looks at me twice. I'm invisible again, and maybe that should feel safe. But it doesn't.

Swiping through my messages, I read through the texts from Mom.

MOM

Haven't heard from you in a couple of days? Everything good?

I know… But I'm your mother, it's my job to worry about you.

Just let me know you're okay. I love you.

Just getting used to the new apartment and the new job. Totally not an upcoming episode of Forensic Files. I love you.

I don't wait for a response before closing out the text messaging app. At this time in the morning, I'm certain she's asleep—and probably has been for at least a few hours. I pull up my Cillian King note app, and read the two bullet points I left myself before adding a third.

Don't let him get the upper hand.

It's just after three a.m. when I finally step into my apartment. The door clicks shut behind me, and I lean against it for a second, letting the silence settle into my bones. I drop my bag by the wall and kick off my sneakers, then move toward the bathroom through the dim space.

I run the water—steaming, punishing hot—and the mirror fogs up almost instantly. Quickly, I strip from my clothes, letting the hoodie and joggers fall to the floor in a heap. When I sink into the tub, the heat stings at first, then soothes my aching muscles. I lower my body all the way in, until only my face is above the surface. It feels like a baptism, like maybe if I sit still long enough, I'll sweat Cillian out of me.

But it doesn't work. Alone with nothing but my thoughts, I can't stop thinking about him. There was something different about the way he touched me—lightly, but with intent—like it meant something. And that's what scares me.

I know men like him. *Hell, at this point, I should have an honorary PhD in cocky alphahole.* Born into power. Fed on privilege. Hardened by the weight of it. Men like him don't ask. They take what they want. But Cillian... Something about him is different. Calculated, sure. Dangerous, definitely. But there was something in his eyes when I turned him down. Not anger. Not entitlement. *Curiosity?* Like I'd surprised him. Maybe not giving him what he wanted and was expecting only further grabbed his attention and fueled his interest.

The bathwater grows cool, and my resolve fades. I pull the drain and stand, wrapping myself in a towel. I'm beyond ready for bed, but my brain is still far too loud for sleep. Instead of climbing beneath the sheets, I slip into an old T-shirt and pour myself a glass of cheap white wine. I curl up on my small loveseat beneath the living room window, tucking my knees to my chest and pulling the throw blanket up as I stare out at the city beyond my window.

I can't help but wonder what Cillian is doing... I wonder if he's home and still thinking about me. *Fuck, Madison... What the hell is wrong with you?* This isn't who I am. I don't get distracted. I don't fantasize. I don't wonder *what if* about men with sharp suits and smoother lies. Still, I can't help but imagine his hands again—warm and strong, resting right where they shouldn't be. The way he looked at me in that private room, like I was the only person who existed in his world.

I sigh and take another slow sip of wine from the glass sweating in my hand.

This is not going to end well.

The club feels is still humming beneath the surface, like it's alive and breathing. It's only been open one night, and already it seems to be a raging success. The air is thick with perfume, sweat, and the sharp tang of champagne mixed with money. Upstairs in the VIP suites, a few girls are wrapping up with the high-rollers who wouldn't leave without one last dance—and a denial of requests they'll never get fulfilled here. The cleanup crew is already moving through the club like shadows, collecting glassware and brushing glitter from tabletops.

When the last drunk bastard stumbles out the door, the house lights up as the music dies down; King's Temptation is quiet again. It's just us—me and my brothers watching the last flickers of neon pulsing against the black marble floors

Enzo leans against the edge of the bar, rolling his sleeves up with that smugness he wears when he knows something went well. "Not a bad first night," he boasts, eyeing the tally sheets. "Six figures on paper. More off. We're already making money hand over fist."

Thumbing through receipts beside him, Nikolai lets out a pleased sigh. "Two of the booths paid cash straight out. The VIP suite room didn't even ask for change of ten grand. *That's* the kind of clientele we need more of."

"Judge Ralston showed," I share, scanning the now-empty VIP balcony above. "I had Scarlet keep him company."

Enzo whistles low. "He's got some vigor left in him for a man of his age."

"He left smiling," I mutter. "Next time, we make sure he walks out owing us a favor."

"He'll owe us plenty." Nikolai's eyes flick to mine. "He already reserved a VIP suite for next week."

"He liked Scarlet that much, huh?"

"No." Nik shakes his head and arches a condescending brow at me. "He wanted to ensure the most coveted dancer of the night wouldn't be tied up all evening again." My jaw clenches at his words, even though I shouldn't care. But, of course, it's her. *Raven. Madison.* Whatever name she's using when she sets men on fire without touching a match to them.

The three of us finish up, leaving the aftermath of opening night chaos to the well-qualified staff we hired. When we step outside, my Aston Martin is already waiting at the curb for us. The three of us slide into the car, and I glance in the rearview mirror. "Did you get the footage I asked for?"

Nikolai nods. "Sent it just before we left." His expression sharpens with interest. "Do I even want to know?"

Enzo raises an eyebrow. "Footage? What footage?"

"Raven's dances," Nikolai answers without looking at me, his tone flat. "Every one she did tonight, including in the VIP suite." I shoot him a displeased glare in the rearview mirror at his overshare, but it does nothing to stop him from talking. "Please tell me I'm not going to spend what's left of this night *listening* to you watch her give you a lap dance on repeat like some obsessed teenager."

Enzo snickers from the passenger seat, a smug smirk spreading across his face as he mimics jacking off.

"That's *not* what it's for," I bark, more tightly than I intend. Nikolai and Enzo both give me *that* look. They know me too well, but they also know when not to push. The rest of our short ride home is filled with financial details and small security concerns that need to be addressed.

After letting Enzo out on the floor below us, Nik and I head into our shared penthouse. It's cold and far too quiet after the loud evening at the club. I head upstairs and shed my shirt the second I'm through my bedroom door—already annoyed with the spicy citrus scent of her perfume still clinging to the fabric. It's ingrained in my skin, too—like a fucking ghost. *No wonder I can't stop thinking about her.* I drop the shirt to the floor and strip off my pants as I head for the shower.

The water scalds my skin, but I don't care. I stand beneath the spray with my skin burning red, my thoughts still racing a hundred miles an hour. The echo of her voice in my head like a song I can't get rid of as I rerun every second of her perfect body pressed to mine, every smirk and fleeting glance when she knew she had my attention. *Because she did... All fucking night.*

When I finally step out, towel off, and pull on a pair of loose lounge pants, I feel no better than I did when I walked through my front door. Still wired. Still restless. Still thinking about her. I sit on the edge of the bed, grab my phone from the nightstand, and pull up the footage.

Nikolai labeled each clip clearly: Raven - Main Stage, Raven - Booth 6, Raven - VIP Suite 7. I tap the last one. *There she is.* It's surreal, watching it play out from above, me sitting lounging against the back of the couch like I'm in control, when I damn well wasn't. She had me the second she climbed onto my lap and looked at me like she couldn't care less how badly I wanted—*no, want*—her.

Only, I can't stop watching her. I watch clip after clip, zooming in on her face and memorizing every inch of her sun-kissed skin before returning to footage of the two of us in the VIP suite. There's a moment, a fleeting second where she smiles, and her eyes betray her. Just a flicker. The smallest crack. But the truth behind her mask. I saw it, even at the time —it just didn't quite register. She was really smiling. Not working, performing, or pretending to be enjoying herself, but genuinely smiling as she flirted with me.

I tap through the other clips, watching them again, and noticing she's different with the clients—not less seductive, but less present. Her laughs are shallow, not bubbling over her lips. She's still flawless and lethal, but completely disconnected. Unlike how she is with me: sharp, alive, and real.

I sit there far longer than I should, cycling through the footage, slowing it down, watching for every small reaction.

Every twitch of her lips. Every breath. That fucking sway of her hips I can't tear my eyes from. I study her like I'm trying to solve her. *Maybe I am.*

The sky is already beginning to lighten, and the sunrise creeps into my room. Yet, I'm still wide awake. After opening the other folder Nik emailed me, I skim through her tiny human resources file until I find what I need. I type her number into my phone. I shouldn't. I fucking know I shouldn't, but my fingers move on their own. I type a single message—no name, no greeting. If she wants to play games with me, she can figure it out for herself. I hesitate for a moment and then press send before tossing the phone onto the bed.

I pull the blackout curtains and climb between the sheets, hoping to get a few hours of sleep. Instead, I lay with my head on the pillow, waiting for her response.

CHAPTER 9
madison

My phone buzzes on the coffee table, its vibration cutting through the silence in the apartment and abruptly waking me from my sleep. The sound is sharp against the quiet hum of early morning traffic outside my window. I blink, groggily. The sky glows faintly, violet and ash streaks of dawn fading as they're overtaken by the early morning sun.

I must've dozed off.

My neck aches, stiff from the awkward angle I'd fallen asleep in. Sitting up, the soft throw blanket slides from my shoulder, and the half-empty wine glass still in my hand sloshes dangerously. I set it carefully on the coffee table and rub at my eyes, still heavy from my slumber. When I lift the phone, I expect it to be my mother—again—probably to check if I remembered to lock the door when I got home.

But the number flashing on the screen isn't hers. Instead, it's from an unknown number.

UNKNOWN

You look better when you aren't pretending to smile.

My breath catches in my throat as recognition immediately pulses through me. There's no name, but I know exactly who it's from—that smug, arrogant man. Even through the sterile light of the phone screen, my body reacts to him. I can practically feel his presence sliding over my skin and his warm breath blowing behind my ear. I reread the text, and picture him sitting in a penthouse apartment—shirtless, brooding, and impatiently waiting for my response.

Why is he shirtless in your thoughts, Madison?

Because I can't help myself, my thumbs slide over the screen as though they have a mind of their own. I smirk at the three words—pleased with myself—and hit send.

You tipped better.

The dots appear immediately.

He really was waiting for my reply.

So it was the money that made you smile, then?

I chuckle, stretching out my legs and pulling the throw blanket back around my chest. My lips curve as I type back.

It's adorable that you pretend it surprises you.

He doesn't respond right away, and for a second, I think I might've bruised his ego. I'm about to put my phone down when the familiar three dots reappear on the screen.

No…

Adorable was that sound you made when you pressed against me and whispered, 'Daddy.'

Heat spikes across my cheeks. My lips part in disbelief, and I actually look around my empty apartment like someone else might be witnessing my embarrassment. The memory he referenced flashes bright behind my eyes. The clench of his jaw as he fisted the plush leather of the couch, and his excitement twitched beneath me.

Fuck… He's shameless.

I roll my eyes and rise from the loveseat, padding barefoot to the kitchen. The cool hardwood floor causes my toes to curl. I pour the wine down the sink, quickly rinse the glass, and fill it with icy tap water. Taking a generous gulp, I try to cool the sudden warmth in my chest.

He is far too smooth and confident. It's not fair for the rest of humanity to even call what he does flirting. I'd bet money he could teach a masterclass on how to incinerate women's panties.

My phone buzzes again, pulling me from my thoughts.

Tell me, Madison. That rule of yours… Is it one you're willing to break?

I lean on the counter, wine glass still in hand. Him using my real name does something to me. I shouldn't care that he's interested in me—not Raven—but I do. I stare at the screen for a moment longer before slowly typing back my reply.

> Client rule. Boss rule. Take your pick. Both are still in effect.

His reply is instant.

> So if I fire you, does that solve the problem?

I snort, loudly and unguardedly. My laughter echoes throughout my tiny apartment. Of course that's his solution. *Just erase the boundary.* He's ridiculous.

> I'm not that easy, Mr. King.

> But you are that tempting.

> And again, it's Cillian.

> ...or Daddy, since it sounds so sweet when you say it.

I chew the inside of my cheek, staring at his words—my pulse skipping, and my stomach flopping. Every fiber of my being is screaming that I should stop this. *Put down the phone, Madison. Walk away before this goes too far.*

> Bold of you to assume you've earned that privilege, Mr. King.

> Such a bratty mouth...

Damn him. He doesn't miss a beat.

> Since you like it, you're going to love hearing me keep telling you no.

This time, he doesn't reply right away. I sip my glass of water and find that suddenly *I'm* the one waiting impatiently for a response.

> You danced for several men after me. If it's a no, answer me this…

> Why am I the one you're texting at sunrise?

Because you watched me all night like you wanted to ruin me.

Because when you touched me, I didn't feel bought—I felt seen.

Because, as much as I shouldn't, I like the way you talk to me.

> Because you have my number.

His dots appear. Stop. And appear again.

> You know that brattiness of yours is going to get you in trouble, right?

> With who?

> Your Daddy.

> I have it on good authority, he doesn't like bratting.

I go still—the breath leaving my lungs. As I curl back up into the loveseat, I pull my knees to my chest and notice that my heart is hammering like I've just run a half marathon. My thumbs hover over the screen, but this time he's actually left me speechless.

His dots appear, but his reply is much slower. *He's thinking…*

> I like watching you, Madison.

Though his words should be creepy, they're not. I tilt my head back and stare at the ceiling.

Who is this man?

> I won't be at the club for a few nights, but be a good girl.

> Because I WILL be watching.

CHAPTER 10
madison

I move through the low-ceilinged back corridors of the club with sweat-damp hair pinned loosely at my neck and my heart still racing from my last stage dance. The air here is stale, thick with the mixed scents of everyone's perfumes and the deep echo of the bass that never stops. It's already been a long shift, but at only ten, there are still quite a few hours to go. I pull my sheer halter top tighter and run a hand over the curve of my hip, feeling the fabric ride up slightly as I give my makeup a quick check in the mirror.

Pleased with my appearance, I head back into the club. My steps stutter slightly when I spot Cillian in the owners' booth. He didn't lie—it has been days since I've seen him. Actually, it's been days since I've heard from him at all. He's been completely silent since our sunrise text exchange after opening night. With the complete lack of communication, I've been wondering if maybe he'd finally gotten the message and was backing off.

I was wrong...

His eyes lock on me as I step onto the stage for my third dance. Holding his stare, I strut toward the pole and grip it firmly. Pushing my ass out, I slide down the pole—slow and sensual. Cillian leans forward, his gaze is still—fixed and unblinking— as he watches me. He undoes the top buttons of his crisp navy shirt, loosening the collar, before rolling the sleeves up to his elbows. I'm so focused on him, I forget to engage with the men surrounding the stage. I dance for Cillian.

The music swells as I wrap my leg around the cool metal and slide my hands apart. After pushing from the floor, I ballerina-spin around the pole. My body moves without thought, arching as I gracefully place my toes onto the stage to stop my spin. My heart is pounding, but this time it isn't solely from the effort I'm exerting. I'm so engrossed in Cillian that I barely notice my song coming to an end. It isn't until Britney joins me on stage and reaches for the pole that I realize my set is over.

I step into the shadows and walk the long route toward the bar for a bottle of water. There's a strange pressure in the air tonight, and it's not just Cillian. The club feels tense. Security is much heavier than usual, positioned throughout the club and guarding doors that don't typically require guarding. Enzo King passes through the crowd not far from me, grousing into his phone with a low, clipped voice.

When I'm walking past the owners' booth, Cillian flashes me a quick smile before diverting his attention to Nikolai King and the men he's approaching with. All of them are dressed a tad too tacky—cheap, flashy suits that are trying far too hard—to be the type of clientele this club draws. They slide into the seats of the owners' booth. Almost immediately, a couple of girls provide bottle service and stay to sit on the laps of the King brothers' guests.

One of the regulars demands my attention as I wait for the bartender to assist me. Painting my well-practiced faux smile on, I bat my eyelashes and give him what he wants. I promise him a private dance in VIP and excuse myself to change into the lacy outfit I know he likes—the one that results in a large enough tip to cover a month's worth of rent. Toying with his tie as I turn away from him, I'm surprised to find the owners' booth has emptied so suddenly.

As I pass by yet another security guard, I make my way into the back of the club. I turn the corner into the staff corridor and freeze mid-step when I hear what sounds like a rather heated conversation coming from down the hall. Nikolai's voice is the first I recognize—deep and slightly irritated. Ensuring I'm quiet, I move closer toward the light. Heavily-accented voices spill through the slightly cracked door at the end of the hall.

Enzo answers in the same short tone I heard earlier, —"We are the ones taking all the risks. If the cops were to stroll in here right now, we're going to jail, and you're just some poor drunk bastard that wandered into the wrong room."

Nikolai adds, "The minute you're out the door, I'll scrub the security footage and erase any evidence you were ever here."

The way they talk—like they've done this a dozen times—tells me this isn't a fluke. Whatever this deal is, it isn't some one-time risk. It's a system—efficient and clinical.

"Just the weapons this time?" Cillian asks, his tone sounding more a confirmation than a question. I don't hear an answer before he continues, "Half rifles. Half compacts. Mix of US and Russian stock. One crate of suppressors. All of it clean—no scratches, no serials, no heat."

"Unfortunately, an accident on the FDR has delayed tonight's delivery. It'll be about an hour later than we had planned," Nikolai informs the room.

"I informed our security the moment we knew," Cillian's familiar voice flits into the hall. "They'll keep the staff and our guests away from the deal."

"You guys okay to wait an hour?" Enzo asks.

Shoes scuff against the floor, and I suck in a startled deep breath, worried I'm going to get caught somewhere I *definitely* shouldn't be. A deep, mature voice—with an accent I can't quite place—mutters something in Spanish and chuckles deeply before responding, "I'm sure we can find something to occupy the time."

"What's your poison?" Nikolai asks, his voice moving closer to the door.

I step away as he receives his answer. "Thin, good fucking tits, pretty, brunette, and young."

They pull open the door as I step into the side hall that leads toward the dancers' dressing room. I lean against the cool wall, close my eyes, and let out the breath I didn't realize I was holding.

Their footsteps echo in the confined space as they walk toward me as Enzo chirps, "I'm pretty sure you'll love Rav—"

"No," Cillian barks his interruption before clearing his throat and softening his tone. "She wasn't feeling well and went home early."

Nikolai glances down the hallway I'm standing in. A smirk pulls at his lips, and he arches an inquisitive brow when his gaze falls on me. He slaps Cillian on the back, drawing his attention to where I stand. Fighting back laughter, he teasingly scoffs, "So, Raven went home sick, huh?"

My heart hammers as I breathe through my nose and scrunch my face in faux confusion. Cillian stares at me, striding past without so much as flinching at being caught in his own lie. He's so calm, moving through his dark world, like a man who doesn't have to answer to anyone. It's a stark contrast to the way he interacts with me—impulsive and reckless. I wait for their footsteps to disappear into the noisy depths of the club before pushing myself from my perch against the wall.

Tucking my hands into the curve of my waist and keeping my head down, I rush down the short corridor. I step into the bright glow of the dressing room, avoiding eye contact with the guard posted just inside the door when I pass through. Quickly, I take a seat at my station and lift my tube of red lipstick, only then do I notice that my hand is trembling. I squeeze the gold tube harder and wrap my other hand over it in an attempt to steady my nerves.

Everyone assumes the danger in a place like this comes from the men who touch too long or don't take no for an answer. They don't see the ones who are *always* the real threat—the quiet ones in charge. The ones who never raise their voices because they don't need to. The dangerous men running back-alley deals in secret.

Regaining my composure, I touch up my lipstick and reapply a fair amount of shimmer to my cheeks and collarbones. I stare at my reflection and swallow hard as I take a deep breath. Exhaling, I watch my face morph—my fake smile spreading across it like a mask.

The rest of my shift passes like usual—lap dances, wandering hands, inappropriate offers, and one surprising marriage proposal, promising to give me a better life. The latter is a lie I've never once seen turn out well for any of the girls who've accepted such an offer. I am beyond ready to leave for the night by the time two a.m. rolls around. I briskly walk down the hall to change and grab my things. Half the hallway lights have already been turned off, and the narrow corridor is much darker than usual. But I don't need the glowing overhead flourescents to see Cillian is there—I can feel him.

He steps from the shadow like he's been waiting for me. He doesn't say a word. Doesn't smile. His gaze holds mine for a moment before his eyes rake down my body. I'm far too tired, physically and mentally, to play with him tonight. I keep walking without the faintest ease of my pace, not wanting to give him my attention. As I pass, his fingers brush along the small of my back, light, almost absent, but completely intentional.

I tense briefly—unsure if it's a warning for eavesdropping or a thank-you for playing into his lie—and painfully fight the urge to glance over my shoulder to find out. "Good night, Madison," he mutters, barely above a whisper as I leave him in the hall. Those three words are all it takes to almost make me break my resolve and give him what he wants. Almost.

CHAPTER 11
cillian

I shouldn't have touched her. Not that first night. Not last night. And I definitely shouldn't want to feel her skin against mine again tonight, yet here I am... Desperate to have the delicious citrus of her perfume filling my lungs and clinging to my clothes again.

Fuck.

Moving across the floor like a shadow, I ignore the women who are trying to catch my attention and the men who nod respectfully or out of fear—some mix of both. I don't stop for any of them. I need a drink, something to burn the thoughts of her from my mind. Something to kill the slow, feral ache growing in my chest. After slipping behind the bar, I pour a few fingers of whiskey into a tumbler, ignoring the bartender's raised brow—he knows better than to comment.

"Everything good, Cian?" Nikolai's voice cuts through the low thrum of the music from beside me. His shirt sleeves are rolled up to his elbows, his black tie loosened, and a grin tugging at the corner of his mouth.

"Fucking peachy," I answer dryly.

His eyes narrow. "So... that dancer..."

"Which one?" I ask, diverting his line of questioning because I know exactly who he means.

"You really need me to say it?" Nikolai smirks. "She got under your skin at the bar, but you're watching her like a fucking addict."

He might be quiet, but fuck... he's always two steps ahead. My face contorted in a scowl, I shoot him a warning look. "You got something to say?"

"Hey... Not judging"—he raises both hands in mock surrender, waving a white bar towel in one of them—"She's... well... She's something fucking else."

"She's just a dancer."

"She's not *just* anything," Enzo adds, appearing on my other side, sipping a Negroni.

I glance between the two of them, noticing that we have garnered the attention of the bar-back and at least two of the customers across from me. "This isn't the place for this conversation."

I head toward the owners' booth, my boots heavy against the polished black floors, just like my thoughts. Security parts the velvet rope as I approach. I sink into the velvet chair at the end, as far away from the buzz of the club as I can get. Enzo and Nikolai follow, because, of course, they do.

"We don't keep secrets from one another," Enzo admonishes, taking the seat beside me. *That's rich...* As though I have no control over them, I roll my eyes at him. "Except *that*. And I apologized. And you know I fucking love her." I can't argue with him, because I know with certainty he's going to make himself my brother-in-law as well as my brother-in-arms sooner rather than later.

"Don't pretend you're not already involved with her." Nikolai chuckles. Everything in this place—every light, every curve of marble and velvet, every dancer, song, and smile—it's all calculated and controlled. A machine we've built to serve a very specific purpose: indulgence for the wealthy, sanctuary for the corrupt, and a perfect mask for laundering the bloody money on our hands. There's no room for distractions—especially petite brunette ones with lips I want to taste and curves I can't stop thinking about running my hands over. As though he can read my thoughts, he goes on, "Between the way you look at her and your obsession with her security footage, she's clearly something to you."

"She's not—" I stop myself, because denying it feels stupid. And they're both already staring at me with knowing smirks. They know me. Better than anyone. They're not just my friends. They're my brothers. They've seen what I do when I get obsessed with something. *Or someone.* They've both been watching me unravel since the first night Madison stepped on our stage—both of them would need to be blind not to see that Madison has clearly gotten under my skin.

And more so, I *am* obsessed. *Completely and utterly...* My compulsion has ventured well past watching security footage. I've delved into her past. She's smart and educated—and could be doing so much more with her life than working the pole, giving drunks lap dances, and having strange men slipping bills into her panties. She's better than this life. *Better than **my** life...* She doesn't belong here. *But fuck, she fits in seamlessly well.*

"Deny it all you want," Enzo interrupts my thoughts, "but it's obvious as fuck to everyone in here."

Fuck...

She finishes a lap dance on the main floor, and I cross the room before she has a chance to get involved with another customer. I place my hand on her shoulder as I approach, and she startles slightly. "We need to talk."

She spins around, staring up at me with big, dark, unreadable eyes and exclaims, "Now!?"

"Yes." My response is firm, not offering any opportunity for discussion.

With a slight shrug of her shoulders and an overt roll of her eyes, she lets out a heavy breath. "Fine."

The simplest of requests, and it's met with bratty defiance. She's the first person I've met in a long time—*excluding my sister*—who has the gall to constantly push back to practically everything I say. It's aggravating as hell, but she challenges me, and part of me loves that nothing with her is easy.

I steer her toward the hallway near the DJ booth and past the heavy doors that lead to a private stairwell. Beside it is a small office that we barely use—soundproof and windowless. I unlock the door and gesture for her to go inside. For a moment, she looks at me curiously before stepping into the small room. After pushing the door shut behind us, I lean against it and fold my arms across my chest. The tension between us in this confined space is palpable. She slowly turns to face me. "You shouldn't be here," I mutter.

Madison raises a brow and snarks, "Here... as in this room? Or here, as in the club?"

"Both," I exhale.

"That's not your call."

"The fuck it's not," I unintentionally raise my voice at her resistance.

She crosses her arms in response. "Fine. It's your club. If you don't want me here, then fucking fire me."

"I don't want you fired," I grit.

She sucks in a deep breath. "Then what *do* you want, Cillian?"

I love the way my name sounds rolling off her tongue. It's sinful, and I want to hear it again—only louder, screaming it as she comes with those long legs wrapped around my waist. *Fuck... Reel it in, Cillian.* "I want to know what the fuck you're doing." I rush forward before I can stop myself, and for the first time, her armor falters. She cowers ever so slightly before quickly regaining her confident demeanor.

Lifting her chin and refusing to back down, she insists, "I'm working."

"The way you dance, you could've worked anywhere." I shake my head, quickly losing myself in her dark eyes. "And who in their right mind busts their ass to earn a dual master's in Psychology and International Studies to work the fucking pole?"

Her eyes widen at my confession that I've dug into her past beyond the minimal information she listed on her résumé. "If you must know, this pays a lot more," she sasses. "I'm fucking good at it. I might as well take full advantage of this body I was given."

I stare down at her, my breathing growing heavy. "This place is a house of wolves. And you walked in with a sweet smile… All defenseless and acting like these men wouldn't bite."

"*They* didn't bite," she firmly insists before softening her voice. "*You* did."

I exhale, slow and ragged.

She's right.

"I'm trying to protect you," I respond, finally.

She laughs, and I can't miss the animosity in it. "From what? This place? Your world? Or *you*?" I don't answer, because I'm not certain anymore. I step closer, and this time, she doesn't move. Reaching out, I brush her hair from her face, my fingers lingering at her temple. Her breath stutters. *She might be denying it, but she wants this.* I can see it in the tight line of her jaw and the way her gaze keeps dropping to my mouth.

"I don't play games," I confess softly.

"That's a lie," she whispers with a slight smirk, her tone nearly playful.

"Not with you. I think I've been pretty clear about what I want. I'm desperately trying to respect that you don't want what I do."

She swallows hard and gestures at the small space between us. "Then what is this?"

"It's a line," I clarify. "One I'm fighting not to cross, but you're making it fucking impossible."

She leans in just enough that her words blow over my jaw. "Then why does it feel like you already did?"

"Because I did." Hell, I ran past it the moment I grabbed her wrist and dragged her away from men willing to spend a fortune for a minute of her time. And I want to go even further, but I know how this ends. My world swallows innocent women like her whole. My mom and Eavan are a testament to how bleak it can be for them. I lost one far too soon and did deplorable things to save the other. I can be the monster who ruins her or the one she's afraid of. Those are the only options—there is no middle ground—and they both feel like she loses. There is no safe option to allow myself the indulgence of her, but I'm so fucking selfish in my need for her that, at this moment, I don't care.

I'm going to fucking destroy her...

My hand trails down the side of her face, and I wrap it around her throat. "The dances. The texting. Even this," I gravelly whisper, using the firm hold around her slender neck to walk her backward until she is pressed as firmly against the door as I am to her. She stares up at me, her pouty lips parted just enough to be inviting. "They aren't shit compared to what I'm thinking about right now." Leaning in until I'm a breath from kissing her, I continue, "Or what you are."

CHAPTER 12
madison

The coolness of the door is jarring against my bare skin. My breath hitches, and I'm uncertain whether it's from the icy steel at my back or the way his declaration rippled down my spine.

I don't breathe. At least, not properly. Not in a way that reaches my lungs. I can't, with his fingers laced around my throat and his heated breaths feathering over my mouth. With him this close, I don't know if I'm frozen in fear or in want.

The line between us has grown so fucking thin, you probably need a microscope to find it.

His fingers, wrapped around my neck, aren't pressing or tight. They're controlled, not forceful. They're desire wrapped in reverence, it's dominance. He's touching me like I'm already his, like he's trying to memorize the way I feel in his hands before he pushes this moment too far.

And God, I want him to.

His eyes not leaving mine, he stares down at me with the insistence of someone who knows what surrender looks like—waiting for a sign of mine. My heart is pounding so loudly, I'm certain he can hear it as clearly as I can. He definitely can feel it thudding beneath his fingertips.

I tilt my face a fraction toward him, leaving my lips a mere breath from his. A thousand reasons not to race through my thoughts, all shouting at me to stop this and walk away. But they're grossly overshadowed by the lone thought of wondering what his lips will feel like pressed against mine.

Madison... Don't...

My lips brush against his. The dusting flutter is so soft, it barely qualifies as a kiss. "We shouldn't..." I whisper. But even as I say it, I know it's already too late.

His whiskey-scented breath blows over my lips as he parts his. "Then tell me to stop." Each word vibrates against my trembling lower lip, and every bit of resolve washes from me. Internally, I scream at myself to be smart. *Don't throw it all away for one measly kiss.* But my hands betray me. They fist into the fabric of his shirt, crisp and still warm from the heat of his body. My fingers curl so tightly, it's like I'm drowning and he's the only thing that can pull me to the surface.

We crash together, our mouths meeting with hunger and defiance. His lips are demanding and desperate, like he's waited years for this moment, not days. I kiss him back with every ounce of fight in my soul. Not gently. Not cautiously. Nothing about this is slow or sweet. It's reckless and wild—

nothing but pure, unadulterated desire. It's everything I've tried to pretend I didn't want.

His tongue plunders my mouth as I moan into his with need, and I let myself forget everything—who I am, where we are, and what this will cost me. I just want to feel. *I just want him.* I don't care about anything except the way he's holding me and claiming my mouth like he can't get enough. Like I've ruined him just by existing. His hands slide to my thighs, and he grips them tightly. He hoists me up, and I instinctively wrap my legs around him .

One of his hands runs over my ribs and along my side, tracing every inch with his palm before roughly kneading at my breast. The other firmly grips my bare ass, holding me in place as he grinds his ever-hardening length against me. *And fuck... it feels good.* My whole body tingles with electricity, and I can barely think.

He drags his tongue up the length of my neck before sucking my earlobe into his mouth. He nips at it with his teeth, and my body reacts without thought—my legs tightening around his waist as a breathy moan rattles from my lungs. Squeezing my thighs, I slide myself along his thick shaft, trying to relieve the ache between them.

My hands slide up his chest and tangle in his thick copper hair. I fist it hard enough to elicit a pleased groan from him. "I knew you weren't a good girl," he teasingly mutters against my neck, his tone low and deep. It sounds so filthy whispered in my ear that it vibrates along my skin and straight to my pussy. His palm slaps against my ass cheek, and I yelp at the sudden, unexpected burn. I grind against him even harder, mewls and whimpers spewing from me uncontrollably as I work myself to the brink. He spanks me again and roughly squeezes the cheek. I grunt with delight as he asks, "But you like how bad girls get treated, don't you?"

"Yes…" I breathlessly moan my response without hesitation. A devilish smirk pulls at the corner of my lips, and I tug roughly at my fistfuls of his hair again, needing more of what I know he'll give me. His hand strikes my skin again with such force that tears well in my eyes, and all I can think is how badly I want him to do it again.

Adding another searing handprint to my already red ass. "Yes, Daddy," he sternly corrects.

"Yes, Daddy," I muster, blinking back tears and teetering on the edge of my release.

"You're so fucking wet that you're soaking through my pants." Thrusting against me, he moans into the crook of my neck, "That's it, firecracker. Come for me."

He roughly squeezes my hot, tender cheek, and I pull back until his hazel eyes are boring through me. My chest heaves, and my lower lip trembles as I stare at the green flecks in his golden pools—the intimacy of his gaze hurling me to the edge. "Let me watch you fall apart." He wraps his free hand around my throat and tightens his fingers. "And then I can watch you break all your rules as you let me sink inside you to pick up the pieces."

His words slice through the near-euphoric haze, and my hands fall from his hair. *This can't happen.* Not here. Not now. Not like this. And definitely not with him. I plant my palms on his chest, firmly, and push just enough to garner his attention. His body stills immediately with his lips hovering inches from mine. Holding our stare, he loosens his grip.

"I can't..." The words catch in my throat as I slowly unwrap my legs from his waist. Breathless and fumbling to find my footing in my stilettos, I lightly shove him away from me, needing to put distance between us. My fingers slide across my swollen lips as he painfully takes a few steps backward. I can barely look at him, because the sight nearly undoes me. Cillian looks wrecked. His brows are drawn in confusion. His chest rises and falls like he's run a marathon, blowing heavy breaths over his now red-stained lips. Following every move I make, his eyes roam over my body with need.

I can't breathe. I need to get out. Now. Before I change my mind and do something even more stupid. I turn and wrench open the door with such force that it slams into the wall with a sharp echo. My heart in my throat and his handprints painted across my ass, I bolt down the hallway.

"Madison," he calls after me. His voice is pinched, like he's not sure whether to chase me or let me go.

I don't answer. I just run straight into the dressing room. Quickly I kick off my heels and pull on my shorts, an oversized T-shirt, and my sneakers. I push through the side door into the alley and keep walking as the pounding in my chest drowns out the sounds of the bustling city around me. I don't stop until I'm down the block and far from Cillian's sight.

Leaning against a brick wall, the night air is cool against my flushed cheeks. I press my hands to my face and try to slow my breathing. Try to *think*. But there's nothing but *him*—his mouth, his hands, and the way I melted into him like I belonged pressed against his body. And the worst part? I want to go back. I want to race into that room for more. I want him. But giving in to that desire could ruin everything.

I close my eyes and suck in another deep breath, but all I smell is him—spicy musk, heat, and want. Dragging my palms along my face, I groan into them.

What the fuck did you just do, Madison?

I walk home instead of taking the subway—wandering the city streets alone like it'll somehow calm the fire he lit inside me. It doesn't. Instead, it only gives me more time to think about what I've done.

When I finally reach my apartment, I toss my keys into the bowl by the door, strip out of my clothes, and head straight to my bathroom. I step into the icy spray of the shower, but it does nothing to wash him away. As I lean against the tile surround, I close my eyes and swear I can still feel his breath on my neck and his deep voice whispering in my ear. *Come for me... Let me watch you fall apart...*

Pressing my fingers between my thighs, they sink into my still-wet pussy with ease. I work them inside me and over my clit, and I vividly imagine it's his mouth and hands, eager to provide me the release I denied myself. I come fast and hard—breathlessly screaming his name, with my knees buckling. Riding my hand to prolong the euphoria, I hate how much of me aches for more. It was too easy to give in to him, and the worst part is that all I can think about is how badly I want to do it again.

And that's fucking terrifying.

CHAPTER 13
cillian

I stand frozen in the middle of the room, chest heaving like I've been gutted. *Because I have.* Her heels roughly click against the tile floor as she rushes to put space between us, echoing louder than the chaos still ringing in my thoughts. Her sweet, sultry—and fucking addictive—scent still clings to my clothes, and I can still feel the heat of her on my palms. I stare at the empty threshold for what feels like an eternity. "Madison..." I call after her, choking on the single breathy word.

Everything in me wants to follow after her. My body fucking aches to. I could catch her. It wouldn't take much. A few long strides down the hallway and I'd have her pressed up against the nearest wall again—bruising her lips with her legs wrapped around my waist, where they fucking belong. But I don't move, because I know what will happen if I do. I won't stop this time. And neither will she. If I put my hands on her again, we *will* finish what we started.

Crossing the room, I swipe my hand down my face and growl under my breath. I slam the door shut, and the sound reverberates through the room, violent and final. "Fuck!" My hands ball into fists at my side, both of them still tingling. It's not from adrenaline—although that's there too—but from the way she felt in them. The way she moved in my hold, her body begging for more as she surrendered to me. The way her lower lip quivered as she teetered on the brink of coming in my arms.

She wanted it. Fuck... she *needed* it.

I stalk toward the wall and throw my fist into it with a roar, hard enough to put my hand through the drywall. The pain grounds me for a second, maybe two. That's the only reprieve I get before the images of her flood back into my thoughts— sharper and more vivid than before.

Her legs wrapped around me, flexed tight as she ground her slick panties against the throbbing cock beneath my zipper. The slight tug of her fingers tangled in my hair that accompanied every breathy whimper spewing from her parted lips.

With my forearm planted against the wall above the hole I made, I rest my forehead against it. My cock aches, needing more of her. I close my eyes, and the thoughts of her are so real that I can practically feel her pressed against me. An unfettered groan rattles from me as I run my palm over my throbbing cock and find my pants are soaked with her arousal.

Madison flexes her hips and slides her slick, panty-covered pussy along my length. I wrap my fingers around my cock, and I stroke myself through my wet pants, mirroring her movements in my fantasy. *Her lower lip quivers, a breathy scream trembling over it as she falls apart for me.*

Tearing at my zipper, I hastily pull my cock from the confines of my pants and spit into my palm. My fingers circle around my length, and I smear my saliva along my shaft. *I tear her panties to the side and drive into her. I take her hard and fast, her hips meeting each of my brutal thrusts.* I tighten the grip on my cock and fist myself vigorously, needing to rid myself of the need for her. *Madison's lips part, spewing breathy grunts as I repeatedly drive the entirety of myself into her.* "Come for me," I grunt, my stomach taut and my hips thrusting needily to meet my fist.

A scream rises from her lungs, and I crash my lips against hers. Sloppily kissing her mouth and fucking her without abandon, I swallow her bliss as I continue to violently work myself to my own release. "Am I being a good girl for you, Daddy?" she pants through our kiss.

"Yes," I groan, fucking my hand like a crazed man. My moans fill the small room until my cock is pulsing in my hand and the ribbons of my release are splattered over the wall before me. "Fuuuuck..." I drag in a breath, but it does nothing to steady my rapid breathing.

When I tuck my cock back into my pants, I should feel better. But I don't. My hand was a poor substitute for the wet pussy I was so close to being inside of. I rake both hands through my hair and flop onto the office chair behind me—still breathing hard, my cock still as rigid as fucking stone, and wanting her worse now than I did before. I stare at my cum painted across the wall like I'm trying to read fucking tea leaves—trying to solve the answer to the question I've been asking myself since the night I met her.

What the fuck is she doing to me?

I've fucked plenty of women, shamelessly left their beds still warm, and never looked back. *This* isn't that. Madison is not just some girl I can bend over the nearest surface and forget by morning. I've known that since the first second she shot me down—and only been reminded every subsequent time she told me I'm not nearly as charming as I think I am.

I'm not confused about what this is; I'm a fucking wreck because I know. I don't want just one night. I want *her*. I want Madison with all her mess, fire, and complete with smart-ass bratty retorts. I need her sweet whimpers and the way her eyes bore through me as she fights this thing between us. I'm going to watch her fall, even if she claws the whole way down.

Lifting my hands to my face, I bury my face in them and let out a long, exhausted sigh. I knew what I was doing the second her lips brushed against mine and I slammed her up against that door. But not once did I stop to think about what it would mean for her, and now I've got no one else to blame for the situation I've put myself in. She still works for me. And thoughts of Madison—*my Madison*—up in one on that stage or in one of the VIP rooms infuriates me. Thinking about her grinding against strange men like she did on me, or their eyes devouring every inch of her perfect body, has me seeing red. I know myself well enough to know that I'll end up dragging some asshole out by the throat before she makes it through half a shift. *No way in fucking hell is that happening.*

Grabbing a handful of tissues, I clean my release from the wall and think about a fix I can live with. I can't fire her. She'd never forgive me. She'd probably think it was punishment for not fucking me. *I couldn't forgive me for that.* Her hours, though, I can limit them—pull her from the private rooms where men get too handsy, too bold, too confident, thinking their cash buys them a piece of what they're watching.

She can dance, but she'll do it when *I'm* there; when I can keep my eyes on her. Not a man in this place will think about laying a finger on her when they know I'm watching. I'll get Chloe to frame it logistically. She can say the roster's full, or that we're switching up themes—whatever bullshit we need to feed her. She'll hate it. She's far too proud not to, but she'll forgive me. *I hope*. I won't risk seeing her on the security feed grinding on some drunk bastard who doesn't know how to look without touching.

I clench my jaw and pull my phone from my pocket to text the shift manager. It's probably not the right thing to do, but until she realizes she's mine, it's the *only* thing I can do.

THREE DAYS LATER

I storm from Chloe's office, and the music swallows me the second I step into the hallway, but it's not enough to drown the thundering in my chest. My heels hit the tile floor with sharp, angry clicks—loud enough to be heard over the bass rolling through the club. My anger flushes up my chest and burns over my cheeks with every step I take.

The other night was a mistake—one I've come to the thought of more than a couple of times the last few days. But that doesn't mean Cillian King now gets to make the rules for me like I'm some sort of possession he suddenly controls. I've spent all day thinking about him being that close to me again.

Only, after my meeting with Chloe, it's so that I can slap that cool arrogance right out of his mouth.

I head straight to the dressing room, flames of irritation still simmering under my skin. The other girls glance up when I enter, but no one says anything. They know, even if no one says it out loud. Word travels fast in places like this. And I'm certain none of them are upset that I'll be working shorter shifts or that my VIP suite clients need to be pre-approved by management—a fact I first learned when I overheard Chloe tell one of my regulars, "Raven isn't available tonight."

I'm being sidelined. Or more correctly, I'm being claimed—by *him*. He's implementing rules about what I can and cannot do in the club, like he owns me. And I've had enough. Struggling to maintain my composure, I reapply my lipstick and stand abruptly from my dressing station. I rush out of the dressing room and down the back hall to where Cillian disappeared as I entered Chloe's office. He's coming out of the security office when he sees me, and I swear he freezes like he didn't expect me to come for him.

"King," I snap, my tone definitely not appropriate for addressing my boss—or a King brother.

His brow arches slightly, and with the corners of his mouth twitching upward, I can tell he's trying to hide his amusement. "Madison."

I close the distance between us. "Why in the hell are you shortening my shifts and limiting my VIP time?"

He studies me with an unreadable expression before finally answering, "Thought you could use the break."

"You *thought* I could use a *break*? That's cute." My scoffing laugh is short and sharp, my hands balling into angered fists at my sides. "Seriously? *That's* what you're going with? I don't sleep with you, so you pull me from rotation. Did you really think I wouldn't say anything?"

"You don't need to work the VIP rooms," he states simply.

"That didn't answer my question."

Staring down at me smugly, he counters, "It's the answer I'm giving."

"The other night, it was a mist—" My voice cracks before I can finish my lie. *It was wrong, but it wasn't a mistake.* "I'm not your responsibility. I'm not your problem."

His eyes flash before narrowing slightly. "That's where you're wrong. You are very much *my problem*." His voice drops—low and rough. "I'm not going to watch every greedy asshole sneaking inappropriate touches just because it comes with a good tip."

"I never asked you to watch," I spit. "You're not my protector, and you sure as hell aren't my owner."

"That's where you're wrong." He moves closer, his broad frame casting a long shadow down the dimly lit hallway. The air grows thick, and I find myself suffocating on the intoxicating scent of his cologne. "I don't share what's mine, firecracker."

The words hit me like a slap across the face, rattling me to the core. *His.* My throat tightens as my heart rises from my chest. He brushes one finger along my jaw—just enough to set my skin on fire—and I'm frozen against his touch. His eyes are locked on mine, as unwavering as his declaration. "I'm not yours," I retort, sharp as glass.

Cillian's finger hooks under my chin, tipping my face toward his as he closes what little distance there was between us. His gaze drops to my mouth as his thumb dusts along my lower lip. "Not yet."

"Not *ever*." The words feel like a lie as they spew over my lips. "I'm not a thing. You don't get to claim me and control what I do just because I kissed you, Cil—"

"Kissed?" He smirks and drags his thumb back across my lip with enough force to smear my fresh lipstick. His hand runs along my side and over the swell of my hip and down my thigh. "Call it what you want, firecracker, but you were seconds from coming with these gorgeous legs wrapped around my waist." The image flashes through my thoughts and flutters in my pussy.

"And I stopped that, just like I'm stopping this." I shove him back, my palm hitting his chest hard enough for the slap to echo down the hall. While he barely moves, the distance is enough to breathe again. "You're going to have to get used to hearing no."

"No." His steady voice is joined by a devilish glint in his eyes. "I won't."

"So fucking smug and cocky."

"Not cocky." He shakes his head. "Confident. So confident that the rules stay in effect, because *my* girl will not have strange men putting their hands all over her."

Almost too soft to be heard, I mutter, "Arrogant asshole…"

"I'm pretty sure you have a set in a few minutes, and I don't think your boss will take kindly to you being late." Cillian flicks his finger under my chin and winks at me. Slowly turning on his heel, he walks away from me. He makes it a few feet before calling over his shoulder, "And, Madison, if you're trying out cute names for me, I much prefer Daddy over asshole."

"Smug fucker," I mumble under my breath, hating how badly I still want him, even when I fucking despise him. Back in the dressing room, I ignore the grumblings from the other girls. I quickly retouch my makeup with calm, deliberate precision, making sure every line is sharp and every detail is perfect.

If that cocky fucker is going to watch everything I do, I'm going to give him something to see.

I strut onto the stage with my over-the-knee stiletto boots clicking against the shiny surface, wearing nothing but a sheer black mini dress and a G-string—leaving nearly all of me on display. The spotlight falls on me as the music rises, and the room stills the way it always does, but I don't dance for them. I dance for myself. If I'm being honest with myself, I dance for him, too, defiantly showing him what *doesn't* belong to him.

Cillian is exactly where I expect him to be—in the owners' booth, half-shadowed by the lights of the club and swirling a drink on the table. I grip the pole above my head and slide my ass down the length of it. His eyes don't leave me—not for a second. *Good*. Dropping to my knees, I hold his gaze and crawl across the stage until I'm leaning over the edge. I daintily wrap my fingers around the tie of the man sitting before me and abruptly yank him toward the stage. Holding the silk firmly, I roll onto my back and seductively thrust my hips. The man leans over me as I pull at him harder, his face only inches from mine as I lift my feet into the air and slowly spread my legs into a wide V.

Watching me, Cillian's fingers tighten around the glass with such force I expect it to explode in his hand. His jaw clenches, and his knuckles grow white. He stands from his seat hastily—ire filling his eyes and flaring his nostrils—only to be dragged back by Nikolai's firm hand. Angered words pass between them as I place the man's hands on my hips. Cillian's heated gaze sears through me as I drag the client's hands along my skin. Defying him should be satisfying, but it isn't. He's raging with anger, but seeing how desperate he is to keep me to himself has me burning with desire.

Fuck... This man is going to ruin my life.

It's been three nights since I've gotten any sleep. Every time I close my eyes, I see Madison on that stage, that sheer black dress clinging to her perfect body like a second skin. What Madison did up there wasn't dancing. It was a fucking torturous declaration of war. Her eyes found me in the crowd like she was aiming a loaded gun at my restraint as she defied me like the little brat she is. She held my stare as a dare, putting that asshole's hands on her and punishing me with every sway of her hips, letting him touch what's *mine*. It was her way of punishing me for sidelining her, and fuck if it didn't work.

I pull my phone from my pocket again, checking for a reply. Still nothing. Not even the courtesy of a read receipt. She's ignoring every damn message I've sent since our confrontation the other night. That does nothing to stop me from sending another.

> As much as I dislike your public display of defiance, you have no idea what being ignored is doing to me.

Still nothing from her. I'm so consumed by thoughts of correcting her behavior that I've been sipping the same drink for the past hour, which is now warm and watered down. I'm too busy replaying every second of our last encounter. Every insult, her palms on my chest as she shoved me away, and the infuriating glare from her chocolate-brown eyes that burn brighter when she's furious.

She drives me fucking insane.

Yet, Madison was so fucking adorable when she was angry with me—all attitude and fire. I wanted to grab her and kiss her until she forgot why she was mad. I wanted to shove her against that wall and show her how wrong she was about me, about this. About us. Soon enough, she'll realize that every time she pushes me away, all she's doing is daring me to claim her for real. I don't want to control her. I want to *claim* and *protect* her.

I spot her at the bar, wearing a deep crimson number that I love on her—one with the low back and thin gold chains that frame the curves of her hips. She's with one of our VIP guests —a high-paying, low-mannered drunk who is one strike from being banned from our club. He's flush with old money and feels entitled to the attention he buys with it. His hand grazes her hip, and she might not flinch, but I can see the subtle shift in her posture. She nods with a polite smile—that well-rehearsed one that doesn't reach her eyes.

Her eyes wander from him and flit to me for a second with a flicker of a smile. I've been starved for her attention for days, and that tiny gesture stuns me like a sucker-punch to the gut.

"Jesus Christ," Nikolai snarks from beside me, shaking his head. "Is that all it fucking takes?"

I drag my gaze off her long enough to glare. "What?"

He swallows back a gulp of his vodka, giving me a knowing stare. "You've been walking around like a moody fucking bastard for days. She shoots a half-smile at you for two seconds, and you're grinning like a fucking fool."

"Fuck off," I mutter, watching Enzo chuckle into his glass.

"He's not wrong," Enzo adds. "You've been unbearable since she left you in the backroom with blue balls."

I really need to stop telling these assholes everything.

"Just take the fucking invitation and go talk to her," Nikolai encourages.

I finish my drink and cross the floor with slow, measured steps. She sees me coming and excuses herself from the suit she was talking to. I follow her through the crowd and toward the back of the club. By the time I reach her, she's in the back hallway, alone, near the dressing rooms, tying the sash of her robe around her waist.

"Following me now?" she asks, barely glancing up from the knot she's tying.

"I need to talk to you."

Lifting her face, she cocks a brow and sassily asks, "To apologize?"

I shake my head in response; I can't apologize for something I'm not sorry for. "You look good tonight." I fumble through the words like a fucking teenager.

"Don't flatter me, Mr. King. I'm not in the mood."

"We've talked about this," I correct her. "It's Cillian. Or Daddy. And I'm not flattering you. I'm being honest."

"Honesty?" She scoffs, her voice rising. "Honesty is admitting that you were out of line when you pulled me off the floor and rescheduled my shifts."

"You want honesty? Fine." I step so close to her we're almost touching. I drag my knuckles along her jaw and confess, "Honesty is that I'm fucking obsessed with you—unhealthily and viscerally. I think about you every fucking second of every day. The thought of another man being this close to you—putting his hands on you—fills me with a rage so deep there aren't fucking words to describe it."

Madison's breath hitches, and she stares up at me. Her mouth gapes slightly, and I realize that, for the first time since I've met her, she is at a complete loss for words. She lifts her hand and places it lightly against my chest. "I... Cillian..." She chokes on her thoughts and stammers.

"Cillian." Nikolai's deep voice billows down the hallway with urgency.

I turn—pissed at the interruption—and bark, "What?"

He strides toward me quickly, his expression hard and pinched. "Security caught one of the cashiers in the basement taking his liberties with our cash—wads of hundreds shoved down his pants. A quick check of the footage showed this was not the first time. Enzo is with them now."

"Where are they?"

"Out back," he answers before leaning close and lowering his voice. "They're shoving him into a car and taking him to the warehouse."

I glance back at Madison and place my hand over hers still resting on my chest. "Don't go anywhere," I softly command. "We're going to finish this the second I get back."

I stalk off without another word.

The drive is quiet, the hum of the engine barely masking the chaos brewing in my head. I should be thinking about what we're going to do to the idiot we caught stealing from us. But I'm not. As usual, I'm thinking about her and that look in her eyes as she struggled to find a response.

I pull into the warehouse lot, headlights slicing through the darkness. The concrete and steel building before us is where our enemies confess their sins. No priests. No forgiveness. We take our atonement in blood.

When we step inside, Nikolai and I find Enzo and one of our security guys standing next to the guy already zip-tied to a chair. He's young and scrawny, sweating like a pig. While he tries to look tough, he's shaking so hard that his knees are knocking.

"Do you know where you are?" I ask, unbuttoning and rolling up my sleeves.

His throat bobs with an audible swallow. He nods, sweat trickling down his face, the color draining with it.

"And do you know why you aren't leaving?"

Another nod.

"Good."

Without wasting time, I grab a utility knife from the rack beside me. It's old, and the blade is rusty, but it'll do what I need. The first cut is quick, right across his chest, just beneath the collarbone. He jerks and grimaces at the shallow cut. The next is slower and deeper. A scream rattles from him, the pained cry echoing off the metal walls as he begs for forgiveness. Ignoring him, I drag the blade through his flesh again. Blood splatters across the floor, and the metallic scent of it begins to fill the room.

I continue to carve him. His blood is hot and thick as it coats my hands and splatters over my boots and the floor. It doesn't bother me. I've done far worse. Yet, tonight is different. This isn't just punishment for theft. It's a punishment for *me*.

I carve him open, piece-by-piece, methodical and detached. It doesn't bother me. I've done worse. But tonight, this is different. I'm trying to relieve the ache in my chest that I can't reach. No matter how deep I dig the blade, I don't feel vengeance.

His cries turn wet and pathetic as I continue to slice through his skin until it hangs from his body in tattered threads. I drive deep with the blade and drop it to the floor as he painfully draws his last sputtered breath. Nikolai tosses me a towel without saying a word and wipes the blood from my hands. Enzo makes a call to someone to come take care of the body.

I step from the sweat-and-fear-laced air of the warehouse and inhale a sharp breath as I stare over the jagged skyline of the city. With my blood-stained hand, I pull my phone from my pocket and I check the time. *11:02 p.m.* Madison should still be at the club for a few more hours—if she listened for once.

Waiting for my brothers to join me at the car, I make myself a promise—one I'm not sure I'll be able to keep. If she lets me in, I'll burn down the fucking world to protect what's mine. But if she keeps pushing me away... God help the next poor bastard who crosses me.

After Cillian left me floundering for words in the hallway to go do what was clearly some questionably shady shit, I've spent my night making the rounds in the club. He may have forbidden me from working VIP, but with Chloe gone for the night and Cillian not here, I use the opportunity to spend some time working the floor and mingling with clients.

Hudson—*or Handsy Hudson, as all the girls call him*—has been vying for my attention since I left him high and dry at the bar earlier tonight. He waves me over, and like a good girl, I saunter toward him and sit low on his thigh. His hand wraps around my waist, and he roughly drags me up to his hip as I try to maintain my smile through the sudden discomfort. He reaches into the pocket of his jacket and pulls out his black card, holding it between two fingers. Tapping my fingernail against it, I whisper, "Sorry, sweetheart. Lap dances are cash only."

"I want you upstairs. Executive VIP." He arches a brow and obnoxiously waves the card before my face, his boozy breath blowing over me. I glance around the club, looking for an excuse—a tall, broody red-headed one that has banned me from going upstairs. *A rule I actually want to listen to right now.*

Playfully pulling the card from between his fingers, I wink. "I'm off VIP, but I'll get one of the other girls for you."

"I didn't give you my card to buy a ten-grand-an-hour dance with one of the of the *other* girls. I want you, and I don't think your bosses will take too kindly to you turning me down."

I broaden my smile and take his hand as I rise from his lap. Pulling it onto my shoulder, I lead him through the crowd and upstairs. The VIP lounge is much quieter than usual tonight —far fewer security as well. He opens the door, and we both step inside. Muted lighting spills amber across the carpet and gleams off the glass tabletops, giving everything a hazy, surreal warmth. The private rooms dull the pulsing bass from the main floor into something almost soothing—if not for the way my stomach twists as the door clicks shut behind us.

It's just Hudson... He's been here every night for two weeks, and he's harmless enough. His wallet is thick—like his cologne —and he thinks his money can buy him whatever he wants. I've danced for him plenty on the main floor. And while he does live up to his nickname, I usually don't mind him. This is the first time I've ever been truly alone with him, and he seems... different.

He's slumped on the couch when I turn to face him—his tie half undone, and his fingers working at a few of the buttons beneath it. "Pour me a glass of Scotch before you come park that beautiful ass on my lap." More Scotch is the last thing this man needs, but I do as he requests.

A cocky smirk spreads across his flushed face when I hand him his whiskey. "Miss me, baby girl?" he slurs, the drinks he had downstairs quickly catching up with him.

I smile, just the way I'm supposed to. "Always."

"Come on then. Let's make up for lost time." He pats his thigh, encouraging me to sit.

I slide onto him, my knees straddling his thighs, and my hands resting on his shoulders with practiced ease. My hips sway in time with the soft beat of the music playing overhead. I start slow—just a subtle grind. He grins, wide and far too eager, as his free hand finds its way to my waist.

Gently, I lift it and place it on the couch beside us, and tsk, "You know the rules, Hudson. Hands to yourself."

"And you're not supposed to be upstairs." He chuckles, eyes gleaming darkly. "Apparently, rules are meant to be broken."

"Not this one."

"C'mon, baby," he flirtatiously slurs his plea. "It's just me. Whatever your price, you know I'm good for it."

I let out a soft faux laugh, running a finger down the line of his spread collar. "And I'm good at what I do, but you still don't get to touch."

He groans dramatically and throws his head back. "You're killin' me."

"Just doing my job." I keep my tone light and playful, as his grip tightens around his glass. He downs the rest of his drink in a single swallow and slams it onto the table beside us with such force I'm surprised it doesn't crack.

"You know what I think?" he darkly whispers, leaning so close I can't miss the sourness on his breath. "I think you *like* teasing me. I think you get off on it."

I laugh—more for self-preservation than show—but the second it leaves my lips, I can tell how forced it sounds. "That's the fantasy, right?"

"You dance like you want it," he mutters. "Like you *need* it." My body tenses, just slightly, but I force myself to keep moving. This is far from the first time a drunk man has made an overt pass at me. If I'm being honest, I've heard worse. Only, those men weren't looking at me the way Hudson is: hungry, mean, and dark. He reaches for me again—this time higher—his fingers brushing against the side of my breast as I bat his hand away more firmly than before.

"Hudson," I warn, "hands off."

"Jesus fucking Christ. You're wound tighter than usual," he grumbles with an eye roll. His hands roughly grip both my hips, and he pulls me flush to his erection. Grinding it against me, he snarls, "I know exactly how to help you relax."

I blink blindly—trying to maintain my composure—and lift from his lap with a smile still plastered across my face. "I think your dance is over."

"What?" His voice rises. "I paid for an hour."

"You paid for my time. Not my body. You can see the club manager about a refund."

"You're a real spoiled fucking brat with an attitude problem. You know that?" He shifts forward on the couch, his eyes darkening in a way that causes the hairs on the back of my neck to stand on end.

I take a step backward, putting space between us and slowly moving toward the door. "You're drunk, Hudson. Sit down. Sleep it off. And I'll pretend this never happened."

He stands, and my nervous discomfort spikes into fear. He suddenly seems much taller and broader. The room feels too small, claustrophobic. Yet the door seems miles away. I retreat with each step he takes toward me. "You think you're better than me?" he growls. "Sauntering around this place like you're a fucking goddess. Like you don't know what you really are."

"Don't do this, Hudson." My voice cracks, betraying me as I blindly reach for the doorknob.

"You're just a whore, and I think you need to be reminded of your place." He lunges, and I can't avoid him. Grabbing my wrist with one hand and my waist with the other, he yanks me toward him.

"Let go!" I scream, struggling as he tries to drag me back to the couch. I twist my arm and shove against his chest with all the strength I have, but he doesn't let go.

"You owe me, you little tease," he growls in my face. "Don't act like you don't know what happens up here."

I slam my knee into his upper thigh, just short of my intended target. He grunts, and the blow catches him off guard. His grip loosens just enough for me to pull free and stumble away. I make it two steps before his large fist connects with my cheek. Blinding, white-hot pain cracks through my skull like a gunshot as my mouth fills with warm, liquid metal. *Blood.* Still dazed, I lift my arm too slowly to defend myself from his second swing. My jaw is on fire, and my ear is ringing as my body jolts to the left. The floor rushes up to me, and we collide in a crash that knocks the air from my lungs. My face hits the tile, and the lights blur.

With my vision blinded by tears, I can't tell if he's standing over me or if he's backed away. *Get up, Madison.* My limbs feel heavy and distant, refusing to listen as I try to push myself up from the floor. I can hear Hudson grumbling something as he shuffles, but my heartbeat thuds so loudly that I can't understand him.

Blackness curls at the edge of my vision as I fight to stay awake, even though I'm certain I don't want to be for what I know is coming.

Cillian is going to lose his fucking mind when he finds out.

When I finally reach the club, I park in the alley and make my way through the back entrance. My boots are still splattered with blood, and my hands are still stained—red streaks running through the deep grooves of my knuckles. It's not normal for me to come here after we go to the warehouse, and I should've gone home to clean up and change before re-entering the club. But there wasn't time—not after I promised her we'd finish this when I returned. And I *need* to finish that conversation.

I scan the club floor, weaving through the patrons and dancers, but there's no sign of her. I check with the bartender —he doesn't remember the last time he saw her. Heading back where I came from, I push open the door to the dressing room and ignore the quick pause in conversation that happens as soon as I enter. "Anyone seen Madison?" I ask, my voice rough.

They blink at me with collective blank stares. "Who?" one of them finally asks—some new girl whose name I need to learn.

"Raven." I grit my teeth. "Have any of you seen Raven?"

"Oh. Her. No, not for a bit," a blonde—Diamond, if I remember right—answers, gesturing at the vanity next to her. "But her stuff is still here."

I turn without another word and head straight for security— my chest tightening. The hallway seems longer than usual, the hum of the club fading behind me, drowned out by the thunder of my pulse. I slap the door open and barge in, already barking orders. "Pull up the floor cams. Dressing room. Bar. VIP. All of them."

Mark doesn't ask why. He scrolls through the feeds as I lean over his shoulder, scanning every screen with ruthless precision. I spot her and instantly see red. She's in VIP with Hudson. The sleazy bastard has his hands on her. His grin is as fucking wide as her thighs straddling his lap, and every inch of my self-control burns away.

"Zoom in," I demand. Mark hesitates, and I shout, "Now!" He does, and the feed sharpens just as Hudson grabs her hips. She climbs from his lap, wearing her uncomfortable smile but trying to play it cool. I lean closer to the screen, blood already roaring in my ears. Her lips form words I can't hear, but I can read the intent. She tries to create space, but he follows until he's looming over her. I watch the scene playing before me like it's in slow motion until he hits her. The first blow is bad, splitting open her lower lip. The second is far worse, and I watch her crumble like a rag doll. My heart leaps into my throat as her body slams against the floor. *She's not getting up.* "Where the *fuck* is security?"

"I... um..." Mark fumbles for his headset to call them as I bolt from the office. I make my way up the back stairs two—maybe three—at a time, needing to get to her. Racing across the VIP floor with my eyes focused on the end of the hall, a single thought races through my head. *He hurt her, and he's going to die.*

I reach the room and kick the door open so hard it nearly flies off the hinges, and my heart sinks the second I see her. Madison is on the ground, trembling, blood streaking the corner of her mouth, and one eye already swelling. Her eyes are barely open, fluttering like she's fighting against the darkness. Hudson is standing over her, his pants splayed, and his cock in his hand.

Rage doesn't begin to describe what I feel as I rush toward Hudson. He opens his mouth, but I don't give him the opportunity to speak. I throw my fist against his jaw with a sickening crack. My second punch breaks his nose, and the third shatters his cheekbone. He stumbles backward—blood already gushing from his face—and I grab the front of his shirt to keep him upright to slam my fist into his mouth again. Blood splatters across my shirt, and two of his teeth clatter across the tile floor like dice.

He staggers to the side, and I go with him. Raining down punches in quick succession the moment we hit the floor. His head flails from side-to-side with every blow, but I don't stop. I *can't* stop. I hit him again and again, feeling the sickening crunch of cartilage and bone under my split knuckles. I want him to break beneath me, paying for what he did.

"You fucking hurt her," I snarl, grabbing him by the collar and roughly lifting him from the floor like the fucking trash he is. His face is unrecognizable—swollen, bruised, and covered in blood. I drive my fist into him again. "You put your fucking hands on her like she was yours—"

"Cian!" Nikolai shouts from behind me, but I ignore him. "Cillian—"

"—like you thought you had the right—"

"Cillian!" Enzo shouts, gripping my shoulder and pulling my attention from what's left of Hudson. I slam his head into the floor for good measure and climb from his limp body as Madison lets out a pained groan. My hands are shaking from the adrenaline coursing through my veins—or maybe from the fear that she isn't okay—as I crawl across the floor to her.

Kneeling beside her, every ounce of rage bleeds from my body. What it leaves behind is so much worse—regret and pain. She's still slumped on her side, her chest rattling with shallow, shaky inhales. I brush the hair from her face, my stomach twisting at what he did to her. "Oh, Madison..." My voice breaks as I use the cuff of my sleeve to gently wipe the blood from her lip.

Her lips part, and a harrowing whimper blows over them as she tries futilely to open her eyes. I slip my arms beneath her carefully—one under her knees and the other cradling her back—and lift her from the floor. Madison's body folds into mine, and something in my chest crumples at the feeling; like even though she's hurt, she belongs here. Her head lolls against my shoulder, and her soft breath ghosts over my throat. I press my lips to her temple and murmur, "It's going to be okay."

She stirs a little, and I lightly shush against her forehead as I carry her toward the door, hoping to soothe her. Enzo quickly covers her with his jacket for some modesty, then walks before us, clearing a path to the stairwell. Nikolai follows, quietly telling security to clean up the blood and to dispose of the bastard still crumpled on the floor.

Her lips move, vibrating against my collarbone as she mumbles something so softly that I'm not able to make out. I pull her tighter and press my lips to her temple. My voice shakes as I whisper the words I should've said the second I found her: "You're safe, firecracker. Daddy's got you."

Daddy's always got you...

CHAPTER 18
madison

The world rocks and sways like I'm on a dinghy boat tossing in the ocean as I struggle to open my eyes. A steady heartbeat thuds beneath my ear, heavy and fast. Tires hum against the pavement, and the low rumble of an engine nearly drowns out the thump beneath me.

I'm not sure whether I'm dreaming or dead.

A warm arm wraps around me, strong and unyielding—but gentle and familiar. The rich, spiced scent of his cologne registers as my foggy brain tries to catch up to what is happening. *Cillian.* His chest rises and falls beneath me, and my trembling fingers curl involuntarily into the front of his shirt. "Cillian…" I lift my head just enough to slur, "Where… are you taking me?"

"Home," he answers without hesitation.

I blink, trying to focus. Streetlights blur past us in amber streaks, flashing through the windshield. We're in a car. His car. And I'm in his lap—in the driver's seat.

Maybe this is a dream...

Pushing from his chest—slowly and awkwardly—I try to slide toward the passenger seat, but his arm tightens possessively around me. "No." His voice is low and benevolent, almost a growl. "I've let you push me away long enough." My heart stutters at the way he says it. Every word laced with regret, like what happened in that room was his fault.

The city outside the car dissolves into a parking garage. We spiral upward, level by level, until he eases the car into a reserved spot near an elevator. The moment the engine edge cuts off, I nudge his shoulder and try to move from his lap. "This isn't my home," I mumble, the soft words echoing in my head like a snare drum.

"No," he agrees softly. "It's mine."

"I can go to my own place," I insist, though the words are flimsy and halfhearted. "I'm fine. I just need—"

"You can," Cillian interrupts, cradling me in his arms as he opens the door to the car. "But I'll be coming with you. You've been in and out of consciousness the whole ride. There's no way you're being left alone tonight."

I want to argue, but I know his concern about a concussion is valid, and I don't have anyone else to come watch over me. "Fine." I sigh as he carries me toward the elevator. "But I can walk."

"You can." He uses his hand beneath my knees to push the button to call the elevator. "But you're not going to."

With my arms around his neck and my head resting on his shoulder, he cradles me in his arms for the elevator ride and the short walk into his penthouse. *Holy shit...* His place is all shadow and glass—high ceiling, low lighting, charcoal furniture, and rich woods. It's gorgeous; everything about it looks ungodly expensive.

He carries me toward the windows showcasing the sprawling city skyline and lays me on the leather couch with the utmost tenderness. My body sinks into the cushions, the room spinning slowly. "I'll be right back," he whispers, his footsteps quickly fading as he walks away from me.

Gently, he brushes the hair from my face, startling me. I open my eyes to find him kneeling beside the couch with a cold compress wrapped in a towel. He presses it to my cheek, and I flinch—both from the cold and the pain. "Sorry." He carefully readjusts the compress. "But this will help the swelling."

My gaze roams over his unsavory appearance. His knuckles are cut and bruised, but they're nowhere near bad enough to account for the amount of blood on his hands and shirt. Needing to know, I hesitantly ask, "Did you kill him?"

His expression remains unreadable and tight, just like his lips that don't part to answer. I close my eyes again, and the cold seeps into the ache beneath it. Cillian holds his hand steady, his thumb lightly tracing an absent-minded circle over my temple. This tenderness from him is so foreign that, for a second, I wonder if he's concussed, too.

Cillian slides a blanket from the back of the couch and drags it over my body. He pulls it up to my collarbone and smooths it over my shoulder, his fingers lingering for a moment before dusting my tender jaw. Bending over me, he presses a soft, reverent kiss to the center of my forehead. "Yes," he whispers, the lone word vibrating against my skin.

"Cillian... Don't..."

I can't hear this...

I close my eyes as he continues his confession, "Knowing what he was going to do to you, I should've done far worse." A breath leaves my lungs that I didn't know I'd been holding. Battered and bruised, lying on the couch of a hardened killer, I somehow feel dangerously close to safe. His lips brush against my forehead again, then to the bridge and tip of my nose.

He places a tender kiss on the crack in my lip. I wince at the discomfort, but I don't pull away. I should. I *know* I should. I need to maintain what little control I still have. But right now —sitting in the dark with his hand cradling my cheek like I might break apart—I forget why I've been pushing him away so hard. Or maybe, I just don't want to pretend I don't want this anymore.

"I hate how you make me feel," I whisper with my eyes still closed.

"I know." His warm breath blows over my lips. "I hate how you make me feel, too. Absolutely fucking powerless."

Shifting my weight, every muscle in my body screams, and I sit up. My fingers curl around the front of his shirt like they did in the car. I pull myself toward him, sliding from the couch until I'm straddling him on the floor. Brushing my tender lips against his, I whisper, "You're going to ruin my life."

Cillian's lips flutter against mine as he lightly shakes his head. "No. I'm going to take care of you, firecracker. Daddy will always take care of you." His hand cups the back of my neck, fingers threading into my hair as he pulls me in. He kisses me slowly and intentionally—nothing like the wild desperation of that night in the office. He moves with the confidence of a man who knows he owns every breath I take. It's patient, commanding, and laced with tenderness—steady and sure— like he already knows I won't pull away. Not this time.

He parts his lips, his tongue darting between them, coaxing mine open, and I eagerly let him in—all my resolve dissipating. His tongue caresses mine in a slow, commanding dance, as if he's taking his time savoring every broken piece of me. I can tell he's holding back and trying to be gentle, but I don't want gentle. I want *him*—every rough, jagged piece. My fingers weave into his hair, and fighting through the pain, I pull his mouth more firmly against mine.

A groan rattles low in his throat, rumbling against my chest and spreading fire down my body. He tugs at my locks just hard enough to make me gasp. Swallowing it, he deepens our kiss. It grows needy and sloppy—his hands roaming my body as I grind against him. "Please... don't stop, Daddy."

Lifting us both from the floor like I weigh nothing, he breathlessly growls, "Not a fucking chance."

CHAPTER 19
cillian

I can't get enough of Madison's lips or how she feels in my arms. Carrying her across the penthouse—her thighs locked tightly around my waist—I can't bring myself to pull my mouth from her. Her fingers lacing through my hair and brushing over the shaved nape, she repeatedly moans into my mouth as her tongue dances with mine. Her body instinctively knows where we're going.

The spiral staircase creaks beneath the thud of my boots as I climb it quickly but carefully. I can't go slow, not with her hips rolling subtly against mine—teasing me through my pants. Teasing us both. Her lips trail from my mouth to my jaw, wet and needy. The flutter of her breath blows against my throat as her heaving chest rises and falls against mine.

Fuck...

When I enter the bedroom, I kick the door shut and carry her in without flicking on a light. The ambient glow of the moon casts shadows over the bed and the navy walls. I set her down gently—splaying her across my sheets in nothing but her sheer lingerie—salivating over the offering laid out before me. She stares up at me with need, her hair fanning across the soft gray sheets. Her lips are red and swollen, and the flush of her cheeks burns through the bruise on the right.

I tear off my shirt and crawl over her. Planting a hand beside her head and hovering above her, I watch her deep brown eyes dilate in the dark as her hands roam over my bare chest. With her legs wrapped around my waist again, a smirk tugs at the corner of her mouth when she uses them to pull me down.

I crash my lips against hers, giving her what I know she wants. Our tongues brush together as I claim her mouth—swallowing every metallic-tinged moan and whimper as her split lip bleeds into our kiss. Her hips lift as she silently pleads for more. Moving her hands between our bodies, she fumbles for my belt. One at a time, I grip her wrists and pin them above her head. When both are in one of my hands, I shift my weight and fully settle between her thighs, my rock-hard cock resting firmly against the warmth of her panty-covered pussy. She's firmly pinned beneath me, completely helpless. "You've made me wait, and now I'm going to return the favor. If you want to come, you're going to need to be a good girl." I pepper the words up and down her neck with a trail of wet kisses before whispering against her ear, "Are you going to be a good girl for Daddy?"

She whimpers, nodding before the words even form. "Yes, Daddy."

"Use your words, firecracker." My free hand slides beneath her sheer crop top, and my fingers graze the underside of her pert breast. "I want to hear you say it."

"I'll be good," she exhales. "I promise."

"I don't want promises," I murmur, my lips brushing against hers. "I want obedience." I roll her nipple between my fingers, and her breath hitches as I tease the bud until it peaks. She arches her back—pushing harder into my touch. Her hands strain against my grip, but she doesn't fight me. She doesn't want to. She wants to surrender, and I'm going to claim every fucking inch of her until no part of her questions who she belongs to. I'm going to take my time teaching her what it means to be mine. *Finally mine.*

I release her wrists to pull her shirt over her head in one smooth motion. "Goddamn," I mutter, tracing the curve of her waist, her ribs, and the valley between her breasts as I sit on my knees solely to take her in. *She's perfection.* "You are absolutely fucking gorgeous."

Leaning down, I suck her peaked nipple into my mouth while my hand firmly palms her other breast. She's so sensitive and responsive. Every suck and swirl of my tongue pulls another soft moan from her lips, and I already know I'm going to be addicted to that beautiful fucking sound. I nip at the tender flesh, and a surprised groan rattles from her, making my aching cock throb.

I trail kisses down her stomach, relishing in the way her restless body pulses beneath me. Swirling my tongue around her navel, I breathe in the scent of her arousal—sweet and intoxicating. I hook my thumbs beneath the thin strings of her panties, and she lifts her hips obediently for me to pull them down. With a flick of my wrist, I toss her damp panties to the floor. When I push her thighs apart, I growl at the sight before me—she's fucking dripping.

My breath blows over her inner thigh, and she whimpers desperately, needing my touch. I kiss my way up her soft skin. She cries out when I reach the fleshy skin at the apex of her thighs, sink my teeth into her, and suck until I leave my mark inches from her cunt. I tenderly run my lips over it, deliberately pausing before dragging my tongue up the length of her slick slit. The sound that spews from her is absolutely feral. I groan into her, lapping the arousal from her glistening flesh. Her hips roll, moving my tongue right where she needs me. I let her bring herself to the edge before pulling back and pinning her hips to the bed with a firm arm across her waist.

Dipping my tongue lower, I stroke around her entrance and push inside her. Teasingly, I drag it up to her clit and torturously circle it with slow swipes. Her clit quivers against my tongue, and I know she's so fucking close. I'm met with a disapproving whimper when I pull my mouth from her sweet cunt again.

I deny her time and time again, edging her until she's a sweaty mess and my cock aches to be inside her. "Please…" Madison painfully pleads, her hands gripping the sheets with white-knuckled fists as I refuse her again. "I… I can't…"

"I've tortured you long enough," I groan with a smile against her pussy, and her whole body jumps. "Ask Daddy nicely."

"Please let me come, Daddy."

I flatten my tongue and press it to her clit. Gripping her hips, I hold her against my mouth while I lick and suck at her—fucking worshipping her with my mouth as she writhes beneath me. "Let me hear you fall apart," I gravelly whisper against her clit as I plunge two digits into her. Curling them against her walls, I feast on her like a starved man until she gives me exactly what I want. Her fingers thread through my hair, tugging it hard as she hurtles toward ecstasy. She shatters completely, her hips jerking and thighs trembling against my face. The breathy moan rattling from her is high and choked. It echoes around the room as I unbuckle my belt and shove my pants just low enough to free my cock.

She watches me through half-lidded eyes, her lips parted and chest heaving. I crawl back over her and press the thick head of my cock against her entrance. "Do you still want this?" I ask, my voice pained with need.

"Yes..." she pants. "More than anything."

Staring down at her, I command, "Tell me."

"I need you inside of me."

I thrust into her with one deep, slow stroke, and the gasp that flies from her is half-pain and half-pleasure. I pause long enough to feel her stretch around me, adjusting to my size. I pull back and drive into her again, harder. She clutches at my shoulders, her nails digging through my flesh as I roughly bottom out inside of her again. And again. Hiking her leg over my hip, I roughly palm her ass, my short fingernails dimpling her flesh. I repeatedly plunge into her warm, tight cunt, and it swallows my cock like she was made to take me.

"Come again for me, firecracker," I growl, bracing one hand beside her head and sliding the other between us to rub her already sensitive clit. Her mouth falls open, and her eyes flutter as her back arches from the bed. "That's it... Come while Daddy fucks you."

Breathy cries blow over my face, and she falls apart for me—clenching around my cock so hard that I see stars. Fighting the need to spill into her, I roughly fuck her through her release, prolonging her bliss. I savagely chase my own release, quickly pulling another orgasm from her, until mine slams into me. It is blinding and violent, my hips sputtering against her as cum spills from my quivering cock. I collapse over her, panting against her neck, still buried deep inside and unwilling to move.

I kiss my way to her perfect lips as I struggle to catch my breath. Brushing the sweat-matted hair from her face, I claim her mouth again, softly and with intent. I pull back—still breathless—and whisper against her lips, "You're mine now."

And I'm not letting her go.

A jackhammer rattles my skull as I wake slowly. Every flutter of my eyelids causes the throbbing pain to radiate behind my eye. When I sit up, everything aches—and not just in the satisfying just-had-my-back-blown-out kind of way. Although definitely in that way, too. My face feels like it got hit by a truck, but my pussy feels like it had one drive through it.

Shit!

Last night...

Cillian...

My heart slams against my ribs, and my stomach twists into a knot as a cold wash of panic rolls through me like a crashing

Oh, God...

I did it...

I actually fucking did it...

I slept with Cillian King...

I close my eyes and drag a hand down my face, wincing when I brush over the bruise beneath it. "Fuck," I whisper to the ceiling, my voice hoarse and small.

What the hell did I do?

This wasn't supposed to happen—*I* wasn't supposed to let this happen. No matter how good it felt—or how mind-shatteringly, toe-curlingly, soul-wreckingly good it was—it doesn't change the fact that what we did broke *all* the rules. This is going to complicate everything. And the worst part? I would eagerly climb back into bed with him. Not caring in the slightest that he's a walking red flag with a moral compass that spins like a roulette wheel.

As I climb carefully out of his bed, I wince when I become acutely aware of the soreness between my legs—definite evidence of how thoroughly he claimed me. Cillian was dominating and demanding, sex with him is deliciously rough. Yet afterward, he wrapped his arms tightly around me, stroked my hair, and dusted his fingertips along my spine as we talked about everything and nothing. As I grew tired, he kissed the bruise on my cheek and the crack in my lip with such tenderness it almost broke me.

He was still Daddy, but not the commanding, rough version who savagely tore orgasms from me. The man who murmured sweet reassurances, with me curled into his chest, was soft and tender. He watched me like I was precious and wanted. *Like I was his.* Wandering around his room and looking for my clothes, that's the part of him I remember most from last night. I find my sheer crop top at the foot of the bed and my panties in a wad on the floor. After quickly dressing, I glance down at my body.

Great... World's classiest outfit for the Just Got Laid Parade goes to Madison Roark.

I crack open the door and freeze when I hear two deep and familiar voices—Nikolai and Enzo. *Shit.* They've seen me dressed like this often, but this is different. I can't exactly waltz downstairs in see-through black mesh and barely-there panties like I'm auditioning for stage time at the club. My hand curls around the doorknob, and I debate pushing the door shut and hiding out until the house clears.

"Good morning." Cillian crests the top of the stairs. He's shirtless, with gray sweatpants slung far too low, and his hair perfectly disheveled. I saw and felt him last night, but in broad daylight, this man looks like a fucking god. His gaze skates over my outfit, and an amused smirk pulls at the corner of his mouth. "You plan on hiding up here all day?"

"I... um... don't have any clothes."

"I quite like you without them," he quips, utterly unbothered. Before I can respond, he slips into the walk-in closet, emerging shortly after with a pair of massive gray sweatpants and a black hoodie. He hands me the sweatpants. I yank them up my legs and tie the drawstring twice, hoping I can keep them up. Cillian lifts the hoodie and pulls it over my head. It swallows me whole—the sleeves dangling over my hands. Slipping his finger under my chin, he tips my face up toward his and places a gentle kiss on the tip of my nose. "But I like you like this, too."

He lifts the floppy sleeve of the hoodie and fishes out my hand, threading his fingers through mine. He tugs me gently toward the door. I hesitate for a second, but his grip doesn't falter, and he leads me down the stairs without any reluctance. Pulling me close, he wraps his arm around me and walks us toward the scent of coffee and eggs wafting from the kitchen.

"Damn, Cillian," Nikolai drawls as we approach. "I knew you liked it kinda rough, but that's a little too far." I laugh before I can stop myself—a short, surprised sound that erupts from my chest—and I slap my hand over my mouth.

Cillian groans and shakes his head. "Jesus, Nik. She's right here."

"And?" Nikolai grins, shrugging his shoulders. "It's a compliment. She's still walking. Sorta."

"Barely," I mumble.

"Ugh... Gross." The dry, feminine—and unmistakably judgmental—voice draws my attention to the other end of the counter. "I do not need to hear about my brother's kinks before I've had caffeine."

Nikolai chuckles, unbothered. "Please, Eavan. You've got no room to talk, sweetheart. I've lived through *way* too many nights of you and Enzo going at it like you were trying to break a headboard in surround sound."

Coffee in hand and one leg crossed over the other, she lifts a perfectly groomed brow. Enzo chimes in from beside her, "Behave, princess." With a shit-eating grin, Nikolai takes a ridiculously large bite of the pastry in his hand as Eavan rolls her eyes at him.

Her gaze rakes over my face with concern—actually, they all

do. "Seriously," her tone is soft, and the concern in her eyes is genuine, "are you okay?"

"Okay?" Nikolai scoffs, slinging his arm over my shoulder like I'm suddenly one of them. He gives a gentle squeeze before turning me in his hold. His other hand dusts along my jaw as he carefully inspects the bruises marring one side of my face. His touch is unexpectedly gentle, calloused fingers brushing just enough to check for swelling and broken bones, not enough to cause more pain. Content upon finding nothing serious beneath my marbled skin, he smirks. "That first punch barely fazed her."

"That second one, on the other hand..." I playfully exhale. I can't help it, but I smile, a real, genuine smile. It's absurd, all of this—sore cheeks, sore thighs, and what should be an awkward-as-hell morning-after breakfast—but this feels warm and welcoming.

Cillian slides a hand over the small of my back as he helps me take a seat at the island. He hovers for a second, placing a soft kiss on the top of my head before grabbing me a plate of eggs. What he sets down in front of me is questionable at best— somewhere between overcooked and "maybe I should ask Nikolai for the rest of his croissant"—but I murmur a thank-you and pick up my fork. He pulls out the stool beside me, his thigh brushing against mine as he takes his seat.

The others fall into easy conversation as we eat, and continue long after we finish. I should feel like an outsider in this tight circle, but I feel like I belong. *Like family.* The absurdity of the realization catches me off guard. *They definitely aren't the people I thought they were.* Cillian's hand finds my knee beneath the counter and gives it a tender squeeze, as if he knows what I'm thinking. Maybe he does.

At my insistence—even though he made it very clear I could stay and subsequently refusing to allow me to use public transportation—Cillian throws on a shirt and grabs his car keys to take me home. As we walking to the foyer, Enzo calls, "I grabbed your purse before we left the club. It's in the foyer."

"Thank you," I shout toward the kitchen.

Eavan joins us in the foyer and opens her arms without hesitation, and I step into her embrace. She smells like espresso and leather mixed with jasmine. Her hug is firm but warm, the kind that makes your chest loosen in places you didn't realize were tight.

"Call me if you need anything. Seriously," she insists softly. I nod, something thick catching in my throat. She steps back, green eyes sparkling as she teases, "And if you ever want a support group for people who've slept with my brother... It's just you so far... but I'll make T-shirts."

I can't help but snicker, immediately feeling Cillian's unamused stare. "The two of you are going to be fucking trouble." He shakes his head.

With Madison's tiny hand in mine, the dull thud of our footsteps against smooth concrete echoes in the near-empty parking garage. Fluorescent lights flicker overhead, casting harsh pools of pale light that bounce off the slightly damp floor. The sharp scent of rain from this morning's brief storm still clings to the air, mingling with the faint tang of gasoline and car exhausts.

She leans slightly into me as we approach my car, her steps uneven, betraying the soreness I know is running through her body. I don't say anything, but my hand finds the small of her back to steady her. Even now, after everything, she feels fragile. I want to be the rock she doesn't have to worry will falter.

When we reach the car, I open the passenger door, take her hand, and help her into the low seat. She slides in slowly, tugging the edge of my hoodie over her thighs. I crouch slightly, brushing my fingers lightly over her waist as I click the seatbelt and pull it snug. My beard grazes her cheek as I stand, and I catch the faint hitch in her breath. I close the door, then circle the car—unable to hide the smile spreading across my face—and slide into the driver's seat, the familiar leather cool beneath me.

She doesn't question when I pull from the garage and head south of Midtown without asking for her address. The drive is slow and quiet at first, tires whispering over damp asphalt as we drive to her apartment. My hand settles on her thigh, thumb tracing lazy, absent circles against the baggy sweatpants. I don't realize I'm doing it until I catch her watching me out of the corner of her eye with a tiny grin pulling at the corner of her mouth.

"You know," she murmurs, her words are tentative, like she's uncertain what to say, "your sister's really sweet."

I chuckle, a low sound. "Yeah?"

She nods. "Nothing like you," she deadpans.

A laugh bubbles up, rough and unexpected. "Ouch."

She shrugs, trying to maintain her composure, but a tiny giggle escapes her. "Eavan has always been one of the most important people in my life. Always will be." The words come more easily than I expect. "She was so tiny when my parents brought her home. And I might've only been a child, but I knew immediately what my job was as her big brother."

Madison listens in silence, but with her full attention, turning slightly to face me as I try to keep my eyes on the road instead of her.

"Our father was, well... too busy for her. For both of us, really. After we lost our mom, I swore to her that I'd protect her. I did a shit job of it for a few years," I confess, unable to mask the guilt in my tone. "But there is literally nothing I wouldn't do for her." *Nothing.*

Madison's hand slides over mine, and she squeezes it gently. "I don't have a doubt in my mind how much you mean that."

"I've already lost one person I couldn't live without," I continue, my thumb brushing along the back of her hand. "I won't let that happen again. I don't care what it costs me." She saw my darkness last night, she knows I'm not bluffing.

Her gaze never leaves mine as her throat bobs with her hard swallow. "You aren't what I expected," she murmurs. Silence falls over the car, but I don't push. I wait patiently for her to form her thoughts and continue. "It's no secret what kind of man you are... I just never imagined there would be such a huge heart tucked inside such a ruthless man."

"You're mine now, firecracker," I share, my voice low but sure. "You need to know beyond a doubt, there are no limits to what I would do to someone who would dare hurt you." I see the flicker of emotion behind her eyes, something between fear and fierce trust.

Eyes narrowing slightly, Madison studies with curiosity, or maybe realization. "It's not just a dirty word in the bedroom for you, is it?" she asks quietly, a hint of wonder in her voice. "You really are a Daddy."

"No." My tone deepens. "It's not just a bedroom kink for me. It never was, especially with you. That word. It means something. It's not about control and domination. It's about responsibility and care—, making you feel secure enough to give yourself to me without ever questioning whether I'll hold you or hurt you. I want to make sure you feel safe enough to fall apart and know that I'm going to be there to help you put the pieces back together."

She blinks, lips parting slightly.

"It means I take your safety personally," I continue, barely able to pull my eyes from her to focus on the road. "I want to protect you from the world, but also from the shit that gets too loud in your own head. It means I'll carry the weight for you. Even when you're too fucking stubborn to ask for help."

A shaky breath escapes her, but she doesn't look away. She stares at me, like no one's ever said anything like this to her before or vowed to worship her the way she deserves. "You barely know me," she blurts, just above a whisper.

"I know more than enough," I confess, reassuringly squeezing her thigh. "I've been fucking obsessed with you since the night we met in the bar. I want to give you the world, firecracker. You don't have to do anything but let me."

Her eyes shimmer as they well slightly with tears. When she finally speaks, her voice cracks around the edges. "I've never had someone want to take care of me like that."

"You do now." My words aren't a promise; they're a vow.

We drive in silence for the final few blocks to her apartment, the world outside blurring past, muted and distant—like we've slipped into a separate pocket of time where only the two of us exist. The hum of the engine fills the space between us, steady and grounding. Neither of us says a word, but her hand stays on mine the whole time, her thumb brushing over my skin like she's reminding herself I'm real.

I pull up to the curb before her building. It is old—red brick mottled with ivy and well-weathered by time. The windows are streaked with rain, catching the streetlights in long silver trails.

Rushing, I round the car and open the passenger door, extending my hand to help her from the seat. I pull her onto the sidewalk beside me, and my hand instinctively finds the small of her back as I lead her inside. She doesn't pull away, not in the slightest. She leans into my touch like it's something she needs more than she'll ever admit.

My hand still on her back, the stairwell creaks beneath our feet as we climb the steps to her apartment, echoing softly in the narrow space as we reach the third-floor landing. She digs through her purse for her keys, her hands fumbling a little, betraying nerves she's trying to keep in check.

"I didn't say it last night..." she begins, her voice barely above a whisper. She turns slightly, still facing the door, fingers fidgeting with the keyring. Then, slowly, she fits one into the lock and pauses. When she finally turns back toward me, there's something raw and unguarded in her expression. "But... thank you."

Holding her stare, the softness in her eyes unravels me.

"You don't have to thank me," I insist, meaning every word.

"I do." Her chin lifts with quiet resolve. "You came for me. You saved me."

Staring down at her, my voice drops low, steady and unshakable. "I always will."

CHAPTER 22

madison

Sticky from age and neglect, the lock of my apartment door is stubborn as hell when I try to open it. I fight with the key—cursing it under my breath—wrestling with the lock until it finally clicks. "Got it!" I spin around victoriously to find my face flush with Cillian's chest. Looking up, I'm met with his gorgeous hazel eyes staring down at me. Heavy with heat, they bore through me.

"You asked to come home," he murmurs, his voice deep and rough, "and I complied. But I can't bring myself to leave you." The air thickening around us, I push up onto my toes and meet his lips. The hunger that has been simmering between us all morning pours into it. Nothing about it is gentle. It is urgent and demanding—absolutely fucking all-consuming.

My pulse hammering, I clutch the front of his shirt with one hand and fumble for the doorknob behind me with the other. Breaking our kiss, I pull back, a smirk tugging at my lips as I drag him into the apartment. "Then don't."

Wrapping his arms around me, a devilish grin spreads across his face as he lifts me just enough to carry me inside before kicking the door shut behind us. Our clothes don't stand a chance. We tear them from each other like rabid animals, fabric dropping in heaps as we kiss our way deeper into my one-room studio.

I circle my hands around Cillian's shaft, and his breath sputters when I drag my fist up his length. "I want to suck your cock. Can I, Daddy?" I ask huskily as I kiss along his jaw.

"Get on your knees," he commands, his tone suddenly dark. "Show Daddy what a good girl you are."

Without hesitation, I drop to my knees. I place a wet kiss against the soft skin of his tip before flicking it with my tongue. I stare up at him, dusting the thick head against my parted lips and slowly shaking my head. "But I'm not a good girl." I take him into my mouth—tasting his salt and musk— as I quickly swallow every girthy inch to the base. A guttural moan rattles from him, making my pussy ache.

I take my time, dragging my tongue along the underside of his shaft as I ease my mouth up to his tip before slowly swallowing him back down my throat, teasing him the same way he tortured me last night. "You aren't a good girl at all," he groans, his fingers tangling in the hair at the back of my head and guiding me over his length. Fisting my locks, he takes control and leisurely bobs my mouth over his cock.

"Spread your legs for me," he whispers the gravelly command. "Touch that pretty little pussy while you let me fuck your mouth. I want you moaning with my cock in your throat as you make yourself so wet for me that you're dripping."

"Yes, Daddy," I mumble the words around his cock. Doing exactly as he instructed, I spread my knees and press my hand between my thighs. I slide my fingers between my slick slit and rub teasingly slow circles around my clit.

"Breathe," he instructs, and I suck in a deep breath seconds before his hips jerk forward, roughly burying himself in my throat. My eyes well with tears, and spittle runs down my chin as I work myself to the edge, struggling to draw in air. "This smart fucking mouth of yours feels so good." Cillian grits his praise between deep thrusts.

Beaming at me with pride, he slows his pace. I swallow him down—my eyes locked on his—as he dusts his free hand along the side of my face. "Rub that clit, firecracker," he murmurs. "I want you wet and ready for me. The moment I pull out of this pretty mouth, I'm going to lap up every drop of you until you're screaming my name."

His touch is fire, and his words are gasoline. Moaning around him, my slick fingers rub over my clit hungrily as I stare up at him with lust-hooded eyes. I'm mere swipes away from coming when Cillian slowly pulls himself out of my mouth—a string of saliva running from my lower lip to his cock. Without a second of hesitation, he hoists me up and carries me a few feet to the kitchen.

My ass hits the icy countertop with a thud, but he doesn't give me a chance to react. Before I can suck in a breath and exhale a gasp, he has me splayed across the cool surface and is burying his face between my thighs. "Fuck... I love your sweet pussy," he moans and groans against me—the vibrations over my clit causing me to claw at the hard surface beneath me.

He sucks my clit into his mouth and firmly massages it with his tongue. I come fast, breathlessly crying out, "Yes... Fuck... Oh, God..."

Abruptly standing—his beard stained dark with my arousal—he grips my hips hard enough to leave bruises as he slams into me with a growl. "God isn't making you come, firecracker. Daddy is." He pulls out slowly and roughly plows into me again. "You scream for Daddy"—he repeats the savage motion—"and I'm going to fuck your tight pussy until you get it right."

He drives into me with fast, feral thrusts, each so punishingly demanding that I come for him again. Pulling me up to his chest, his arousal-dampened beard drags against my skin as he sloppily kisses my neck. Teetering at the brink, he sinks his teeth into the crook of my neck, and the sudden burst of pain throws me over the edge. "Da... Daddy!" I scream, my thighs quivering as I fall apart in his arms.

Still buried deep inside me, he pulls me from the counter. He palms my ass as I wrap my arms and legs around him, sliding up and down his thick length. "You feel so good wrapped around me."

I work with him, flexing my hips as he moves me. "You're so big and stretching me so tight."

"But look at you," he pants, his voice thick with lust and praise. "Taking every last inch of Daddy's cock so well."

We move through the apartment, desperate and needy. Every surface becomes our playground: the counter, the wall, my tiny loveseat overlooking the city. My skin tingles everywhere he touches, his hands rough and claiming. His breath is hot against my neck, as he commands and praises in equal measure. I come for him again and again, until I'm soaked with sweat and every muscle in my body aches.

Lifting us both from the loveseat, he carries me toward the bed. "You're mine. Every inch of you."

"I'm yours, Daddy." The words escape my mouth and pass over my lips without thought.

His...

The way he talks to me—like I'm his and only his—flutters in my pussy... And my heart. *And apparently turns off my already malfunctioning brain.*

It ignites something in him, something feral. His gaze narrows, and his soft, golden eyes suddenly burn with fire. He takes me to the floor and quickly slides back inside. Cillian drives into me hard and deep, every thrust more brutal than the last. Each of them claiming my offering—claiming *me*. I cling to him, my nails digging into his back as he takes me unrelentingly hard.

We move together, wrapped in sweat and each other. My face buried in his neck, I moan against his skin. When I come, it crashes through me violently, like something ripped loose from the inside out. Vulnerability. I didn't just let Cillian fuck me. I gave myself to him.

"Such. A. Good. Fucking. Girl. For. Me." He grits each word between thrusts, his face contorted with the agony of a man on the edge. Slamming into me—hips sputtering and jaw clenched—he spills his release into me as a guttural roar rattles from deep in his lungs. His chest heaving, he exhales, "*My good fucking girl.*"

Collapsed on the floor in a heap, we're a tangled mess of limbs, the world falling away until there is only us in this moment.

Rolling onto my side, I fold my forearms across his chest and plant my chin on them. Glancing to our left, a small chuckle escapes me when I see the pristinely made bed. "Guess we didn't quite make it, huh?"

He smirks, brushing damp hair from my face with a possessive tenderness. "It's still early, firecracker." His voice is dark and certain. "And I'm not leaving until I claim you there too."

The evening's city lights filter through the thin curtains, casting a kaleidoscope of hazy light and shadows over the room. We're sprawled on her bed, my back resting on a pillow against the wrought-iron headboard, and her head resting on my thigh. Aimlessly running my fingers through her rich chocolate hair, I stare down at her. She's quiet and calm; it's a strange kind of peace I haven't felt in a long time. I brush my thumb over her uninjured cheek, watching her eyelids flutter closed as she sinks deeper against me. Her scent clings to me, soaked into my skin—bright citrus and spice. Every breath fills my chest with her.

I didn't plan on staying this morning. I told myself I'd drive her home, make sure she was okay, and give her a tiny bit of space to recover. For a day or two—or at least a few hours. But standing on her doorstep, the pull between us was magnetic. I literally couldn't bring myself to turn around and walk down those three flights of stairs. Fuck, even if I did make it down to the entrance, I would've barreled back up them before reaching the sidewalk.

What really fucks me up is how good today felt. Not just the sex, though that wrecked me in a way I'm still recovering from. It was everything in between. The two of us barefoot in her kitchen, making dinner and arguing about what kind of music to play while she danced in my T-shirt. We talked for hours, sharing stories about our childhood and our families, but each of hers felt like it had holes she wasn't quite ready to fill.

A day of nothing but boring domestic shit. We didn't go anywhere. We didn't do anything big. And still, I felt... content. *Normal*. And that shit scares the hell out of me. Yet, I enjoyed every minute of it. I could spend every fucking day like this with her and not get tired of this kind of life.

My phone buzzes on her bedside table, a sharp reminder of the other world waiting for me. I ignored it a few minutes ago, not wanting to disturb Madison as she was falling asleep—and hoping it was a false alarm. Sliding my fingers from her hair, I move as little as possible when I stretch my arm out. Enzo's name is flashing on the screen, and I know before answering it that there this isn't going to be good news.

I swipe to answer. "Yeah?"

Enzo doesn't waste time. "We've got a problem. Surveillance. Someone has eyes on the club. Maybe our apartments, too."

I sit up straighter, my body instantly alert. "What kind of surveillance?"

"Cameras. Nik found two hidden in the back of the club. Somebody got inside—and we're not sure how deep."

"FBI?"

"Has to be. They're quiet, clean. And Nik can't find any trace of them being planted on the security feed."

"Any idea what they've seen?"

Enzo sighs. "No clue. We don't know if they were planted yesterday or during construction. Fuck. There were about a thousand guys in and out of this day and night before we opened and nearly as many every night since."

My jaw tightens, and I let out a heavy sigh. "All right. I'll call in a favor. Judge Ralston owes me for keeping his activities at the club quiet. If there's a warrant, he'll find it."

"We better move fast, Cian. If they're in this deep already, we're fucked. Life without parole puts a real damper on shit."

I hang up and look at Madison. Her eyes are closed, and she's sleeping peacefully. Tenderly I lift her head and slip from beneath her, managing to slide from the bed without waking her. I pull the blankets over her, and she stirs for a second, but quickly falls back into slumber. Quietly fumbling around her tiny apartment in the dark, I find my clothes and dress. Before leaving, I kiss the top of her forehead one last time—tracing the soft lines of her battered face with my fingertips. "I'll be back. " I promise the words against her skin.

Slinking out of her apartment, I borrow her spare key so that I can lock the deadbolt. I pull my phone from my pocket and send Madison a quick message, knowing she keeps her cell on silent, so it won't disturb her. Then a second to my brothers to let them know I'm on my way.

Rain slicks the roads, and the city lights cast a haze of neon across the pavement on my drive to the club. I drive faster than I should, weaving through cars as I make my way uptown. My mind races with the weight of how this could be the beginning of everything crashing down around us.

Walking into the club, everything looks like business as usual—girls on the stage and drinks flowing like Mardi Gras. But it doesn't feel like any other night. The mood is sharp and electric. Enzo is pacing near the bar—his face tight and a half-empty whiskey glass on the counter beside him. Nikolai meets me with a grim look when I join them, his arms folded across his chest and his eyes still narrowed.

"These are what we've found so far." Nik slides a glass of water with three cameras no bigger than my fingertip at the bottom across the bar.

"Do they have audio?" I ask.

"I don't know. I sent a picture to Hawk. It's his area of expertise."

In disbelief, I shake my head. "And there's really nothing on the security footage?"

"I have guys skimming through it again," Nik informs me. "But it's weeks of footage, and so far, nothing stands out."

"Fuck," I mutter, raking a hand through my hair. "We think any of the staff were in on it?"

"Too early to know." Enzo shakes his head. "But we vetted the fuck out of every person we put on our payroll to make sure this shit wouldn't happen. It has to be a customer or from before we opened."

"Check them all again. Just to be safe." I know we went through everyone with a fine-tooth comb, but shit gets missed. Loyalties change. People get desperate. "Run backgrounds, credit checks, family ties. I don't care if it's the bartender's dog walker—if they breathe near this place, we need to know everything about them."

Enzo gives a sharp nod and pulls out his phone.

"I texted the judge on my way over," I add, my fingers tapping along the edge of the bar. "But I'll call him first thing in the morning. If a warrant was filed—sealed or not—Ralston will find it. He owes me."

"And if it wasn't a legal search?" Nik watches me with those unreadable, ice-cutting eyes.

"Then we've got a bigger problem." I heavily exhale at the thought. "If this is covert... or not the Feds... It could be another family. Could be someone trying to make a name by taking us down. We're gonna have to look at every inch of our operation. Everything."

"Jagger and Hawk were already on their way into town," Enzo adds. "They'll check the security and sweep the apartments and the club when they arrive in a few days."

Nik folds his arms. "And if we find more bugs?"

"Then we stop talking and start fucking hunting. No one crosses the Kings and lives to talk about it."

CHAPTER 24
madison

The room is still dark when I wake—the edges tinged with that fragile, pre-dawn gray. My head is still fuzzy from sleep, and my limbs heavy under the warmth of the blanket. I drift through half-dreams as I struggle to fully come to. Stretching across the bed for Cillian, my hand seeks his warmth. Instead, I find empty sheets beside me, cool to the touch, like he climbed from my bed hours ago. It suddenly feels vast without him—the imprint of his body gone, leaving a hollow I didn't expect to notice so sharply.

Curling up on my pillow where he slept, I bury my face in it and catch the lingering trace of him—the sharp, spicy warmth of his cologne clings to my sheets. I breathe him in and call softly into the shadowed apartment, "Cillian?" The only response I receive is the steady hum of the refrigerator.

I reach for my phone on the nightstand, only to remember I left it on the kitchen counter last night. After slipping off the bed, I wrap a sheet around me when the cool air hits my skin. I move slowly, my body still aching and sore from last night, both from Cillian and that asshole, Hudson, as well. I lift my phone from the counter, the screen lighting up with a mess of missed messages and notifications.

CILLIAN

> Sorry, firecracker. I had an emergency. Let me know when you're up.

I smile softly, staring like an idiot at the screen as my thumbs pad against the screen.

> I'm assuming you find it easier to sneak out when the women you bed are still sleeping.

His response appears almost immediately.

> If it wasn't my brothers, Satan himself couldn't have pulled me out of your bed.

My smile deepens as a strange warmth blooms in my chest. I've dated plenty of men who talk a smooth game, but Cillian isn't like any of them. He isn't all surface charm. His words are never just words. When he speaks, it comes from the depths of his soul. I can feel it in the way he holds me. How every moment with me stirs something fierce inside of him. He isn't just saying he wanted to stay—he truly meant it. For all his rough edges and the darkness of his cruel world, he craves this, the quiet and softness that the parts of me I've shared somehow bring him.

His next message arrives before I get a chance to respond.

> It's early. Go back to bed. I have some things to take care of. I'll be back to get you this evening.

I want to argue and tell him I'm not tired or that I need him back in my bed, but I don't.

> Yes, Daddy.

> Good girl.

Not being a good girl, I don't listen. I stay in the kitchen with my back pressed to the refrigerator, trying to breathe through the swell of something that feels too much like longing. *Like falling.* I scroll through the rest of the messages. Seven more. Three from my mom. Four from an unknown number.

I open the first message from Mom, the time stamp glowing 12:14 a.m.

> MOM
>
> Haven't heard from you in a couple of days and can't sleep. Just wanted to check in. Call me when you're up, okay?

The second at 12:33 a.m.

> I'm worried about you, Maddie.

It's followed promptly by the one that nearly breaks me.

> I know you can handle yourself, sweetheart. You always have. But just… be careful, okay?

Too fucking late.

My chest tightens as I stare at her words, caught between wanting to laugh and the urge to cry. She doesn't know. She has no clue how far over the edge I am. For as cautious as I've been, I jumped over that cliff without a parachute. Without a single regard for the consequences I'm going to be forced to face. And to top it off, I'm falling fast and hard.

> Work has me busy. I love you and I'm okay. I promise.

I hit send, and the lie lands like a rock in the pit of my stomach. I'm not okay.

I'm not remotely okay.

Swiping across the screen, I pull up the messages from the unknown number.

UNKNOWN

> You didn't come home the other night

> Where were you, Madison?

> I can't protect you if I don't know where you are and what you're doing.

> I'm watching you very closely, little girl.

My stomach drops, and my chest heaves, a wave of nausea building in the base of my throat, at the cold truth staring me in the face from behind the glow of the screen. The high of last night—*of Cillian*—evaporates like mist under the heat of daylight. I stare at the messages before me, and the weight of what I've done settles heavily in my chest. My fingers curl around the phone, white-knuckled, as my pulse ticks louder in my ears.

I barely remember who I was before Cillian King touched me —before he buried himself inside me and made me his in a way that no man had before him. This wasn't supposed to happen. *He* wasn't supposed to happen. I've made mistakes before—cold, calculated ones. But this? This is different. I can't just up and walk away from this. This mistake has a heartbeat and consequences that could destroy us both.

After sliding into the driver's seat, I fire off a quick text as the engine purrs beneath me.

> On my way. I'll be there in 20. We're having dinner with my family. Anything you want to wear is fine.

Her response buzzes before I can even shift into reverse.

MADISON

> My face…

> I don't want to go out in public yet.

I figured as much. Skin the shade of muddled berries clings to her jaw—a reminder of the hands that made the mistake of touching her. It'll be at least a few more days before it fades enough that makeup could cover it.

I know. My place. Enzo is cooking.

I'm not taking no for an answer. I'll drag you out naked over my shoulder if I have to.

She opens the door the moment I knock. She's wearing a dark teal summer dress—the kind that clings just enough to hint at her amazing curves beneath it. The thin shoulder straps dip to the low but tasteful V, displaying just a hint of cleavage. It cinches at her waist, and the hem brushes below her knees. Her hair is loose and tousled—messy in the perfect way—and shielding some of the bruising on her face. She looks effortlessly gorgeous, and it almost takes my breath away.

Not bothering with pleasantries, I roughly pull her into me and kiss her. Not just a kiss. I claim her mouth with mine, slow and deep, until I feel her melt against me. Her fingers curl around my collar like she's trying to ground herself. She pulls back, breaking our kiss with a look in her eyes I can't quite place. "We should go," she mutters, breathlessly.

I can't argue with her—even if something about this feels off —because if we don't leave, we're seconds from being back in her bed.

The ride to my place is quiet. Too quiet. Madison stares out the window, eyes distant, as the city passes in a blur of lights. Something's definitely different from when I left her early this morning. I can feel it in the way she's struggling to hold my gaze. I keep one hand on the wheel and place the other on her thigh.

"You okay, firecracker?" I keep my voice low. Barely looking at me, she gives a small shrug. I try again, softer this time. "Talk to me. You can tell Daddy anything."

That gets a reaction. She lets out a soft breath and turns her face slightly my way. She forces a smile. "I'm fine," she says quickly—*too* quickly. "Really. It's nothing. I'm just tired." I watch her as I drive. Her eyes flicker to the passing lights, and her fingers tap lightly against her thigh, nervously, distracted—or both.

I fight the urge to press further as we pull into the parking garage. Her fingers lace with mine as I help her from the car, and she falls against my side—everything suddenly feeling right again.

Enzo went all-out. The penthouse smells like garlic and slow-simmered tomatoes when we step through the door. So good, you'd think we'd walked into his nonna's house. The kitchen table is already set with thick white plates, stemless wine glasses, and linen napkins none of us ever bother using. In the center, there's linguine tossed in a silky pomodoro sauce with fresh basil and shaved parmesan, crispy veal cutlets accompanied by lemon wedges, roasted zucchini bathed in garlic butter, and a loaf of crusty bread.

Eavan kisses my cheek before dragging Madison into a hug. Madison hugs her back without hesitation, but there's tension in her shoulders as we all take our seats around the table.

Nikolai raises his glass. "Christ. I thought this was just dinner, not a wedding feast."

"You're welcome," Enzo mutters, sitting down and grabbing the bottle to refill his glass.

Plates are passed around, and Madison is still distant, focused on her plate and quietly listening to the rest of us. Eavan pulls her into a conversation about going shopping later in the week, and she slowly becomes the sassy girl that I'm used to—chiming in with small comments, bratty quips, and a soft laugh here and there.

By the time we finish the third bottle and are all the kind of full that turns conversation lazy, I find Nik staring at me, head tilted and eyes narrowed like he's trying to solve a riddle.

"Why the fuck are you staring at me like that?" I bark.

He leans back, smirking. "You're here with this beautiful woman, but I can't help but wonder if she's really your type."

I glance at Madison and blurt, "What are you talking about?"

Nik lifts his glass, grinning now. "Twice in the past few months, I've walked in on you on the floor. Lying on top of men with their cocks out." Madison chokes on her wine. *Jesus fucking Christ.* "I just can't help but wonder if there's something you aren't telling all of us."

Everyone laughs as I snap, "I was *beating the shit* out of both of them."

"If memory serves me correct"—Enzo shrugs, ever the instigator—"you sucker-punched me, and *you* were the one who tapped out."

"You were going to fucking strangle me."

"He's into breath play. That was foreplay," Eavan deadpans, already pouring more wine. Madison laughs full and unrestrained, a rich, hearty sound that bubbles up from her chest. Completely authentic, like it couldn't be faked even if she wanted to.

With the night getting late, Enzo and Eavan disappear to their apartment beneath the penthouse. Nik vanishes shortly after, and I lead Madison out onto the terrace. We curl up on the chaise, her body tucked into mine. She shifts against me, her voice soft. "I should be good to return to work by Friday."

I glance at her. *Friday?* The thought sits bitter on my tongue. "We can discuss it."

She laughs—sharp and not amused this time—as she pushes out of my hold. Clearly annoyed, she snips, "A couple of nights together doesn't mean I'm quitting my job for you."

My jaw clenches. "You need time to heal. And honestly? You're mine. Every inch of you is mine. I don't want other men seeing you like that. And I sure as fuck don't want them touching you."

Her eyes spark under the terrace lights, piqued but defiant. "Discussing it doesn't mean you get to dictate."

I lift her hand slowly, brushing a kiss across her palm, and her breath catches. "We *are* discussing it. I didn't say 'no,'" I murmur. "But I can be pretty persuasive." She rolls her eyes—fighting the smile tugging at her lips—as I slide over top of her, the weight of my body pinning her gently, one hand trailing up her thigh.

"Good," she whispers. "Because I'm not making this easy."

My hand slips beneath the soft hem of her dress, fingers brushing over her inner thigh, slow and deliberate. She bites her bottom lip when I graze the edge of her panties.

"Would you rather I make my argument with my fingers or my tongue? Both are quite compelling."

Chewing at her lips, she mutters, "Fingers."

Groaning low, I slip her panties to the side. I lift my hand, bringing my fingers to my mouth. I suck them in and coat them thoroughly with my saliva before easing two of them inside her. She arches off the chaise with a sharp gasp, her nails digging into my shoulder.

I keep my strokes steady, deep and deliberate, teasingly curling against her G-spot. Kissing along her jaw to her neck, I gravelly whisper against her skin, "You think I want to share this? You think I can stand the thought of men ogling what's mine?" I add my thumb to her clit and apply more pressure against her walls, eliciting a beautiful fucking whimper from her as it pushes her over the edge. "Or of you dancing half-naked for strangers when you could be here, doing this with me?"

Working my fingers through her orgasm, she's on the brink within seconds. She moans, hips grinding into my hand as she falls apart for me again. "They don't deserve to wonder if you come as sweet as you do, much less dare to do so with *my* pussy on their lap." Working my hand a little rougher and nipping along her neck, I force her to come for me again. "You belong here. With me."

After pulling my fingers from her, I draw one of them into my mouth and suck the sweet tang of her from it. Her face turns toward me, she's breathless and her eyes are burning. I feed her my other coated finger, and she swirls her tongue around it, eagerly cleaning her arousal from it.

"Watching and listening to you come has me so fucking hard for you," I rasp against her ear.

"Good," she pants. "Because it's my turn to provide a counterargument."

CHAPTER 26
madison

Standing from the chaise, my legs are still trembling, and my body is on fire, every nerve still humming. But all I can think about is pulling him inside and getting him under me, over me, or anywhere I can have him if it means he's buried deep inside me. I reach for his hand to guide him back toward the penthouse, but he doesn't budge from his seat.

Turning to face him, I find him staring up at me with a smug grin plastered across his face, like he already won. "We're not going inside, firecracker," he murmurs, his voice low and thick with lust. "You want to argue about showing off that gorgeous fucking body? Then show Daddy—and the whole fucking city—how badly you want it."

My breath catches. I glance around, the skyline stretching around us like a wall of glittering eyes. Dozens of illuminated windows shine from the surrounding buildings. My pulse thrums in my ears thinking about how many people could be watching, but I know he's testing how far I'll go.

I swallow hard, then reach beneath my dress and hook my fingers under the waistband of my panties. Slowly, I slide them down my legs, drawing them over my thighs, my knees, and past my calves. I step out of them one foot at a time and hold them out to him. The cotton is soaked through. He playfully pulls them from my fingers and lifts them to his nose, inhaling deeply with a contented sigh that sends heat spiraling to my core. His eyes rake over my still-clothed body, his voice gravel-deep. "That's a lot of clothes and not a lot of skin. Not exactly pleading your case."

Without breaking eye contact, I undo the invisible zipper running along the side of my dress, grip the hem, and pull it over my head in one smooth motion. I toss it toward him and let it fall to the ground at his feet. Naked, I lower myself to my knees before him.

I teasingly exhale, "Oh, Daddy..." With nimble fingers, I reach for his belt and unbuckle it slowly, taking my time unzipping his pants. His cock springs free, thick, veined, and already aching for me. I drag my tongue along his length, from base to tip, not once breaking our heated stare. "I haven't even started."

I take him into my mouth, tongue swirling and lips tightening around him. I hollow my cheeks and work him deep, feeling the way his thighs tense under my hands. A sharp groan spills from his lips as I swallow his cock—one hand tugging gently on his balls and the other gripping his thigh. "Fuck. That slutty little mouth of yours feels good," he roughly praises, and it only makes me hungry for more. His fingers fist my hair, pulling hard enough to sting, and I moan around him.

On the edge of release, his cock twitches in my mouth. I let him fall from my lips with a wet pop. I stroke him slowly, watching the saliva coating him glisten in the moonlight as I climb into his lap. Straddling him, I align his thick head to my entrance. With one slow motion, I sink over him until he's buried deep inside me—gasping at the sudden stretch and fullness. "I'm going back to the club."

My hips roll, grinding me over him. "I'm doing it for *me*. Because *I* enjoy it." His large hands slap my ass, both cheeks stinging as he roughly palms them.

"And you're going to let me," I grit, riding him hard and sliding myself over the entirety of his length. Planting my hand on his thighs, I lean back, and his eyes travel down my body to the unfettered view of where we meet with a growl. "All that work gives me the endurance to fuck like this—" I manage to push out the words as an orgasm rattles through me, my whole body shaking.

Throwing my arms around his neck, I slow my pace but grind harder. His jaw is clenched as his head tips back, each of his ragged breaths blowing against my neck.

"I'm doing it because I've never let a man tell me what to do," I breathlessly whisper against his ear, "and I don't plan on starting now."

He snarls, and his strong arms lock around my waist. In one quick, brutal motion, he flips me beneath him. My back hits the cushion, legs still wrapped around his hips as he looms over me, his face carved in shadows and fire. His hand wraps around my throat, and he tightens his fingers. "You're wrong, firecracker," he groans, thrusting deep enough to steal what little breath I could manage through his tight grip. "You *will* listen to Daddy, or you'll be punished."

He fucks me slow and rough, like a man possessed. Each thrust is deep, deliberate, and savage. My body arches for him —skin burning and heart hammering like thunder. "I'll compromise," he hisses. "You can dance. When I'm there. But the first asshole who so much as puts a fucking finger on you?" He pulls out and slams in painfully hard. "I'll drag him out back and put a bullet in his fucking skull."

I shouldn't like it. I should be furious at his possessiveness, the territorial demand he has over me. Instead, I'm unraveling. Coming undone for him—not just my body, but *me*. Because it's not only about control. It's about how far he'd go for me.

His mouth crashes over mine, stealing air and my ability to think, kissing me like he's starving and I'm the last thing he'll ever taste. The way he's pounding into me—deep and unrelenting—has me crying out into his mouth, my back bowing off the chaise as his cock drags against the rawest parts of me. Every stroke is devastating. Every thrust feels like he's fucking the air out of my lungs, like he's cementing his claim into the very center of me.

With a growled breath, he pulls from me and flips me again, forcing my chest to the chaise as he yanks my hips up. Ass in the air and legs trembling beneath me, I barely have time to gasp before he's slamming back into me from behind, burying himself deep with a force I've never felt before.

"You wanna test Daddy?" he barks, his fingertips digging into my hips as he drives into me again and again. "Then take every inch of this cock like the needy little slut you are."

The force of his hips meeting mine shoots jolts of ecstasy straight through me, each thrust seemingly harder than the last. My fingers grip onto the cushion, knees spread wide to steady myself as I whimper through the overwhelming pleasure. The friction, the fullness, and the filthy stretch of him pounding into me in this position—it's almost too much. *Almost.*

He slaps my ass, the sting blooming instantly before he grabs the flesh tight in his grip. "Fucking perfect," he growls. "So fucking beautiful—back arched, dripping wet, ready for me to fuck you however I please."

My body shakes from the force of him. When his fingers find my clit, I scream into the night. The orgasm trembling through me is so strong that my arms crumple beneath me, and my face falls into the cushion. His handprints blaze across my ass and thighs, and I push backward, needing to meet his vicious thrusts. "That's it, firecracker. Look how desperate you are to take Daddy's cock."

He folds himself over me, pinning me to the soft cushion. He groans against the side of my neck as my pussy flutters around him, and I sob through another grueling wave of euphoria. "My dirty girl likes being filled and owned, doesn't she?" he snarls. "Tell Daddy you love it."

"I... I love it, Daddy," I breathlessly stammer through my pleasure-filled sobs. Gasping and shaking beneath him, my nails claw at the cushion for some semblance of control. "My greedy little pussy... can't get enough."

My climax slams into me so hard I scream—the sound ripped from my chest yet muffled by the cushion under me. "Nobody else will ever make you come like I do, because that greedy little pussy belongs to me." His hips slam against my ass with a guttural roar, thrusting deep and stilling as he pours into me. "Mine."

Struggling to breathe, I exhale, "Daddy's." *Because I am.* No matter how hard I try to fight this, I already know I'm going to give him everything, no matter the cost.

THREE DAYS LATER

"Go back to sleep," I whisper, tenderly brushing Madison's hair away from her face and pressing a soft kiss to her temple.

"It's fine." Madison stirs beside me in the bed, her voice thick with sleep. "I'm up."

Nik's knock on the door was sharp and early, letting me know that Jagger and Hawk arrived a little earlier than expected—too damn early for the shit I know is coming. I pull on my clothes quickly as Madison stretches, her limbs uncurling like a cat under the covers. She blinks slowly, still caught in the haze of sleep. The bruises on her face are starting to fade, but the sight of them still twists something sharp in my gut.

"Who are Jagger and Hawk?" she murmurs, squinting up at me.

I pause at the door, one boot on, the other still in my hand. "Some hired guns we've worked with before. Muscle. We do other business with them, too. Enzo brought them in to keep an eye on Eavan a while back."

Madison sits up a little straighter, the covers slipping from her chest. "Keep an eye on her for what?" she asks, her brows furrowing with genuine curiosity.

"Take a shower and get dressed." I shake my head, ignoring her question. I leave her naked in my bed, staring at me with an unreadable expression.

The air grows thick as I make my way downstairs—the tension and unease palpable. Hawk, Jagger, Enzo, and Nik are all gathered around the kitchen island, mugs in hand. Nik is sipping black coffee. Jagger, as usual, looks like he hasn't slept. Enzo is pacing slowly, his jaw grinding. And is Hawk is scrolling through something on his phone, eyes narrowed at the screen.

"Morning," I mutter, grabbing a mug and pouring myself a cup. I take a sip and am surprised at the bite of it. *Thank fuck.*

"Sorry for intruding so early," Hawk begins. "But it's a lot of space to cover. We figured we'd get started sooner rather than later."

"We'll do a full sweep here first," Jagger explains, pulling out a small black case and flipping it open to reveal an array of electrical devices. "Then we'll move on to the club."

Hawk swipes through his phone, dropping it onto the counter with the photo Nik sent him the other night—the cameras he pulled from the club. "They do have audio. The feed they transmit is short-range. Which means someone is either watching from nearby—probably within a building or two."

"If they're smart, they're rotating through devices and recording feeds, as well," Jagger adds.

I run a hand through my hair. "Start here. I want everything combed through—no shortcuts."

We split off—Hawk and I sweep the penthouse while Jagger and Nik head to Enzo and Eavan's below. We go room by room, tearing apart every vent, every electrical socket, checking baseboards and light fixtures. If there's a pinhole to hide something in, we inspect it.

Madison appears a little after eight, fresh from the shower, her wet hair twisted up, wearing leggings and one of my T-shirts. She watches us silently from the kitchen as she pours herself a cup of coffee, eyes scanning the equipment, the wires, the mess we've made. I can feel the unease rolling off her. "You guys always ransack apartments apart before breakfast?" she asks with a casual smirk.

"That smart mouth, firecracker," I lament, without looking up from the outlet I'm pulling from the wall.

"Another one?" Hawk chuckles under his breath, having been on the receiving end of Eavan's more than a few times.

I shake my head. "What can I say? This place is a magnet for sassy women who like to talk back." I glance toward Madison to find her staring back at me with a pleased smile. *Such a brat.*

By late morning, we've swept every inch of the apartments. Nothing. Not in Enzo's, and not in mine. We've double-checked every frequency. Each of them is clean. *For now.*

The others start packing up their gear, and I pull Madison aside. "Stay," I softly insist.

"You want me to stay locked up like a princess in your ivory tower?" She tilts her head and arches a brow.

"No." I brush my knuckles over her cheek. "I just want you here when I come home."

The fire in her eyes tells me she wants to argue, but she doesn't. "Okay."

"I'll let Eavan know you're here, so you won't be alone all day."

———

It takes us over an hour to cover the office and backrooms of the club. By the time we hit the executive VIP, I already feel the knot tightening in my stomach. "This makes three," Hawk announces, crouched on a ladder, a screwdriver in one hand and a vent cover in the other. He holds up the tiny camera for a second before smashing it between the ladder and the handle of his screwdriver.

"Where else?" The words are like lead in my mouth.

Jagger steps in from the hall. "We just pulled another from the ceiling above the owners' booth. And one more from the rear entrance—the one you use for less-than-savory visitors."

"Like you fucks," Nikolai quips, trying to lighten the mood.

I cross my arms and lean back against the wall, tension creeping up my spine.

"They're watching you," Hawk mutters from the ladder. "Not

the girls. This isn't about getting off on strippers. They want to know what the three of you are up to."

"Targeted placement," Nik agrees. "They're tracking our movement, who we speak to, how long we linger—and I would assume most of all—who comes and goes through that private access."

My eyes drift over the lounge's plush seating and dim lights—a place meant to entertain the city's filthy rich and most corrupt. It's supposed to be ours. Supposed to be off-limits.

"How long do you think it's been going on?" I ask.

Hawk shrugs. "If I had to guess? Since you opened. Maybe longer. If it took us ladders and screwdrivers, it did for them, too."

The thought that someone is feeding intel to whoever is on the other side of these feeds makes my blood fucking boil. I can handle enemies I can see coming, but this invisible threat hiding in our walls makes me feel like I'm the prey, vulnerable in a way I haven't felt in years. "Where are we at on going through the construction workers? And the staff?" I glance at Enzo, who is scrolling through files on his tablet.

He sighs. "About halfway. We've been double-checking everyone's background, bank activity, and family ties. At least three years back for everyone. But it'll take a few more days to finish the rest."

"A few days might be too fucking long," I say under my breath, my jaw tightening so hard my teeth grind together.

CHAPTER 28
madison

The sun's starting to dip outside the massive windows, casting long golden rays across the hardwood floor as I sit cross-legged on the couch next to Eavan. We've been holed up inside all day, just the two of us. Cillian, Enzo, and Nik have been gone since this morning, tied up at the club with Hawk and Jagger.

I didn't want to stay, but Cillian looked like he had enough going on without arguing with me. Although I have to admit, spending the day with his sister has been nice. She's as sweet in long doses as she is in the short amount of time I've spent with her before.

We spent hours on the couch with the TV on in the background, flipping through old movies neither of us really watched. We swapped stories—small, surface-level ones. She told me about growing up in New York, and I told her about my boring childhood in a small town in Virginia. I shared the carefully curated version of my life, keeping my secrets tucked tight to my chest. Sharing more with her than I have with Cillian, I talked about my dad's passing and how I took up stripping to finish paying my way through college. *It's not pretty, but it is the truth.*

The apartment smells amazing—garlic and sweet basil wafting from the oven where our lasagna is baking. It's not gourmet by any means, but we made it with what little there was to work with in this apartment. Eavan claims Enzo will turn his nose up at the jarred sauce the moment he smells it, but dinner will be ready when they all get home. *Home... This isn't your home, Madison.*

We're nestled into the plush leather couch, a near-finished bottle of red wine on the coffee table—both of us working on our second glass.

I take a sip, watching the light catch in the deep crimson liquid. The day has been peaceful, but I feel like I'm crawling out of my skin as I sit beside her. "How do you do this?" I blurt suddenly, unable to sit with the guilt twisting in my stomach any longer.

Eavan's head tilts slightly as she turns toward me. "Do what?" she asks with curiosity.

I swirl the wine in my glass, avoiding her eyes. "Handle Enzo leaving in the middle of the night. And knowing what he does when he's gone."

Her smile is soft but steady. "Simple. I know who he is and what kind of man he is when he leaves our home. But more importantly, I know what kind of man he is with me and his family. The rest doesn't matter."

I stare at her for a moment. Her eyes don't flicker. She means it. Every word.

"It's that easy?" I ask, unable to hide the disbelief in my tone.

"I love him. More than I thought possible to love a person," she replies without hesitation. "So, yes. It is that easy."

Her words are a punch to my chest.

I glance down at my wine, swallowing hard. Could I ever be that sure? That grounded? Could I really live in the gray areas Cillian's world bleeds into—where violence and power sit at the table with loyalty and love?

The guilt gnaws at me, slow, constant. Being here with Eavan, making dinner, drinking wine... it feels like stepping into someone else's life. A better version of mine. A far different future than I was ever meant to want. But I do. *God help me, I do.* It wasn't supposed to be like this. Falling for a man like Cillian King shouldn't have happened. And yet, here I am... making dinner with his little sister and spending the day with her like I belong here. *Wanting to belong here.* And that scares me more than anything.

Eavan doesn't ask what's going on in my head. Maybe she senses it. She's been in my shoes—sort of. Maybe she knows that whatever I'm feeling doesn't have a simple answer.

I glance over at her as she curls her legs beneath her. She's beautiful and composed. But there's an edge in her posture. It's the same one I see in Cillian and the guys, too. They all live like this, always bracing for something to go wrong. I've lived on the edge too, but not like this. Not with people I care about involved.

The oven beeps, loud and shrill, yanking me from my thoughts. Eavan hops up with a smile and heads into the kitchen, grabs oven mitts, and slides the bubbling pan of lasagna out onto the oven. I follow her slowly, still thinking. My thoughts are further thwarted by the sound of heavy footsteps and familiar voices behind me. I glance up as Nikolai walks in first, with Enzo immediately behind him.

Cillian's eyes instantly find me when he steps into the room, and he crosses it with purpose. Before I can even breathe, his mouth is on mine. His kiss is firm and demanding, but also warm and comforting. The tension drains from shoulders with every second his lips linger on mine.

Yeah... Maybe it really is just that simple.

His hand settles on my hip, and I glance up at him as he pulls back. "It smells amazing in here." He inhales, his gaze wandering behind me to the dinner cooling on the island.

"It smells good," Enzo admits. "But definitely not like Nonna's sauce." Eavan and I both start laughing before he even finishes his sentence.

"See!?" she exclaims. "He's a total snob about what he eats."

He pulls Eavan to him and uses his finger to pull her chin up toward him. "I am." He stares down at her with a dark gaze, and I very quickly realize that he is no longer talking about dinner.

"Go. Out," Cillian playfully barks. "The last thing I want to be thinking about while I eat dinner is my best friend's face between my little sister's thighs."

"It's not always my thighs," Eavan quips, clearly pleased with herself when Cillian lets out a disgusted groan.

Nikolai throws his arm around me and pulls me away from Cillian. Lowering his voice, but still loud enough for everyone to hear, he shares, "If he won't eat your ass, I would." My cheeks burn at his teasing of Cillian. *At least I think he's kidding.* I glance between the two of them, trying to make sure.

"Jesus Christ. I will eat her ass," Cillian huffs, possessively dragging me back from Nikolai, and I feel like my entire face is on fire from his declaration. Nikolai, Enzo, and Eavan all chuckle as Cillian drags a hand down his face.

Grabbing a plate, Nikolai winks at me with a smirk. "You're welcome."

ABOUT A WEEK LATER

It feels strange, stepping back into the dressing room of the club after being gone for so long. Long enough that I barely recognize Raven's reflection when I look in the mirror. The bruises are gone—mostly. The last of the yellowing can be covered easily with makeup, and for the first time since that asshole laid hands on me, I don't feel like a walking wound. I bend closer to the mirror, dabbing concealer over the faint shadow still clinging to my cheekbone.

The last few days have been filled with negotiations, whispered arguments, and slammed doors—*and sweaty, heat-filled nights leaving palm prints across my ass as we finalized our* compromise about me returning to the club. But somehow, we came to an agreement.

The rules? Only working when Cillian is at the club. And only when he's available to watch me, or leaves me under the eye of Enzo or Nikolai. Dancing only happens on the main floor. No VIP. Ever. After the way things went last time, I didn't actually fight that one. The rest were the very rules I swore I wouldn't accept, but his arguments were compelling—or at least wore me down. Standing in front of my locker, zipping up my black stilettos and adjusting the straps of my sheer rhinestone dress, I'm about to take the stage under his conditions.

I finish as the opening beats of my chosen song—"Pink Pony Club" by Chappell Roan—pulse through the club. The lights fall over me as I step onto the stage, glittering off my dress like it's a disco ball. I wrap my fingers around the pole, flipping upside down with ease before twisting into a slow spin. Arching my back, I drag one leg down the cool metal until my back is flush with the stage. My body moves with muscle memory, fluid and confident. *Thankfully.* Because my thoughts are on anything but the task at hand.

My eyes flick over every shadowed corner, every booth, and each balcony rail until I find him. Cillian is standing near the back of the club, one hand in his pocket and the other wrapped around a glass. He doesn't smile or give a wave. He just watches with an intensity that makes my heart hum. It centers me. Grounds me.

It's strange, how badly I want his eyes on me now. In the beginning, when I first started dancing here, I used to dread his gaze. It made me feel far too seen and exposed. But now? I crave it—both when I'm dancing *and* when I'm not. There's something in the way he looks at me that makes me know who I belong to. And it terrifies me how much I like it.

My performance comes to an end, sweat glistening across my chest as I swing down into a final pose, legs split wide in a slow descent that ends with my body curved along the stage pole. Applause breaks out, but I barely register it. My attention is on Cillian's heated stare and how he seems seconds from storming across the club and spreading me across one of these tables. A thought I'm not exactly opposed to.

I rise slowly, striding offstage with a sway of my hips, trying to keep my breathing steady. The high of performing still thrums under my skin as I walk in Cillian's direction. I make it three steps across the main floor when a hand wraps tightly around my wrist. My whole body freezes, and the hairs on the back of my neck stand on end. "You've been avoiding me, little girl," a low voice rasps behind me, and I don't need to turn around to know who it is.

Panic pulses through me as he steers me toward a shadowed booth tucked near the edge of the room. I stumble slightly as he takes his seat—my hand still caught firmly in his grip. Not releasing his firm hold, he pats his thigh. The unspoken request is clear: *Dance for me.*

My heart hammering with nerves, I tentatively climb onto his lap. Keeping my movements stiff and minimal, my eyes scan the room again, searching for Cillian, Nikolai, and Enzo.

"Good to see you, Special Agent Roark," Agent Frankford leans close, his breath catching against my ear.. Stunned, I sit motionless on his lap—a tap of his hand on my thigh reminding me to dance.

"What the hell are you doing here?" I hiss through my teeth, keeping my smile wide for appearances.

"You haven't checked in for weeks. And you've been ignoring my messages, too."

It's not a lie. I've been undercover in here for nearly a month, and I checked in like clockwork every day—until the night I found myself sandwiched between Cillian and a steel door. I'm doing everything I can to maintain my professionalism, especially when everything in me wants to fall deeper into Cillian's dark world.

"And that's worth blowing my fucking cover?" I huff, feigning annoyance with him. It's safer than the truth. I can't exactly tell my handler what's really going on. That I'm slipping— falling for the very man I'm supposed to be surveilling.

"Considering we lost the last of our surveillance, yes. We needed to know that you're still alive and see if you've learned anything about the inner workings of their operation."

I almost laugh. *What have I learned?* That Cillian King fucks like a god, protects like a monster, and looks at me like I'm his most prized possession. And let's not forget that I hate myself for how much I crave the warmth of his arms around me when I sleep.

"I haven't got any new intel," I lie, neglecting to inform him about Cillian murdering Hudson or bringing in Hawk and Jagger to thoroughly sweep their lives for bugs. "And I'm fine."

He reaches into his coat pocket and pulls out three tiny cameras, briefly displaying them in his palm before folding them into a twenty-dollar bill. He tucks the wad into the front of my G-string. "Replace the ones they found. Tonight."

I freeze, staring at the weighted bill resting just above my pussy, and my stomach coils with dread. Reaching for it, I stop dead when I spot Cillian over Frankford's right arm. He's moving fast—his eyes locked on me—storming toward us with rage flickering behind his eyes.

"Shit," I mutter.

Frankford sees him too and straightens slightly. Cillian tears me from Frankford's lap, and he rises quickly to his feet, instinctively looking to protect me. Cillian plants a hand on Frankford's chest and shoves him back into the booth, quickly pulling me into his chest. His fingers slide beneath my jaw, tenderly tilting my face up to his. "Are you okay?" He brushes my cheek tenderly with his thumb.

My eyes dart between Frankford's disapproving stare and Cillian's furious concern. I nod quickly and mutter, "Yeah. I'm okay." Frankford watches us, silent, his mouth pressing into a tight line as his eyes track every movement.

Seemingly content with my answer, Cillian leans down, and his lips brush against my ear. "Go get changed. We're leaving." Cillian kisses my forehead, lingering for a moment, and the knot in my chest loosens a bit as the one in my stomach cinches tight. Behind him, Enzo and Nik arrive, both watching the situation unfolding with narrowed eyes.

I don't argue. I back away, feeling everyone's eyes burning into my spine as I follow Cillian's instruction.

In the dressing room, I head straight to a bathroom stall with my heart pounding. I spin the lock and yank the folded bill from my G-string the moment the door swings shut behind me. Unfolding the twenty-dollar bill, I reveal the cameras—so small and easy to hide.

My hand shakes as I hold them in my palm, staring down at the toilet below. This is it—the moment I'm forced to choose. I close my eyes and take a long, shuddering breath. Everything inside me is coiled so tightly that I might explode. My stomach turning, and my head spinning. But my heart? It knows. I turn my hand, and the cameras drop into the water with a soft plunk.

I flush, and in an instant, they're gone. And nothing will ever be the same again.

CHAPTER 30
cillian

My eyes don't stray from Madison—not once—until she disappears behind the curtain at the back of the club. Only then do I let myself look at the man still seated in the booth.

"You aren't welcome here," I snarl, stepping closer to Agent Frankford, the smug FBI agent who dared come to our apartment with his loose-as-fuck insinuations about what we did to our fathers. His smug posture doesn't change, but I catch the flicker in his eyes—he's scared. *And he should be.*

"You think you scare me, King? This place is coming down, and it's only a matter of time before I have you and your brothers in cuffs. Then behind bars, where you belong."

Enzo steps beside me, arms crossed over his chest. Nik flanks the other side, his jaw ticking.

"Big talk from someone sitting in our booth without backup," I grind out, my voice low.

Frankford doesn't flinch. "You might've taken out our surveillance, but we've got people on the inside. You won't see the next one coming."

Enzo steps forward, his face darkening. "Inside, where? Here? At the club? Who the fuck did you flip?"

Frankford doesn't answer—just laughs, his stare focused on Enzo. "You should be worried. By the time I'm done, I'll find a way to arrest that cute little redhead of yours, too. Eavan, right?"

An angered growl rises from my chest, ready to kill him where he sits. But Enzo beats me to it, grabbing him by the collar and yanking him from the booth. Slamming him against the edge of the table, Enzo snarls, "You keep her fucking name out of your mouth." He twists Frankford into a headlock, dragging him through the club. Nik and I quickly follow, pushing past the dancers, staff, and clientele who freeze as we pass.

When we reach the rear hall, I excuse myself for a second—I need to find Madison. I grab two trusted guys from security as I cross the back of the club. She's stepping out of the dressing room when I find her, face flushed and eyes wide. I cross the space in seconds, cupping her face with both hands. "I'm so sorry, firecracker. Something came up." I press my forehead against hers, hating every inch between us.

"That man?" she asks softly, her voice cracking and lower lip quivering.

I silently respond with a nod, not wanting to drag her into this part of my life. "Nate and Sam are going to give you a ride home. I'll call you in the morning."

She nods, but the worry in her eyes is sharp. I kiss her, slow, soft, lingering against her lip when I break away from her. She presses into me, and I force myself to pull away before I can't.

Leaving her with Nate and Sam, I turn on my heel and head toward the rear door of the club. Enzo's SUV is waiting for me in the alley. I climb into the back of his G-Wagon. Frankford is slumped unconscious next to me, blood trickling from his nose. Enzo starts the car without a word, headlights cutting through the dark streets. Nik rides shotgun, silent and unreadable, his fingers tapping a slow rhythm on the grip of his knife.

The warehouse is cold, the only illumination coming from a single overhead bulb that casts a harsh glow over the center of the room. We have Frankford dragged inside and tied to a steel chair, his wrists secured behind his back, ankles bound to the legs before he wakes. When he finally comes to, he's groggy and blinking against the bright light.

"Morning," I quip. "Sleep well?"

He looks up slowly, blood drying above his upper lip. "You don't know what you're doing."

"We do. Of all people, with your theories about us... You should understand that we know *exactly* what we're doing." I crouch in front of him and lower my voice. "Who's your guy inside?"

I don't get an answer—just a blank, stubborn stare from his bloodshot eyes.

"Okay," I nod, pushing to my feet and cracking my knuckles. "Let's get started." My first punch is almost polite—a warm-up with a jab to the gut. It lands just below his ribs, and he grunts as the breath whooshes from his lungs. The second lands on his cheekbone with a sharp crack that sends his head whipping sideways. I land two more on his face, fresh blood now trickling from his nose. "Who's your fucking guy, Frankford?"

Lips pursed, he shakes his head.

Nik steps forward, twirling the knife in his palm. "Let me." He drags the smooth blade along Frankford's forearm—slow and surgical. His skin slices open, blood welling immediately. He grits his teeth and holds back his screams as Nik takes his time adding three more deep cuts. Blood trickles down Frankford's arms, pooling on the concrete behind his chair.

"This doesn't end until you talk," I inform him before landing another punch to his already bloody and swelling face.

"He wants to be a martyr. We can make that happen." Enzo paces behind the agent restlessly. He grabs a pair of bolt cutters from the workbench and holds them up for Frankford to see the steel blades. "This is gonna hurt," he warns, gripping his bloody left hand. "Just be happy I'm starting with your tongue."

"No," Frankford blurts. *Finally.*

I smile and condescendingly tap my palm against his face. "There he is."

Enzo takes his pinky finger. The sound is grotesque—a muffled crunch of bone and cartilage—followed by Frankford's blood-curdling scream. It echoes around the metal walls of the warehouse, sounding like a wounded animal. His body convulses against the chair, the pain suddenly too much.

"Tell us who it is," I insist as Enzo readies to take another finger. "Or we might have to start getting creative." He spits at me, bloody spittle spraying across the front of my shirt. Enzo squeezes the cutters, and a second finger drops to the pool of blood at his feet.

I spend two hours methodically wrapping piano wire around each of Frankford's toes, slowly cinching it tight and sawing through the bone, agonizingly removing them one by one. Drenched in sweat and covered in blood, he trembles above me but stays silent. *He's a stubborn son of a bitch.*

"I'm not telling you shit," he pants between labored breaths.

"Who's your guy inside?" I demand, my fist slamming into his jaw again. "Who?"

We go all night, savagely inflicting pain on him. By sunrise, blood soaks all of his clothes, and his head hangs lifeless against his chest. He didn't break, not even a hint of the name we were seeking.

"Maybe he was just full of shit." Nik wipes his hands with a rag, breathing heavily. "Maybe they don't actually have anyone undercover."

"Maybe," I parrot, staring at Frankford's body. My knuckles are raw, and I'm exhausted. "Or maybe he was so sure of what we have done that he was willing to die to let someone else finish the job."

We all stand around him for a moment in silence. We just killed a Fed. We might as well have wrapped the piano wire around our necks and asked them to cinch it tight.

True to his word, Cillian called me early this morning, informing me to be ready within the hour. He was knocking on my door by 8:00 a.m., greeting me with a soft kiss on the cheek.

His sports car hums beneath us, the leather seats creaking softly as I shift uneasily, watching the city grow small in the side-view mirror while we drive in silence. I can barely pull my eyes from the bruised and bloodied knuckles resting on my thigh. When I do, I look up to find him stealing quick, guarded looks my way.

I clutch the edge of my seat, like it's somehow going to keep me from falling apart. Memories of the furious look on his face when he tore me out of that booth burn fresh beneath my skin, and I know without asking exactly why his hand is so tattered. *Agent Frankford.* The nerves knot in my stomach as we drive further from civilization, fear coursing through me that my handler gave me up at some point last night. I try to swallow down the thought, but my throat feels raw and tight, like I'm swallowing glass.

When Cillian finally slows, we are completely alone. I don't see a single car in the parking lot. "Where are we?" My voice cracks, sounding small and fragile as I slowly turn toward him.

Ignoring my question, Cillian cuts off the engine. He slips from the driver's seat and rounds the car. My heart hammers wildly, and my gut twists tighter as he opens my car door, certain this is where I meet my end. He reaches out a hand, taking it gently and helping me out of the car. When he stares down at me, his eyes are filled with exhaustion. "The other day, you asked what Jagger and Hawk were protecting Eavan from. I want to tell you."

I nod and swallow hard, hoping he can't see my nerves unraveling.

"Here?" The word slips from over my lips, just above a whisper, barely believing where we are.

He threads his fingers through mine, his rough calluses sliding along my smooth palm. "Yes."

The air is thick with fresh-cut grass and moss. Gravel crunches beneath our feet as we walk side-by-side with our fingers laced together—silence quickly settling between us. He leads me through rows of headstones. Sunlight gleams off the polished granite and weathered stone, casting soft shadows across the well-maintained grounds. It's quiet—*far too quiet.*

We stop before a large marble tombstone—the gravesite even

more pristine than the rest of the cemetery. I read the headstone.

Saoirse O'Brien

Beloved Mother

My breath hitches when I see the dates. She died exactly sixteen years ago today. I look up at Cillian, searching his face for something. *Anything.* He rests his hand on the stone, his fingers tracing invisible patterns as if he's trying to touch a ghost.

"It started here," he murmurs, his voice thick with emotion. He looks up from the headstone and meets my eyes, his dark and full of grief. His words are equally as heavy and raw. "My mother..."

He takes a deep, shuddering breath and clenches his jaw tight. "She was taken from me... from us... in the worst way." His voice breaks slightly, but he keeps going, "Kidnapped. Tortured. Murdered by a rival family who tried to use her as leverage to take over my father's empire."

Bending down, he kisses the top of the cool stone before continuing, "My father... he let it happen." His gaze drops to the ground, his voice bitter and hollow as he solemnly shakes his head. "He fed her to the fucking wolves to save himself. To save his power and his money. At thirteen years old, I learned exactly what kind of man my father was. What kind of man he expected me to become—cold, calculated, and merciless. Willing to do the unthinkable."

The already tight knot in my stomach twists further, terrified of where this conversation is going. His jaw clenches as his eyes find mine—his flickering with a determined fire. "I swore I would never let that happen again. And I swore I'd never be like him. But fate is a cruel fucking bitch… I'm more ruthless than he could've imagined."

His eyes not leaving mine, he tells me every sordid detail of the deal his father made with the Irish, Bratva, and Armenian mobs—using Eavan as a bargaining chip to forge them together in the world of human trafficking. Seeing the pain in his eyes when he talks about the hell of a marriage she was being thrust into nearly breaks me. He looks down at the stone again, his muscles coiling. "I was determined to make sure it ended here. With us. That her story wouldn't be like my mother's."

His eyes find mine once more, the weight in them pressing against my chest, a tidal wave of emotion threatening to drown me. "I killed my father. We killed *all* our fathers." He tells me everything. How their father's twisted greed pushed them to forge their families. About the Armenians still coming for Eavan. How Jagger, Hawk, Damon, Gunnar, and his brothers risked everything to save her when she was taken.

He confesses every bit of information I was sent undercover to unearth. Every decision. Every detail. It should feel like a victory. This is the kind of information that would put him behind bars for life—probably take the entire King empire down with him. My mission, my orders, and my duty to the FBI… It's all here, gift-wrapped in raw honesty. But it doesn't feel good—not even close.

This isn't intel. This is Cillian—his pain and his guilt—laying his truth before me because he wants me to know exactly who he is. He trusts me with the ugliest, most inhumane parts of his soul. The atrocities he committed weren't for power or greed. They were a necessity to save the one person who matters most to him in this world. Everything he does is for his family.

Cillian slips his fingers between mine, and tears burn as they well in my eyes, realizing that I have fully accepted him and his place in the darkness of the underworld.

Eavan is right... It really is just that simple.

What they do doesn't matter—why they do it does. His fingers squeeze mine hard, and I almost wince at the intensity. "I would do anything to protect my family." He leans closer, breath warm against my cheek. His voice drops to a near whisper. "Anything."

Without another word, we walk, hand in hand, back to the car. He leans against it and lightly pulls me into him. His eyes search mine—raw and vulnerable—as he cups my face and lightly strokes his thumb across my cheek. "I need you to know, I would do anything to protect you... Because I love you, Madison."

My heart races so hard I'm sure he can hear it thudding as I blink rapidly, trying to hold back the rogue tears now trickling down my cheeks. "You don't really know me." I struggle to push out the words.

"I know enough." He tenderly wipes the damp trails from my face. "More than enough. There isn't a thing in this world that would change the way I feel about you."

Yes... there is...

His arms tighten around me, pulling me into an embrace that feels like it might shield me from the ghosts of my past and the threats plaguing our future. Lifting onto my toes, I press my lips to his and whisper a bit of truth among the web of lies he fell in love with. "I love you, too."

The admission feels like jumping from a plane—terrifying and freeing all at once. Our lips crash together, and for the first time in a long time, I feel like I'm exactly where I'm supposed to be. *And who I'm supposed to be.* He claims my mouth with a soft tenderness, leaving me breathless when he pulls back, teasingly nipping at my lower lip.

"Show me how much you love me, Daddy."

"It'll be my pleasure, firecracker. I'll spend a lifetime showing you how much I love you and learning all the things I don't know about you."

Her breath catches, soft and sharp. My fingers trail down the line of her spine, her body warm beneath the thin, delicate fabric of her loose floral dress. I want to ruin her in the best possible way, leave her dripping in aftershocks of my worship. I lift her chin, needing her to see it in my eyes... This isn't just lust. This is devotion. This is the part of me I've never given to anyone else.

She stares back at me with wide, pleading eyes. And it fucking does me in. Without breaking our stare, I lower my mouth to hers. Our kiss is slow and consuming. Her hands knot in my hair, greedily tugging me closer, pulling me deeper. I let her have all of me. Every breath. Every groan. Every pulse of need in my veins.

I guide her backward, step by step, toward the front of my car. The air between us crackles as I slide the straps of her dress off her shoulders and let the fabric flutter to her ankles in a soft, breathless whisper. She gasps as I tear her panties off her body, tossing the tatters beside her dress. Morning light spills over her bare skin like something out of a dream—golden and glowing—as her thighs back into my Aston Martin.

"Christ, Madison." I run my thumb along her jaw, down to her collarbone, and around the curve of her breast. "You're fucking perfect." She starts to speak, but I press my lips back to hers, silencing her. I lower her gently onto the warm sunbaked hood of the car, and she stretches out beneath me. She splays across it like she was made for this, *made for me.*

I strip off my shirt, letting it fall to the gravel as I lean over her. My hands and mouth explore her every curve, like I'm experiencing her perfect body for the first time.

Her nipples pebble under my tongue as I drag it across her chest, sucking gently, then harder, until her breath stutters. I tease one with my fingers while lavishing the other with my mouth, switching back and forth until she is arching from the car and panting with need. "Daddy..." She whimpers her plea.

"Shhh," I murmur, biting down gently on her pert nipple before softening the sting with a warm stroke of my tongue. "I'm going to give you everything you want, firecracker."

Her hands reach for my belt, undoing it with a speed that shows just how desperate she is. She slides my pants down enough to free me. Her hand wraps around my cock and gives it a firm tug—my hips jerking against her thigh. "Fuck," I hiss, my head dropping onto her shoulder as she strokes me. Her touch is tight, confident, dragging me exactly where she wants me.

She guides the thick, aching tip of my cock to her soaked entrance. Rubbing it up and down her slit, she breathes, "I need you inside me, Daddy."

Her request unravels the last of my restraint, and I sink into her in one slow, relentless push. Her body welcomes me—tight and wet—clutching around me like she was created solely for the purpose of taking my cock. A collective groan rips from our throats as I bottom out.

We move together, slowly at first, savoring every stroke, relishing in every inch I slide in and out of her. Her lips part and lashes flutter. I watch her gorgeous face as she hurtles toward the edge. "You're doing so good," I encourage. "Let me feel that pretty little pussy clench around me when you come."

Her nails dig into my back, sharp little crescents marking me as hers when they drag down my bare skin. "Fuck... Daddy... You feel so good... So deep..." Gasping between moans, she begs, "Please... Don't stop... Harder..."

"You want more?" I growl, hips snapping roughly. Her body jerks with the force, her back sliding along the shiny hood. "You want to be fucked like the naughty girl you are?"

She moans, and the sound bellowing from her is broken and delicious. "Yes, Daddy. Please."

"Look at you," I groan, slamming into her again. "So fucking needy. So wet for me. Say it. Tell Daddy exactly what you want."

"Use your pussy," she cries out, arching beneath me. "Ruin me."

"Be careful what you ask for." I reach down and rub her clit in tight, firm circles, and she quickly comes undone beneath me. "Let me feel that sweet cunt squeeze me as I wreck you."

She shatters around me with a loud, breathless "Daddy!" Her body locks up before pulsing in rhythmic waves. The sound of her unraveling sends me hurtling toward the edge, but I don't follow her over yet. I pull out, slowly, letting her feel every inch slip free. Her breath still ragged, she whimpers in protest.

"Shhh," I hush against her skin, dragging my mouth down her chest and across her stomach. I kiss and nip at her skin until I reach her thigh. With her leg over my shoulder, anchoring her in place, I bury my face in her pussy. The first lick is rough and possessive, and she gasps as my tongue glides from her entrance to her clit. I tongue-fuck her in slow, teasing circles before sucking her clit into my mouth. Her fingers lace through my hair. She yanks it hard, and I groan into her in response.

Wrapping my arms around her thighs, I pull her tight to my face as I demandingly lick her to climax. Her hips buck wildly against my mouth—my tongue unrelenting against her overstimulated clit. "Cillian! Fuck! Daddy!" Her whole body shakes in my arms, and she fists my hair painfully tight, but I don't stop. I ruthlessly assault her clit until she comes again—hard—her arousal coating my beard. Her body spasms, and her voice breaks as her screams echo off the trees around us. I stand and grip her hips, resting myself against her soaked entrance. She stares up at me with unfettered need. "Please."

"Are you begging for mercy? Or more of my cock?" I rasp, dragging the tip along her drenched cunt.

"More... Please, Daddy."

"Are you sure?" I ask, my voice dark with need. "Because I'm going to fuck you so hard it hurts."

"I don't care," she pants. "I need you."

I savagely thrust back into her, burying myself to the hilt. Her eyes roll back, and her thighs tighten around my waist. I fuck her. Relentlessly. Every stroke shakes the car, pained whimpers and moans pouring from her lips as she scars my back with her nails.

"Take it," I growl. "Take every fucking inch. Show me who you belong to."

"You... Fuck... I'm yours, Daddy... Always."

I reach between us and rub her clit again, needing her to fall with me this time. Her entire body clamps down around me, her final orgasm ripping through her like a bolt of electricity. She screams my name, every muscle of her body shaking beneath me. And it's my undoing. I thrust deep one last time, and my orgasm explodes through me. I bury my face in her neck and groan her name as I come inside her, my cock twitching, spilling my release into her until there's nothing left. Exhausted, I collapse on top of her, our bodies slick with sweat and hearts pounding in tandem.

Staying inside her, I kiss softly along her jaw. My lips trail over her flushed skin as we both struggle to catch our breath and come down from our high. "I fucking love you, firecracker," I whisper.

She lies beneath me, fully satiated. She smiles as I brush the matted hair from her face, but I can't miss the flicker of sadness in her eyes before she tucks her face in the crook of my neck. She presses her lips to my skin and whispers, "I love you, Daddy."

CHAPTER 33
madison

Standing in the open doorway of my apartment, Cillian's lips press against mine with fierce urgency. He pulls away slowly, his hand lingering on the small of my back. He stares down at me, his eyes dark and conflicted. "Fuck. I hate leaving you," he confesses, his voice rough and almost breaking. "I'll see you in the morning."

I nod, unable to form words, watching as he slowly turns and walks away. His footsteps echo down the stairwell, each a painful countdown. The sound of the final footstep fades, and I step into my apartment and close the door.

My back leans against it, and I'm unable to move. I slide down the door slowly, crumpling into a heap on the hardwood floor. The cold chills my bare skin, but it doesn't touch the fire burning inside me. The tears I've been holding back for hours spill over, unstoppable, streaming silent trails down my cheeks.

The web of lies I've spun so carefully—the half-truths and facades of cover—he loves them. He doesn't love me. He loves the girl I became to investigate him. It's only a matter of time before he finds out.

I curl tighter, rocking slightly, trying to steady the ragged breaths as I choke on my heavy sobs. I'm not an undercover agent anymore. I gave up the life I was building the minute I flushed those cameras down the toilet, severing the tie for good when I didn't alert anyone to the danger Frankford was in. I gave it all up for him. But when he finds out who I am—a woman with a secret so heavy it threatens to crush us both—he'll never forgive me. My whole world will come crashing down because I'll lose the only thing I have left.

Him. And his amazing family.

The pain and guilt claw their way through my ribs, squeezing until I'm gasping for air.

After what feels like hours, I finally push myself up from the floor. My legs are shaky, my hands trembling as I reach for my purse. The small weight of my phone feels impossibly heavy in my palm. With trembling fingers, I dial the number I know by heart. The first ring echoes in my ear before the familiar voice answers.

"Hi, Madd—"

"Mom..." My voice breaks before I can stop it, sobbing into the microphone.

"Oh, Maddie. Sweetheart." Her voice sounds as broken as mine. "What's wrong?"

I swallow hard, fighting the lump lodged in my throat. "I screwed up, Mom. I screwed up so fucking bad."

"What happened, sweetheart?"

I close my eyes, the tears flowing anew. "I fell... I fell for the one man I knew I shouldn't."

There's silence on the other end of the line. "I don't understand," she shares, her tone filled with confusion. "I didn't know you were seeing anyone."

"I shouldn't have been. It was so fast. And... It just happened," I confess.

"Is he a man from work?" she asks, trying to understand.

"No. I mean... yes. Sort of."

"Maddie. You aren't making any sense."

I swallow hard. "He's my target."

"Oh... Maddie," Mom exhales, her voice laced with empathy and disappointment.

"I threw it all away for him. Everything Dad and I worked so hard for. My chance to follow in his footsteps. I set my entire career on fire because I love him."

"Maddie, you didn't throw anything away," she insists. "You've made a choice. I won't lie and say I agree with it, but you've made a choice."

"Mommy..." I sob, my heart breaking.

"Let me finish." My mother's voice softens, a lifeline in the spiraling storm. "I might not agree with the side you chose. But Madison, I know you. You've fearlessly followed your heart since you were a little girl. I can't promise I'll ever support the decision. But if it's the one your heart wants, I know beyond any doubt that it's the right decision for you."

"He's going to tear my heart to shreds the moment he learns who I really am." But I shake my head, bitter tears dripping onto the floor. "He's going to tear *me* to shreds. He'll never understand."

The phone falls silent for moment. Then, "Oh, Maddie," she soothes. "You're stronger than you think."

But right now, I don't feel strong. I feel broken. I curl into myself, clutching the phone in my hand. The weight of my secrets is suffocating, but hearing my mom's steady voice reminds me of who I am beneath the lies. I'm more than an agent. I'm a daughter, a woman, and capable of love beyond measure, even if it's the kind of love that could destroy me.

I wipe at my tears, my voice hoarse but determined. "I have to figure out how to fix this... or maybe I just have to live with the mess I made."

"Whatever happens, Maddie, you're not alone," she assures me. "You have people who love you. We'll get through this."

I close my eyes, drawing in a shaky breath and remembering Cillian's words from this afternoon. *There isn't a thing in this world that could change the way I feel about you.* I hope to God he meant what he said, because I'm about to put them to the test.

CHAPTER 34
cillian

The elevator doors slide open, and I step into the penthouse, expecting silence. Instead, I'm met with the sharp eyes of Enzo and Nikolai. The second I step from the foyer into the kitchen, Enzo barks, "Where the fuck have you been?" His voice is low and sharp, laced with worry and anger. "I've been trying to reach you for hours."

"I was with Madison. At Mom's grave." I empty my pockets, dropping my keys and phone on the counter. "I turned my phone off. What's so urgent?"

Staring at me from across the room, Nikolai says, "Madison."

"Yes, Madison. What's the problem?"

"Madison," he exhales heavily. "Madison *is* the fucking problem."

My face contorts with confusion as I stare back at him.

Enzo slams a folder on the granite countertop, and the papers inside fan out as it slides toward me. "She's the man on the inside." The words hit like a punch in the gut, knocking the air from my lungs. My legs unsteady, I drop onto one of the barstools.

I stare, numb, as I lift the dossier. "Where did you get this?"

"We've been digging deeper into all our staff," Enzo informs me. "And while she might be your girl, Madison is part of our staff."

When I flip through the pages, I find them full of names, dates, photos—her whole life laid bare.

> *BORN IN KINGSPORT, TENNESSEE.*
> *RAISED IN LOLITA, VIRGINIA.*
> *PARENTS JAMES AND KATE ROARK:*
>   *SPECIAL AGENT WITH THE FBI AND*
>   *SCHOOL TEACHER*
> *GRADUATED HIGH SCHOOL WITH*
>   *HONORS A YEAR EARLY.*
> *QUALIFIED FOR SPORT PISTOL AT THE*
>   *JUNIOR OLYMPICS*
> *PAID INTERNSHIP WITH THE FBI.*
> *HER FATHER WAS KILLED IN A RAID*
>   *WHEN SHE WAS TWENTY-ONE.*
> *STRIPPED AT TEMPTING TASSELS FOUR*
>   *NIGHTS A WEEK DURING HER SENIOR*
>   *YEAR OF COLLEGE*
> *GRADUATED TOP OF HER CLASS*

Then nothing...

After graduation, she just disappeared, resurfacing about a month ago in New York City and right into my life. I shuffle through the papers, desperate to find the answer to the question I can't bring myself to ask. And then I find it...

It's a blurry screenshot of CCTV footage, but I know in my gut it's her. *My* Madison standing beside Agent Frankford, a gun in her hand and determination written across her face.

"Fuck!" The word rips from me—sharp and bitter—as I slam my hands on the counter. I angrily swipe at the papers, sending them raining to the floor. My chest tightens, and every muscle in my body is coiled like a spring ready to snap.

"What does she know?" Enzo asks, his voice heavy as he rises from his seat at the island.

"Everything."

I run a hand through my hair, frustration and disbelief crashing over me. "She knows fucking everything." I spilled every secret I had this afternoon. I poured my heart out to her. My mind is racing. The woman I love is the enemy on paper. A spy who's been living a double life under my roof, under my fucking nose, under me. *How the fuck did I miss it?* I pace, every step fueled by anger and helplessness, my chest aching with what I'm about to lose.

"We'll take care of it." Enzo pulls me from my thoughts. "Tonight. Before it can go any further."

"You won't fucking touch her," I snarl. My words are so fueled with anger that spittle flies across the counter. "Not a fucking finger. If you lay a hand on her, I swear, I'll kill you where you stand. Both of you."

Nikolai shakes his head and scoffs, "You're in love with a fucking Fed, you idiot. She's going to destroy everything we've built. And our lives. I'm not about to spend my life rotting in prison over a tight little ass you can't get enough of."

Seeing red, I storm across the kitchen. My fingers fist the front of Nikolai's shirt, and I shove him into the refrigerator with enough force to rattle the contents inside. "Do not fucking talk about Madison like that. Not now. Not ever."

Enzo pulls me from Nik's throat, throwing me across the kitchen. "Cian, you're my fucking brother, and I love you. But I'm with Nik on this one. I'm not spending my life in prison because you fell for the wrong girl."

"I'll take care of her," I gruff, picking my keys up off the floor. Without saying another word to them, I head back to the parking garage and slide into the driver's seat. My fist slams against the steering wheel, angrily blowing the horn as I turn over the engine to head back to her apartment.

I sit in my parked car at the corner of her block for hours, replaying every interaction we've had, trying to figure out what I missed. I lean back, eyes burning, and hands clenched into fists. When I slip from my car around one a.m., the lights in her apartment have been off for a little over an hour. After grabbing some supplies from my trunk, I make my way upstairs, stand outside her door, and pace for a few minutes before lifting her spare key to the lock to let myself silently into her apartment.

I'll do anything to protect my family... and if that means killing the woman I love and carving my heart from my chest, so be it.

The faint sound of footsteps shuffling outside the door to my apartment pulls me from my light sleep. At first, I think I'm still dreaming. My guilt presenting as restless paranoia. Rolling over and snuggling back into my pillow, I hear it again, distinct footsteps just beyond the entrance.

The lock rattles, sticking with that familiar squeaky hitch in the bolt that I've become far too used to. I sit up abruptly, my heart jumping into my throat. *Someone is trying to get inside.* Smooth and controlled, I slide from the bed keeping my movements quiet, like I was trained. Opening the drawer of my nightstand, my fingers close around the cold, matte steel of my Glock.

The cool hardwood floor bites at the soles of my feet as I cross it silently. Pressing my back to the wall, tucking myself into the shadows of the corner—I flip off the safety with practiced ease as the lock finally gives way a few feet from me. The door slowly opens. A flood of hallway light spills into the single room, stretching long shadows across the floor. Heavy footsteps land on the wood floor, and the door closes as quietly as it opened.

He's inside.

Cloaked in the shadows, the dark figure moves toward my bed. I can vaguely see the outline of broad shoulders, a masculine gait, and the vague shimmer of the blade in his hand. Whoever he is, he knows what he wants and where he's headed.

I raise my gun and slip soundlessly from my corner, my muzzle pointed at the back of the intruder. In three silent steps, I'm behind him. My hands are steady as I press the muzzle to the back of his neck. "Put your hands where I can see them," I command, my voice authoritative and unwavering. "Now!"

He goes still, his posture not faltering. He isn't surprised or afraid, merely resigned to his situation. "Daddy isn't into gun play, firecracker," he gravelly whispers, and my blood turns cold.

"Cillian?" I exhale. He turns fast, disarming me with a sharp twist of my wrist. The gun is suddenly in his hands instead of mine as his knife clatters to the floor. I barely process what's happening before he slams me against the wall with one hand clamped firmly around my throat. His eyes are wild, and his jaw is clenched so tight that the muscles are ticking. The scent of whiskey on his breath, he angrily growls, "I also don't like little girls who lie."

"I... I didn't..." I choke out the words, pressing my hands against his chest as I try to breathe.

He slams the gun—*my gun*—into the brick inches from my head. Hard. Cracks splinter through the mortar and clay, tiny shards and dust raining down to the floor. I flinch, even though I know he won't hit me. He wouldn't hurt me. Not really. *I don't think...*

"Don't fucking lie to me, Madison," he snaps, his voice darker than I've ever heard him before. "Or should I call you *Special Agent Madison Roark*?"

The bottom drops out of my stomach, and my knees go weak. "I wanted to tell you."

"Then why didn't you?" he spits. "All the nights we spent together. All the things I told you. Yesterday... *Yesterday*! When I laid everything bare... At my mam's fucking grave. And you just stood there, pretending."

"I wasn't pretending." My voice cracks. "I've never pretended with you. Not once. I love you."

He barks out a humorless laugh. "I'm just your fucking *target*."

"You aren't. You never were." Tears stream hot down my cheeks, blurring him in front of me. "I chose you. Weeks ago. I betrayed the Bureau. I walked away from everything. For *you*."

"We'll see."

He steps back, and I suck in a breath like it's the first I've ever taken. My relief is short-lived. He yanks the belt from his jeans in one fluid motion, the leather hissing through the loops. Before I can move, he's behind me, wrapping it around my neck and threading it through the buckle. My fingers reach for it as he pulls it tight. Not enough to cut off my air completely. But enough that I struggle for every shallow breath.

Enough that I know who's in control.

The muzzle of the gun presses into my ribs. "Walk," he demands. Frozen with fear, I don't move. I can't. "*Now!*"

He tugs at the makeshift leash around my neck, tightening it. I stumble forward, my bare feet dragging across the floor as I struggle to keep up with him. My hands tremble at my sides as we reach the edge of the bed. I look back at him, my eyes silently pleading for my life. "You don't have to do this," I whisper.

"You determine what happens here," he says coldly. "You're going to tell me everything. Get on the bed."

I hesitate. And he snaps the belt again, pulling it even tighter. I choke and climb onto the mattress, sinking on my back against the pillows, my eyes never leaving his.

"Hands above your head."

I do as he says, lifting them slowly to grip the bars of my headboard. He reaches into his pocket and pulls out a thick zip tie. The plastic bites into my wrists as he cinches it tight, binding me to the wrought iron. He sets the gun beside my head, like a warning, and threads the loose end of the belt around the bars above me. The noose around my throat restricting me to only taking shallow, measured breaths.

I'm helpless.

And he knows it.

He climbs onto the bed and straddles my waist, caging me in with his body. His eyes scan every inch of my face for the truth. Pressing the muzzle of the gun to my temple, he demands, "Talk."

And I do. I spill everything. My recruitment. The assignment. How I was placed on this case months ago with the intent of blending at the club. That he wasn't part of the plan. Getting close to him wasn't what the FBI planted me for. How I fell for him. And never stopped falling.

"I couldn't betray you. Even when I thought I might have to, I couldn't do it." I breathlessly fight for every word, my voice hoarse and desperate. "I burned my world down for you. I torched my career. My team. I walked away from the life I worked so fucking hard for, because none of it mattered anymore. Nothing matters. Except you. I love you. My heart doesn't care that we practically just met. I love you so fucking much it hurts."

He stares down at me, expression unreadable. For a long moment, all I can hear is my breathing and the quiet creak of the belt buckle with every shallow rise and fall of my chest.

"I'll take every secret to the grave," I whisper, tears streaming down my face. "Whether that's tonight or a lifetime from now. But Cillian... I never lied to you when it mattered."

His jaw tightens. I can see the war raging behind his eyes, battling heartbreak, fury, and betrayal.

He's just as wrecked as I am.

He drags his gun down the side of my face and presses it firmly under my chin as he leans in close. His lips hover by my ear. "I should fucking kill you."

His words turn my blood to ice, and I close my eyes, thinking, this is it. *This is how I die.* Cillian slides off the bed slowly, repeating under his breath, "I should kill you... but I fucking believe you."

Before I can speak, he leans down and presses a gentle kiss to my forehead. It's tender and tragic, like he's mourning us. My heart breaks and tears flow hard, my sobs uncontrollable as he disappears into the darkness of my apartment. My breath catches, and my eyes widen when he returns a moment later with his knife.

"Cillian..." My voice cracks. I tug helplessly at the zip ties binding my hands, my wrists aching from the tight, harsh restraints. His gaze roams down the length of my body— something dark flickering behind his eyes. He watches my shirt twisting and riding up my body as I struggle, revealing that I'm bare underneath it.

He places his knife on the nightstand and lets out a heavy exhale. "I believe you, Madison. And I love you." His eyes meet mine, staring through me as his voice lowers. "But my love doesn't erase the consequences."

"Please. Don't do this," I beg, watching it fall on deaf ears.

He opens the nightstand drawer and rummages inside it. My pulse spikes when he pulls out a small bottle of lube I forgot was even in there. Setting it beside the knife, he asks, "What kind of Daddy would I be if I let your betrayal go unpunished? What kind of message would that send you? There must be a price, a punishment worthy of your disobedience."

He removes his shirt, tossing it to the floor and unfastens his pants. Without breaking eye contact, he pushes them down his legs and pulls them over his feet. His cock is already hardening—thick, veiny, and flushed. He drips a generous amount of lube onto his length. Standing over me, he strokes himself, spreading the slickness from base to tip. "I should take you raw for what you did, but I'm not a monster," he shares. "I don't want you screaming in pain. I want you begging for my forgiveness."

He climbs onto the bed and settles between my legs. He pours more lube onto his fingers and presses them to the ring of muscle. He circles my tight hole with his slick fingers—rubbing slow and rough—watching me tense beneath him. My whole body trembles, but only partly from fear. The rest is need, anticipation, and desperation. "Cillian…"

"Daddy," he sternly corrects, pushing his hips forward, leaving the tip of his cock resting against my lubed-up asshole.

"And Daddy always knows exactly what you need, doesn't he?"

I nod in agreement, muttering, "I'm sorry…"

He presses forward, and the stretch is immediately overwhelming. "Don't fight me, firecracker. Relax and let me in," he growls. "You know you need this." He rubs his lube-coated finger over my clit to distract me from the pressure and pushes harder—insistently nudging his way into me.

"It's too much," I gasp when his thick head fully breaches the tight ring and pushes inside. "It's not gonna fit—"

"Yes. It will," he grits, his face contorted in pain, like he's struggling not to roughly drive the rest of himself into my ass. "You're going to take every inch of Daddy's cock in this tight little hole. And when I'm buried inside you, you can tell me what a bad girl you were and how desperately you want to be loyal to the Kings."

He rocks into me slowly, working his way deeper, inch by inch, the burn of being stretched causing my eyes to water. But he doesn't rush. Doesn't *really* hurt me.

"After you beg for forgiveness, you can beg me to fill your ass with my cum. Beg me to claim this perfect little hole as mine, too." He stills with his hips pressed to my thighs, and I realize I've taken all of him.

"Please, Daddy," I plead, struggling to adjust to him filling my ass. "I'm sorry… *so* sorry."

"That's better," he growls, taking me slowly. "Keep going."

"Please… forgive me… punish me…" *Fuck! He hurts so good.* "Teach me… I'm yours, Daddy… I'll be good for you…"

"That's my good girl," he praises softly. Reaching between us, he rubs his thumb against my clit—stroking it in slow, devastating circles. He slips two fingers into my soaked pussy, and I moan at the sudden sensation of being filled in both holes. His fingers curl inside me, and his thumb rubs my clit with perfect pressure. My hips buck wildly beneath him, driving his cock into my ass.

My body tightens, and when my release rips through me, it leaves me gasping, vulnerable, and filled to the brink with the man I betrayed, but never stopped loving. Slowly pushing himself all the way inside me again, he leans forward and presses his lips to mine. "Daddy forgives you."

Pulling his fingers from my pussy, he reaches for the knife on the nightstand. He wraps his arousal-coated fingers around it, and my breath catches. "But the Kings... They aren't as merciful," he shares darkly. "They take their forgiveness in blood."

Reaching over me, he unties the belt from the headboard and removes the tight noose from around my neck. "Do you want to earn their forgiveness too?"

I hesitantly nod. "Yes, Daddy."

"Open," he demands. I part my lips, and he places the leather between my teeth. "Bite down."

He slices through the thin fabric of my T-shirt, spreading it wide and baring my breasts. Stilled and buried to the hilt in my ass, he positions the blade above my right breast, pressing the tip against my flesh. The sting is sharp and immediate as he breaks the skin. He presses the tip deeper, carving a small, deliberate shape.

Biting down on the belt, I cry out in pain, my eyes flooding with tears and warm blood trickling across my chest. I don't stop him. I lay as still as I can, *offering* myself to him with tears pouring from my eyes. Willfully taking my punishment. My penance.

The knife burns, tearing through my flesh as he steadily carves the single word into my skin: ***KING***.

He cuts the zip tie from my wrists and tosses the knife to the floor. I groan as blood rushes back into my hands. Dipping low, Cillian licks the blood from my chest. His tongue is hot and possessive. "Now and forever, you're one of us." He tenderly kisses each of the letters, my blood staining his lips. "A King."

The belt falls from my mouth, and I suck in a sob. "Forever."

Taking its place, his bloody lips crash into mine. He kisses me hard, his metallic-tasting tongue plundering my mouth. Claiming my ass with the same needy desperation, he fucks me slow until my thighs are shaking and his hot release is dripping between my ass cheeks.

CHAPTER 37
cillian

Madison's tiny apartment smells like sex and blood. Her breath is soft and uneven beneath me as I pull from her body, every muscle in my frame tight with exhaustion from the restraint needed to take her ass without hurting her. We're both a mess. My hands and her chest are stained red, but all I can see is the raw wound I carved into her flesh, the mark I gave her. The branding she *asked* for. The word gleams across her skin.

KING.

My empire. My family. My name.

She let me brand her like property. Proof of her devotion—to me and my family—permanently etched into her previously unmarred skin.

But now… now she needs care.

"I'll be right back," I promise, climbing off the bed. As I cross the small space to the bathroom, I leave her spent, shaking, and exposed.

The bathroom light is blinding after the dark. I squint through the brightness as I tear open the medicine cabinet. Bottles of feminine face products, her birth control, and cotton pads clatter into the sink as I rifle through it. I open and close every cabinet until I find what I'm looking for: a tiny first-aid kit tucked beneath the sink.

I return to the bed with my hands full; the first-aid kit, a warm bowl of water, and two clean washcloths. She stares weakly, looking up at me with glassy, hooded eyes. "What are you doing? she asks, her voice hoarse and so fragile that I feel it in my chest.

"I might be rough with you, firecracker," I confess quietly, kneeling beside her on the bed and dipping the cloth into warm water on the nightstand, "and demanding with my punishments when you deserve them." I glance up at her. Her lips tremble, but she doesn't say a word. "But no matter how hard I am on you… I love you. And I want to care for you. Nurture you."

I clean her thighs and her stomach. I take my time—reverent, not rushed—like I'm bathing her in my love with every soft stroke of the cloth. She winces slightly when I press the damp rag between her ass cheeks, where my cum lingers in sticky white streaks. .

"I know," I murmur. "I know it's sore, baby."

When she's clean, I set the cloth aside and open the first-aid kit. I uncap the peroxide and pour it into my palms first, rubbing my hands together until they sting with the antiseptic. I've done this dozens of times before. For Enzo. For Nikolai. Even for some of our men, when a job went sideways. I've stitched up bullet and knife wounds. But this is different... This is my Madison.

"This is going to hurt," I warn.

She nods without hesitation. I hold her gaze as I tilt the bottle and let it spill over her wounded chest. She sucks in a sharp breath, and her body arches off the bed, her jaw clenched tight.

"Shhh," I soothe, leaning down to blow softly across the burn. "Daddy's got you. And you're doing so good for me."

Bubbles fizz up over the carved word, pink and angry—but clean.

I gingerly pat it dry with the clean washcloth, dress it gently with the gauze, and tape it to her skin with slow, meticulous care. She watches me in silence, her eyes glassy and bloodshot. When I finish, I close up the first-aid kit and place it on the floor.

Standing beside the bed, I trail my fingertips up the center of her throat. The belt marks are faint but visible. I can see where the pressure left shadows on her skin: a map of my dominance. I kiss each one.

Inspecting her wrists, I find them both raw from the zip tie. I lift them to my lips and whisper apologies against the tender bruises I left behind. Not because I regret punishing her, but because I know the weight of being punished by someone you love.,

I climb back into bed and pull her gently up to my chest. Instinctively, she curls into me, her head tucked beneath my chin, her fingers fisting the sheet and her breath warms my skin.

"You're mine," I whisper into her hair, kissing the top of her head. "And there's nothing I won't do to keep you safe. Even from yourself."

She makes a soft sound—a soft whimper—and I wrap my arms around her a little tighter.

"You don't know what you've done to me, Madison." My voice is a dark rasp. "What I feel for you... This isn't a fairytale love. It's a fucking obsession, devotion so deep it borders on madness."

Her fingertips dig into my chest as she pulls herself tighter to me.

"I'll kill for you. I'll bleed for you. I'll forgive you again and again if I have to. But make no mistake, firecracker, I'll never let you go."

She shifts against me, and I can feel her heart racing, the thud beating against my chest.

"You're the first thing in my life I didn't want to ruin," I softly confess. "And yet... that's exactly what I did with you. I took your life. And selfishly, I'd do it again—without hesitation—if I knew that it meant I'd get to have you."

A soft sigh passes over her lips, her body melts into mine, and I realize she's asleep. I stare at the ceiling as her soft breath blows across my chest, my fingers absently stroking the length of her spine.

She's going to destroy everything we've built.

I'm not going to prison over a tight little ass.

Enzo's voice and Nikolai's warning ring in my ears. They won't understand. They won't care about the depths to which I love her or the lengths she would go to prove her loyalty.

They'll only care about her badge. Her secrets. Her lies. And the threat she poses to them.

I don't sleep—not for a long time.

Tonight, I punished her, forgave her, branded her, and reclaimed her.

But tomorrow...

Tomorrow, I'll have to fight for her.

Madison shifts against me, and I open my eyes to find the sun barely filtering through the curtains. Her breaths are light and feathery. She's warm in my arms, her body tucked into mine like she belongs there. Like she always has. I watch her sleep for a moment before pressing a kiss to her shoulder.

Her skin is marked—last night's faint bruises having grown darker. The gauze over her chest is stained crimson and in need of being changed.

She stirs when I move to sit up, blinking groggily. "Cillian?"

"I'm here, firecracker." I brush her hair back and look down at her. "We need to clean you up again."

She nods, but her body flinches as she tries to sit. I wrap an arm around her and help her up gently, guiding her toward the bathroom. She's sore, of course she is. Not a single complaint passes over her lips, not even when I peel back the bandage on her chest.

When we step into the shower, her eyes tighten and her jaw clenches as the warm spray hits her chest.

"You don't have to be tough for me." I dab the tender wound with a clean cloth. Wringing the cloth, I let the water cascade down her chest. It runs pink for a moment before fading to clear. "I know it hurts."

I wash the rest of her, tenderly kissing every mark her punishment left on her skin again.

She presses her forehead against my chest, and the water sprays over us both. My finger tips her head up to meet my gaze, and I brush the wet hair from her face and cup her gorgeous face. Pressing my lips to her forehead, I say the words I've been dreading since last night. "We have to go see them."

She tips her head inquisitively to the side. "Them?"

"Nikolai. Enzo." I pause. "My brothers. And Eavan"

Her eyes widen. "Cillian, they're going to kill me."

"No," I say firmly. "They won't. Not while I'm breathing."

She shakes her head. "If you had the slightest doubt in my devotion to you, I'm pretty sure you would've slit my throat or put a bullet through my skull."

"It might be what I came here for. But for the first time in my life, I didn't know if I would've been able to pull the trigger." I pull her tightly to me. "They knew it too. It's why they wanted to come instead of me."

"That doesn't make me feel better about going to see them."

"We go together. I'll stand beside you. And we tell them everything."

"I already told *you* everything. Isn't that enough?" she mumbles against my chest.

I slip my finger under her chin and tip her face up to mine again. "You were embedded inside our entire operation. They deserve the truth, too. They need to know, Madison. If I'm going to keep you by my side, they need to see you as more than a Fed who got in too deep. They need to see you the way I do."

"And if they don't?"

"Then I'll bleed for you," I vow. "Or with you. But we'll be *together*."

———

The silence in the elevator up to my penthouse is thick enough to choke on. Madison's hand grips mine tightly, her eyes are glued to the glowing floor numbers as we rise. When the doors to the cab slide open, I give her a reassuring squeeze and lead her to the apartment.

When I slide the door open, Nikolai is on the other side. The second he sees her on my arm, he reaches for the pistol in the waistband of his pants. "What the *fuck*, Cian?" He draws and aims directly at my love.

Before Madison can react, I step in front of her, squarely in the line of fire. I raise both hands. My voice calm but sharp, I insist, "We all need to talk. *Without guns.*"

Nik doesn't move. "Are you *out of your goddamn mind?!* She's a fucking Fed—"

"She's *mine*," I snap. "And she's going to speak. And as my brother, you're going to give her the fucking courtesy of listening."

Enzo appears behind Nikolai, his expression hard and unreadable. Eavan's a step behind him, her eyes flicking between Madison and me like she's calculating how fast to call in cleanup.

"Move, Cian," Nik growls.

"Shoot me, then," I press. "Because if you aren't willing to go through me, you aren't getting to her."

He stares at me down the barrel of his gun, his finger resting against the trigger. He lowers the weapon slowly and reluctantly. I let out a heavy exhale as he mutters, "She better start talking."

I nod once and pull Madison gently beside me, lacing our fingers together again. I feel her hand tremble and tighten my grip slightly.

Walking into the apartment, we sit. They don't. Nik glares from across the kitchen like he's still weighing whether prison's worth it. Enzo paces with his arms crossed. And Eavan observes from the pool table at Enzo's request that she not be in the line of fire if this goes south.

Madison swallows hard, then lifts her chin and starts talking. The words flow like she can't get them out fast enough. "I was recruited for this op about four months ago. They wanted someone with a clean record. A fresh graduate who had no Bureau ties beyond Quantico. No known identity. The one thing that nearly kept me from getting into the academy was the same thing that landed me the biggest sting any new agent could ask for. My experience as a dancer made me the perfect ghost to slip into your world." Her voice is calm, even though her hands shake. "At first, it was just surveillance. Profile building. Mapping your financials, monitoring movements. They were looking for a hole in your organization."

She looks at Enzo. Then Nikolai. And finally to Eavan.

"I knew I was fucked the first night I met Cillian, before the club even opened. And it only spiraled from there. I gave them very little. Just enough to keep my cover viable as I struggled not to let myself get involved with him. No real assets. No locations. No drops. No names. Frankford was my handler. He came to the club because I hadn't checked in for nearly two weeks."

Enzo scoffs in disbelief. "You just *stopped*? Just like that?"

"Yes. Because I chose him." She glances at me, and I tenderly squeeze her thigh. "I fell for Cillian. I hadn't admitted to myself whose side I was on, but Frankford forced my hand. He brought new surveillance for me to plant."

Nikolai's eyes narrow at hearing that information. She shakes her head. "I didn't plant them. I disposed of them while you were busy with Frankford."

"Do you know what they have?" Eavan asks, her eyes flicking between me and Enzo with worry.

"Their case is weak as fuck," Madison shares. "That's why Frankford was pressing so hard. He was desperate. The only evidence they've gathered is through me. Through what I've seen and reported, and I gave them jack fuck. Any intel I gathered, I never gave to them. They have nothing, unless they have me."

"That's the *real fucking problem*," Nikolai mutters.

"No." Madison shakes her head, standing slowly. Her voice firm, she insists, "It's not."

She reaches for the buttons of her shirt, and my chest tightens. "Madison…" I brush my hand along her hip, and she turns toward me.

"It's okay." With shaking hands, she peels open the fabric and pulls the white gauze aside, revealing the fresh scabbing of my name—*our names*—carved above her breast.

KING

The room falls silent. Eavan's hand flies to her mouth, eyes wide in disbelief. Enzo and Nikolai both stare at her, stone silent. *A feat for two men who never shut up.*

"I didn't give my life for crossing the Kings." She taps her finger next to the wound. "But I gave my blood. I'll let each of you carve your name across every inch of my skin if that's what it takes to prove my loyalty. I'm not just choosing Cillian. I'm choosing *all* of you."

She looks at them, one by one. "This is the life I chose."

After a moment, she adds, "This is the family I chose."

Nikolai is the first of my brothers to speak. His voice is tight and cold. "You better be telling the truth, Roark."

"I am."

He studies her. For a long, brutal beat. "She's still *desperate*," Nik fires back, his heated stare burning through me. "Which makes her dangerous."

"But she's *ours*," I counter, stepping forward. "Whether you like it or not."

Enzo rubs his face with a heavy sigh. "This is either the dumbest decision you've ever made, or she's one of the most loyal women on this planet."

Eavan's still staring at Madison's chest, visibly shaken. Madison presses the gauze back to her chest and buttons her shirt slowly, recovering her branding. Eavan glances between Enzo and Nikolai whispering, "I told you... She loves him."

A tiny smile pulls at the edge of Madison's lips. Stepping beside her, I place my hand low on her back. "She's not going anywhere. I swear with my life that she is as much a King as everyone else in this room."

I never thought I'd feel so many things at once; relief, exhaustion, pain, and this overwhelming, disorienting sense of displacement. Like the person I was just a few weeks ago is gone. *Or at least the person I thought I was.* Burned away and changed by a man whose darkness wraps around me like a second skin.

This is my life now.

I feel it in every aching inch of my body; the sting of the carved word on my chest, the bruises on my wrists and neck, and the tender ache between my thighs. But most of all… I feel it in the way Cillian looks at me now, not just with lust or love, but unfettered devotion.

And God help me... I want to be his.

After his brothers accepted me this morning—or at least agreed not to kill me—Cillian insisted I move my things into his penthouse. He swears it's to ensure I'm safe from their enemies and the FBI. I'm certain he wants me at arm's length and in his bed every night. Either way, I didn't put up much of a fight. *Or any fight, actually.*

We pull into the secure parking garage of his building in silence, his thumb rubbing slow, calming circles against my palm. It's as if he knows I'm threatening to come apart at the seams, and this one gesture might be the only thing keeping me tethered.

"You okay?" he asks quietly.

I nod, but I don't lie. "No. Not really."

"You will be," he reassures me.

After parking the car, Cillian doesn't ask if I'm ready. He gets out and helps me out of it. He grabs the bags we threw together from the trunk. I just packed some necessities: clothes, toiletries, and the photo of my dad I had tucked under the mattress.

He sets the bags down by the door, then turns to me. "Welcome home, firecracker." The words hit me harder than I expected. Not because he's being sarcastic, but because he means it. This *is* my home now. Not just this apartment. *Him.*

I step forward, sliding my hands around his waist and pressing my face to his chest. His arms come around me instantly, holding me tightly. "I'm scared," I whisper eventually. "Not of you. Just... of all of this."

His hand runs up and down my spine, slow and soothing. "I know."

He leans back just enough to tilt my chin up. His expression is soft. "Do you regret it?"

I look into his eyes and answer without an ounce of doubt. "No. I just don't know who I am now."

"You're mine," he replies immediately. "That's who you are." The way he says it doesn't feel possessive. It feels grounding. "You'll find the rest," he adds softly. "But you're not alone while you do."

He leads me through the apartment and upstairs to his bedroom, the blinds drawn and the room dimly lit. There's a small pile of clean clothes on the dresser: one of his long-sleeved shirts and a pair of boxers.

"You need rest," he tells me simply.

I nod. "I want to shower first."

He pauses. "I'll help you."

It's not a question. He knows I'm still sore and a little unsteady on my feet. And when he reaches for me again, it's with the same reverence he had last night as he cleaned the blood from my skin. In the bathroom, he peels my shirt off carefully, mindful of the gauze taped to my chest. He removes the bandage with equal care, his eyes lingering on the bright red, slowly scarring tissue. Tenderly, he presses his lips to it before lowering to the floor. Kneeling before me, he removes my shorts and panties.

His eyes rake up my naked body. He eyes me hungrily, but I don't feel vulnerable. I feel *seen*.

The shower is hot. He steps in behind me—wincing for a second at the heat—and helps me wash. His hands are gentle as they slide over my bruised skin. Much like his fingers scrubbing shampoo through my hair. He dries me, his movements efficient and quiet.

We return to the bedroom. He replaces the gauze and helps me dress. Silently, he leads me to the bed, and he pulls back the covers for me to climb between the sheets. I half expect him to disappear after he pulls the covers up to my shoulder and kisses me on the forehead, but he doesn't. He drops his towel and slides in beside, pulling me into him and wrapping his arms around me. We lie there quietly for a while, simply holding each other and listening to our soft breaths.

Aimlessly running my fingertips through his beard, I murmur, "Your brothers still don't trust me."

"No," he agrees. "But they will. Eventually."

"Even Nikolai?"

He huffs a dark laugh. "Nik would trust a rattlesnake before trusting a Fed."

"So... no?" I chuckle.

He presses a kiss to my temple. "You earned something today, firecracker. Their respect. You faced them. You didn't flinch. That matters more than you'll ever know."

"I still feel like I could wake up and this will all fall apart. That they'll change their minds. That *you* will."

He turns me to face him fully. His hand cups the side of my neck, thumb brushing lightly over the faint mark left by his belt. Placing kisses across my lips, he vows, "You're mine. And you've already proven what you're willing to sacrifice for that. Now let me take care of you."

I nod slowly, curling into his chest, his heart beating strong beneath my cheek. "I love you, Daddy."

His lips press to the top of my forehead, and I can feel him smiling when he says, "I love you, too, firecracker."

It's been a week since I brought her here. Just one week since she stood before my brothers, peeled back the bandages on her chest, and offered her loyalty even as they stared at her with ire-filled eyes.

One short week...

She moves through the penthouse like she's always belonged here. Delicate feet in soft cotton socks cross the dark wood floors. A large mug of coffee in her hands every morning out on the terrace. A pink throw blanket she insisted upon thrown across the arm of the couch—a bright, feminine splash in our otherwise masculine space.

The bathroom counter now displays her perfume beside my cologne, her addictive citrus scent lingering in the air subtle but ever-present. Her lingerie fills a drawer of the dresser. And her small clothes hang in the closet beside mine. Including her father's ratty FBI hoodie, which I've convinced her to keep on a hanger until Nik is a little less trigger-happy.

Madison Roark is *everywhere*. And I couldn't imagine it any other way. It's crazy how natural this feels. I'm a man who doesn't let people close. Yet somehow, she's wormed her way into every shadowed corner of my life without even trying. *Actually fighting it every time I pressed.* And she fits like she's belonged here all along.

She's curled up on the couch reading. Based on the shirtless man on the cover, I'm pretty sure it's one of Eavan's books. Her hair falls in messy waves over the arm of the couch, and her legs are tucked beneath her, almost hidden by my oversized T-shirt enveloping her small frame.

I lean against the wall, sipping my cup of coffee as I watch her. She might be the most dangerous thing to have ever walked into my world, but she's also the most beautiful.

Her eyes lift from her book when she senses me. "You're staring again," she announces, her lips curling faintly.

"I like watching you." I shrug. She blushes like she still doesn't quite understand what she's done to me.

"And you don't think that's at all creepy?" she teases.

"No." I push off the wall and walk toward her slowly. "It's endearing."

She sets the book down, her eyes following my every step. When I reach the couch, she shifts to make room for me, but I shake my head and drop onto the cushions beside her, tugging her into my lap.

"You're warm," she sighs, curling against me.

I run a hand down her back, my fingers brushing over the light bumps of her spine through the thin fabric of my shirt. She's only wearing panties beneath it. I know that because I helped her dress after our shower before letting her wander off to read.

My hand stills just above the base of her spine. "Comfortable?"

"Mmm," she hums. "I like it here."

Here. With *me*.

I tilt her chin up toward me. "I want to take care of you," I whisper.

"You already do."

"No. I mean, I want to remind you what it feels like to be worshipped. To be mine." Her breath stutters as I slide my hands under her shirt, gripping her waist. I haven't fucked her since the night I took her ass. Not because I haven't wanted to —*fuck, have I wanted to*—but because I wanted to give her plenty of time to heal after how rough I was. Both physically and emotionally.

"Do you trust me?"

She nods. "Always, Daddy."

Without breaking eye contact, I slide my hand between her thighs. The damp fabric of her panties clings to her.

"What did I catch my dirty girl reading?" I teasingly whisper in her ear. "Because you are absolutely soaked."

She squirms, burying her face in my chest to hide her embarrassment.

I hook my fingers into the waistband and slowly peel her tiny panties down her thighs. They're already drenched. She shivers as I dust the back of my hand along her mound.

"I'm going to make you come on my hand," I inform her, pushing her thighs apart. "At least twice. Before I even let you touch me."

She nods again, her lower lip trembling.

I run my hand up her inner thigh and cup her heat, sliding one finger between her arousal-coated slit. She gasps and arches into my touch.

"So needy already," I exhale against her neck. "Have you been thinking about Daddy's hands? Reading that naughty book and thinking about my fingers in your tight little pussy?"

"Yes," she breathes.

I slide a finger inside her, slow and deep. She moans as I tease her with it, barely giving her what she needs. "Eyes on me," I command. "Watch how much I enjoy pleasing you."

She lets out a soft cry and grips my shoulder when I ease a second finger inside her. Her walls tighten around my fingers, wet and pulsing. I move them just right, hooking, pressing, rubbing the perfect spot while my thumb strokes her clit in slow, tight circles.

Her mouth falls open, and she struggles to keep her stare locked with mine.

"That's it," I encourage, a smile pulling at my lips. "Come for me. Let Daddy feel how sweet you are."

She shudders against me, her head falling to my shoulder and her body arching as she comes undone. Her moan is choked, helpless. I slow, giving her time to come down from her euphoria. "I could watch you come all day long." I brush my lips against hers before denying her. I take my time, fingering her slowly and deeply until her pussy is quivering around my fingers once more.

This time, I don't stop. I don't give her a chance to catch her breath. My fingers rub demandingly against her most sensitive spots, as my free hand holds her thighs open.

"I can't," she whimpers. "It's too much—"

"You can." I stroke her clit harder, curling my buried fingers until her hips buck. "And you will. For Daddy."

She convulses in my arms, her orgasm crashing through her with a raw scream that echoes around the apartment. Pulling my fingers from her, she slumps against me, her body still shaking. I kiss the side of her neck and lick the sweat from her skin. "Such a good girl for me."

I turn her on my lap until she's straddling me, peppering kisses across her face while she catches her breath. She reaches between us, her fingers fumbling with the zipper of my jeans. "Someone's eager," I tease with a soft growl.

"I need you," she begs, still trembling. "Please, Daddy."

"Such a needy little thing," I whisper, brushing hair from her face. "That's okay. Daddy's going to take care of you."

She manages to undo my pants and shimmy them down to free me. My cock springs up, hard and with precum gathered on the tip. Without pausing, she lifts just enough for me to kick my pants to my knees and sinks onto me—slowly, inch by inch—moaning as I fill her.

"Ride me. Let me feel how much you need me." Grinding over my lap like she's dancing for me, her lips parted and cheeks flushed, she rides my cock. Slipping my hands beneath her shirt, they roam up her body and cup her pert tits. I lightly pinch both her nipples and her pussy clenches around me.

With her nipple in one hand, I grip her ass with the other. I fight the urge to take control, letting her use me to please herself. Her hips move faster, and her breaths grow rapid, and I know she's right on the edge again. "That's it. Use my cock. Make that little pussy of yours feel so good."

"Yes... Yes..." she pants, the release she's worked so hard for finally crashing through her. Pressing my lips to hers, I kiss her slow and deep. When I eventually pull back, I ask, "Do you feel worshipped and adored?"

"Yes, Daddy," she answers, breathlessly.

"Good. Because now you're going to feel like *mine*," I grit, gripping her waist and roughly pulling her off my cock. I flip her over the arm of the couch with ease, her stomach resting on it, and her perfect ass high in the air. She whimpers as I grab her hips from behind and line up with her entrance. I drive into her hard, quickly filling her pussy with every inch of my cock. She cries out, her hands clawing at the plush fabric beneath her. "You belong to me," I growl, pounding into her. "Say it."

"I'm yours," she gasps.

I wrap a hand around her neck, squeezing just enough. The tight walls of her cunt clamp down around me and her whole body trembles. "You're Daddy's good girl," I grunt between thrusts. My balls slap against her clit with every drive of my hips.

"Please... Please don't stop," she whimpers, her legs starting to shake. I wrap my arm around her middle and pull her against me as I slam into her harder and deeper, chasing the release we both need. She breaks for me, her body tightening and toes curling. I follow her, groaning her name against her shoulder as I spill inside her.

Breathless and shaking, I slowly ease out of her and collapse onto the couch, pulling her with me. She curls against me, her hair damp at the temples, her eyes dazed and sleepy.

"I love you," she whispers.

I kiss her temple, still trying to slow my heart.

"I know," I reply quietly. "I love you, too."

CHAPTER 41
madison

A COUPLE OF DAYS LATER

The morning has been quiet, peaceful. After everything lately, maybe a little too peaceful. I'm tucked into Cillian's side on the couch, my cheek resting against his bare chest while his fingers lazily trace circles along the small of my back. He's wearing a pair of charcoal sweatpants, hair messy from sleep, and I'm in nothing but one of his old T-shirts and a pair of black cotton panties. The soft rumble of the coffee pot finishing its brew fills the silence, followed by the warm scent of dark roast drifting from the kitchen.

It's not glamorous. But it's *perfect.*

He stirs at the sound of brewed coffee, and I mumble against his chest, "Do we have to move?"

Huffing a low laugh, he brushes his lips across the top of my head. "Technically, no. But we *should*."

I look up at him, pouting a little. "Can't we just stay here all day?"

"Tempting," he murmurs, pressing a kiss to my forehead. "But I promised Nikolai I'd go over the warehouse transfer manifests today. And you"—he taps the tip of my nose—"promised to go with Eavan to the spa. And I think there was something about dinner with the whole family."

"Ugh," I groan, letting my head fall back. "Why does being loyal to criminals feel more exhausting than being a Fed ever was?"

"Because now you're doing it without a pension or dental," he deadpans. I laugh. *God*, I fucking love him.

He pushes from the couch to go get us coffee when the front door rattles.

BOOM!

The heavy steel doesn't just open. It explodes into the apartment—torn from the hinges and lying on the hardwood floor. Shouts flood the apartment, "FBI! Hands in the air!"

I'm too stunned to move—to breathe—but Cillian reacts instantly as the thud of boots stomp across the floor. "Get behind me," he growls, shoving me into the couch and covering me with his body as black-clad agents adorned in tactical gear swarm the penthouse: helmets, goggles, bulletproof vests. Dozens of them. All with weapons raised and looking for a reason to use them. *It's like a fucking war zone.*

Cillian lifts his hands slowly. "Easy," he says, voice calm but deadly. "I'm unarmed."

An agent in plain clothes yells something, but I can't hear it over the pounding of my heart. I'm pressed beneath Cillian, half-naked and still shell-shocked. The agent, in his mid-forties, steps closer, but he doesn't look at Cillian. His gaze immediately falls on me, heated and disgusted.

"Can I at least get my shoes before we go?" Cillian smirks, wiggling his bare feet against the hardwood floor. "Maybe a shirt."

"We're not here for you, Mr. King," the agent informs him, looking smug. "We're here for Agent Roark."

I freeze. "Wait... What!?"

Without the slightest sign of emotion, the agent gestures toward me. Before either of us can say another word, hands are already on me, rough and brutal. Firm hands yank me from behind Cillian, dragging me over the couch like I'm nothing. He twists to stop them, reaching for me, but a rifle slams into his chest and shoves him back into the couch.

"Don't fucking *touch* her like that!" he roars, his tone homicidal.

"Get your hands off me!" I scream, but it's no use. They shove me hard, pinning me against the floor-to-ceiling windows. The cold glass bites into my skin as they wrench my arms behind my back. I struggle until an elbow jams against my spine, demanding my compliance.

"Madison Roark," the plain-clothes agent says from behind me as I gasp for breath, "you're under arrest for obstruction of a federal criminal investigation, witness tampering, and the murder of Agent Carl Frankford."

I barely register the words as the cold, metal cuffs dig painfully into my wrists. My vision tunnels. A roaring fills my ears. Frankford. *They think I killed him.*

"No," I gasp. "No, I didn't—I didn't do anything—"

"You have the right to remain silent," he recites, monotone. "Anything you say can and will be used against you in a court of law..."

"Get off her!" Cillian snarls. "You don't have to cuff her like that!"

The same agent slams him away again, gun aimed squarely at his chest. "One more step, Mr. King, and you'll be joining her."

"You *fucking touch* her again—" His voice breaks like he's barely containing the rage burning through him. "You're not going to get away with this."

They pull me off the glass, dragging me past the wreckage of the front door, my bare feet scraping against debris. I look back. Cillian's eyes are locked on mine, jaw clenched, chest heaving. *Helpless.* And it kills me.

"Don't say a word, Madison," he calls after me. "It'll be okay, firecracker. I'll come for you. I swear on my life."

They throw me in the back of a blacked-out SUV, buckling me into the cold leather seat like I'm a threat to national security. They didn't even afford me any dignity. I'm still in Cillian's shirt and panties. The ride is silent except for the soft *click* of the doors locking and the hum of tires on asphalt. Two agents sit on either side of me, stone-faced, guns holstered but close.

I try to breathe. To think. But my mind is muddled.

Frankford.

Witness tampering.

Obstruction.

I've been falling in love while the fucking FBI was building a case against me.

The agent on my left glances over and sneers, "You think flipping for King was smart?"

I say nothing. He smirks, trying to rattle me.

"You're not a Fed anymore, sweetheart. You're worse than a criminal. You're a *traitor.*"

My jaw clenches.

"I didn't kill Frankford," I say, voice shaking. "I haven't seen him since the night he came to the club."

"And yet you suddenly stop reporting. The night *he* vanishes." The other agent leans in. "You want us to believe that's a coincidence?"

"It is."

"Save it for the trial," the one on my right mutters. "Assuming you even get one."

I look out the window, heart hammering. The city whizzes past in a blur, every building flickers like a countdown. FBI Headquarters looms in the distance, and I know they're waiting to make an example out of me.

I've seen war. Dealt with betrayal. My life is riddled with bullets, blood, and death. I've made choices that haunt me— that will plague my soul for the rest of eternity.

But nothing—not a single moment in my violent, vicious life —compares to what I felt watching the FBI drag Madison from me. Barefoot. In nothing but my fucking shirt. Cuffed and trembling. Treating her like she was nothing. And I couldn't do a fucking thing to stop them.

The moment the last of them stepped into the elevator and the door closed on the cab, the silence in the penthouse was deafening. I stood in the foyer—among the splinters of the door frame—and all I could do was clench my fists until it

My chest heaves, and I can't catch my breath. Running upstairs, I dial Enzo as I hastily change my clothes. Despite the early hour, he answers on the first ring as I'm pulling on my jeans. "Where the fuck are you?" I growl.

"Grabbing an iced coffee down the street. What's going on?"

"They took Madison." I loop the belt through my pants and tear a shirt from the hanger. "Feds. Full tactical raid. They came for her."

"Fuck!" Enzo exclaims angrily. "Why?"

"Obstruction. Tampering. Murder of Frankford."

"The fuck?"

"I need every fucking lawyer we have on speed dial at the penthouse in the next twenty minutes. Now."

"I'm on it."

I hang up and pace the kitchen floor, adrenaline pumping hard enough to make my hands shake, calling in every favor I have to see how legit these charges are against Madison.

Twenty-six minutes later, the kitchen is littered with suits. Four of our top criminal defense attorneys sit in front of me, folders open, pens scribbling as they attempt to piece together the legal equivalent of a triage tent.

"She stopped providing intel to the FBI weeks ago," I snarl.

One of the lawyers, a balding man named Reuben, lifts a brow. "Did she ever make any *formal* documentation of her resignation?"

I grind my teeth. "I don't fucking know."

"Doesn't matter. It doesn't help us much if she didn't submit it on paper," another lawyer mutters. "From a legal standpoint, the FBI still sees her as one of their own. A rogue agent. One who killed one of them."

"She didn't kill Frankford," I growl.

"Do *you* know that?"

My eyes flash to the young guy we put on retainer a few weeks back. He's fresh out of law school and apparently stupid enough to say shit that's going to get him thrown off the terrace.

"I know," I snap. "I can pull the feed at the club if you need me to fucking prove it to you. She clocked out and had two security guys drive her home hours before the last swipe of Frankfort's credit card."

"I know that's true," Enzo adds quietly, "but perception is everything right now. And from their side? She's a Fed who ghosted her handler and disappeared immediately after he vanished."

The air in the room thickens.

Reuben leans forward. "We need to make one thing crystal clear, Mr. King. If the FBI is charging her with obstruction and tampering, that's bad enough. But if they're trying to pin Frankford's murder on her—"

"They're not trying," Nikolai interrupts. "They *are.*"

"Then you need to prepare for the worst."

"I'm not letting them bury her."

"No one's suggesting you should," Reuben responds evenly. "But if this goes federal—and trust me, unless we pull a legal

Hail Mary, it *will*—we're going to need more than emotional declarations. We'll need real evidence. A paper trail. Something that discredits their timeline or their assumption of guilt."

"She's the *only* witness they had on the Kings," I mutter. "And she stopped reporting weeks ago. They lost their last play, and now they're retaliating."

"Exactly." Enzo's eyes sharpen. "They're trying to punish her. And you."

This isn't just about justice. It's about control. They lost their hold on her, so now they're making an example of her.

"Do we know where she is?" I ask.

"They'll have taken her to FBI Headquarters in the city," Reuben informs the room. "Holding for processing and interrogation."

I nod once. "Then I'm going there. Today."

Nikolai's head snaps up. "You can't just *walk into* FBI Headquarters."

"I'm not walking in alone."

I turn to Reuben. "You're coming with me."

"I'll file the motion for visitation and emergency legal representation. But Cillian, if they're charging her formally, it's going to get ugly."

"Then we get ugly first."

Two hours later, I'm dressed in a charcoal suit, with Nik driving me toward FBI Headquarters. It's a visit I always thought would've included handcuffs and armed escorts. Rueben sits beside me in a crisp three-piece, carrying a briefcase full of motions, case law, and enough paper to intimidate a small country.

I don't say much. I can't. Because every time I think about her face—about the fear in her eyes when they dragged her out—rage burns through me so hot I can barely breathe.

They touched her. They *handled* her like she was disposable. Like she wasn't worth even the illusion of dignity. And now she's in a room somewhere, alone, cold, probably still in my shirt, and they're trying to break her.

She's strong, I remind myself. *But even the strongest can only take so much.*

"I know this isn't what you want to hear," Reuben says as we approach, "but if they deny us access, we need to remain calm. Losing your temper won't help Madison."

I glare out the window. "If they put one more bruise on her skin, calm won't be in my vocabulary."

Wisely, he doesn't respond.

The black SUV turns the corner, and FBI Headquarters comes into view, stone and glass, towering over the city like a monument to bureaucracy and fear.

I flex my hands in my lap.

"I'm coming for you, firecracker," I whisper under my breath. "I'm going to burn the whole fucking city down before I let them keep you."

The FBI didn't just take me from Cillian's apartment. They stripped me of my dignity. The second they slapped the cuffs on me, I stopped being anything but a criminal.

When we arrive at FBI Headquarters, I find myself being fingerprinted, cataloged, and photographed—every inch of me. The agent notices blood seeping through Cillian's T-shirt, and I'm forced to remove it so they can ensure I wasn't brutalized during my arrest. *The term apparently being considerably looser than I remember during my training.*

After pulling the shirt over my head, without being afforded privacy or a curtain, I am met with cold eyes and gasps as they see Cillian's mark. *The mark I willingly let him leave on me.* Crossing my arms over my chest, I hold their stares and let them gawk. I'm not ashamed of what the crimson letters on my chest mean: I belong to Cillian King.

Satisfied with their documentation, I'm thrown my shirt and a pair of FBI-issued sweatpants, which are cheap and scratchy. Once back in cuffs, I'm led barefoot down the hall to a sterile, windowless interrogation room. My wrists are restrained to the metal loop in the center of the table, and I'm left under the flicker of the fluorescent lights.

I'm joined by a middle-aged man with a loose tie and sleeves rolled up to the elbows. I remember him from my training at Quantico. Agent Warner. He's one of the top interrogators in the Bureau. He's also the same as every other asshole I worked with, cold, smug, and convinced he's always the smartest man in every room.

He leans forward, speaking slowly with a well-practiced tone. "Let's start simple. Did they flip you? Or were you on their side from the beginning?"

I don't answer, and he tries again with a different question. "Where is Agent Frankford?"

I stare straight ahead, my lips pursed and my fingers laced together on the table.

He sighs. "You're not doing yourself any favors, Agent Roark."

"I'm not an agent anymore."

"Not officially," he retorts. "But you sure as hell were when you walked into *that* club. When you started sleeping with the target."

I don't react. *It kills them when you don't.*

"Do you know what the Bureau thinks of you?" he asks rhetorically. "You're a cautionary tale. The golden girl turned moll. I mean, *Christ*, Madison. We trusted you. Frankford trusted you."

Still, I say nothing.

He leans back in his chair. "We've got witness tampering, obstruction, abandonment of a federal post, *and* an open murder investigation. And all of it circles right back to you. You're going to prison. That's not a threat; it's a promise."

My voice is calm when I finally speak. "Then why am I still cuffed to a table instead of in a holding cell?"

A flicker of frustration crosses his face before he quickly conceals it with a smirk. "Because I think you're smarter than this. I think you know we're your only shot at redemption."

I raise a brow and scoff. "Redemption?"

"Do the right thing, and tell us what you know. You flip on King and his associates. You give us enough to build out the case, and maybe—*maybe*—we don't bury your body under the prison."

I look him dead in the eyes. "I. Am. Not. Flipping."

He slams a hand on the table. "You're throwing your whole life away for *him*? A violent criminal? A psychopath who—"

"Loves me," I interrupt, quiet but steady. "And I love him."

Warner stares at me like I've just confessed to being abducted by aliens to repopulate their planet.

"You really drank the fucking Kool-Aid, didn't you?"

"They're not a cult. I wasn't brainwashed. I made a choice."

"And that *choice* is going to cost you your freedom," he retorts, his tone ice cold.

He opens a file folder and flips through the pages—photos, surveillance, a partial transcript of a conversation I once had with Frankford about Cillian, and notes scribbled in red ink beside my name.

"She was clean. Smart. Promising..." he reads the shorthand version of Frankford's notes. "Loyal and fully embeddable... Above average IQ... Something changed. Recommend retraction."

He slides a Polaroid of my chest across the table. The healing scab. **KING.**

"This? This is what changed."

Silent, I stare at the photo as Warner leans toward me again. His voice low, he threatens, "Here's what's going to happen. You're going to sit here until you decide to start talking. You don't get a phone call. You don't get a lawyer. You'll sit. You'll rot. You'll realize we don't need you to be cooperative. We just need you to be an *example*."

Meeting his stare, I hold it unwaveringly. "Go to hell."

He chuckles low. "You're already there, sweetheart. We'll talk again in a few hours. Maybe next time, you'll be ready to tell the truth."

I lean back in my chair as much as the cuffs allow, and he rises from his. He's about to leave the room when a light knock rattles the door. It's quick and urgent. He opens it, and his brows furrow. A young female agent leans in, her voice too low for me to hear. She slides a piece of paper into his hand. He scans it once, then again, eyes narrowing.

"You've got to be fucking kidding me," he mutters, shoving the paper in his back pocket. Warner storms back into the room. With a look of disgust, he reaches forward and unlocks the cuffs.

"Get up."

I blink. "What—?"

"Do not make me repeat myself."

"Processed out?" I ask in disbelief. "I don't understand—"

"You don't have to," he snaps. "Just move."

Still in shock, I stand from the chair. My limbs feel heavy, like they're not mine.

I'm yanked out into a hallway. A firm hand clamps down on my upper arm, steering me like I'm a flight risk. The corridor is long and narrow, the fluorescent lights buzzing above. I try to glance behind me—try to understand *why* this is happening— but no one explains. I'm completely lost... Until I see *him*.

Cillian rounds the far corner at the end of the hall, a pair of my sneakers dangling from his hand. His eyes immediately lock onto mine. He's dressed in a dark suit, flanked by an older man I don't recognize. The hand on my arm drops at the sight of them, and I run. Tears of joy stream down my face, and my bare feet slap against the carpet-tiled floor with every step.

I don't care that I'm crying. Don't care that I look insane. I don't stop. I sprint straight into his arms. He catches me mid- stride, lifting me off the ground as I collide with his chest, sobbing into his collar.

"I told you I'd come for you," he breathes, voice breaking as he buries his face in my hair. "There is nothing in the world that could keep me away from you."

From the second Madison jumps into my arms, my hands don't leave her, not once.

We step through the double doors, and the soles of our shoes slap across the polished marble floors. Her fingers tangle with mine and squeeze tightly, like she's still afraid. Like she doesn't believe she's free. She is—for now—but I know the clock is ticking.

We descend the stairwell to the parking garage together, passing silent agents who pretend not to look, though every single one of them *does.* Their faces are an array of confusion, disgust, and fear. My girl walks tall, like the queen—*or more correctly, the King*—that she is.

The garage is cool and damp as we move through the echoing space. I guide her toward Nikolai's matte-black Range Rover parked near the exit, Reuben a step behind us, muttering legalese under his breath like he's praying to some bureaucratic god.

"Cillian," he calls, catching up beside me, "I told you, I can't guarantee this loophole holds. Once the Bureau regroups, they'll be right back on the case. Unless they have another viable lead for Frankford, they'll come back for her."

"I know," I mutter, already devising a plan to frame some poor schmuck for his death.

"So don't wait." He grabs my hand, shaking it firmly. "If you're going to do this, do it now."

"Don't wait for what? Do what now?" Madison's voice cracks beside me, raw and hoarse. Ignoring her question, I open the car door and gently guide her inside. She turns toward me after sliding into her seat, and I buckle her seatbelt. "I don't want to run, Cillian. I can't spend my life like that."

"Kings don't run," Nikolai imparts from the front seat, glancing at her in the rearview mirror as I climb in beside her. "We reload."

"We're getting married," I say flatly.

Madison's head jerks from Nik's reflection in the rearview to me. "Wait—what?"

"Congratulations," Nikolai chimes, already pulling out of the space with one hand on the wheel.

"Shut up, Nik," I snarl as I lace my fingers through Madison's again. "As my wife, you can't be compelled to testify against me. We're taking care of Frankford. Everything else the FBI has on you revolves around me. The second you're off the hook for *me*, they've got nothing."

Her expression tightens, and she shakes her head. "Cillian..."

I turn in the seat and cup her face gently, my thumb grazing her jaw. With my eyes locked on hers, I ask a question I already know the answer to. "Do you love me?"

Tears well in her eyes. "Yes."

"Do you want to spend the rest of your life with me?"

"Yes," she whispers.

"Then marry me," I softly insist. "Marry me right now, firecracker. Not just because of the FBI. Not just to protect you. But because I want this. I want *you*, with my whole heart, until my last breath. And even then... it still wouldn't be long enough."

She closes her eyes and takes a deep breath like she's trying to steady herself. They open slowly, and I can see the answer in her warm chocolate pools before she speaks. "Yes," she exhales. "Yes, Daddy. I'll marry you."

———

We make our way through the courthouse to Judge Ralston's office—the large corner one on the third floor. He looks up from his desk with a startle when I push open the door. Enzo is sitting opposite him—tapping a gun mindlessly against the desk—with Eavan by his side.

"I told you," Enzo gloats as we step inside, "we just need a favor."

"Favors," the judge snaps, "don't usually involve guns in my face."

Nikolai closes the door behind us. "Don't mind him. He's being dramatic."

"I've got to be in court in thirty minutes—"

"This'll take ten," I cut him off. "We want to be married. Now. We have witnesses. We just need the paperwork."

Ralston's eyes flick between us, taking in both our appearance. With me dressed in an expensive, well-tailored suit, and Madison looking like she just rolled out of bed. *Still beautiful... Even in borrowed clothes and eyes rimmed red with exhaustion.* "Right," he says slowly. "And why should I agree to this again?"

"Because if you do, you'll have the loyalty of the Kings. For life."

Enzo smiles, dangerously. "And that's more valuable than any campaign donor."

The judge sighs, tugging a drawer open and pulling out a faded marriage ledger and a handful of forms. "Fine. Sign this and repeat after me."

The ceremony is fast. I slide the ring from my pinky and push it down her finger. It's still too big. I'll do right by her and get her real ring tomorrow. The judge drones on about solemn vows and legally binding unions, but all I can hear is her say, "*I do.*"

"I now pronounce you husband and wife."

I don't wait. I wrap my arms around her and crash my mouth to hers, lifting my wife off the ground. "You're mine now," I whisper against her lips. "No matter what, you're *mine.*"

She nods, breathless. "And you're mine."

"Thank you." I extend my hand to shake the judge's hand when Enzo suddenly clears his throat.

"Wait." He turns to Eavan, tugging her forward and dropping to one knee as we all stare at him.

"Princess," he begins, his voice unusually soft. "You're my everything. The woman I want to spend the rest of my life with. To me, you're already my wife... The future mother of my children... but I want the world to know it, too."

He pulls a small velvet box out of his coat pocket and flips it open, revealing a large carat diamond ring—classic, but bold. Just like her. "Eavan O'Brien. Princess. Will you marry me?"

"Yes! *Yes*—oh my *God*, yes!" Tears shimmer in Eavan's eyes as she nods frantically.

Judge Ralston groans and repeats the ceremony, legally binding my sister to my best friend—to my brother. Settling back into his chair, the judge glances at Nikolai and asks, "You too?"

Nikolai folds his arms and smirks. "Absolutely the fuck not. Bachelor for life."

Stepping from the courthouse, we're *two* marriages deep, with twenty years of favor-debt handed over to a man who I'm certain regrets having ever taken the bar exam.

This might not have been the magical fairytale wedding she grew up dreaming of, but selfishly, I don't care.

Madison King is wearing a ring.

My ring.

She's mine—my wife.

And no one will ever take her from me again.

The courthouse fades behind us, the echo of our hurried ceremony still ringing in my ears. But as Cillian pulls me close and spins the too-big ring around my finger, a fierce, unbreakable tether forms between us.

"Mine," he whispers against my hair, his breath warm and rough. "You're mine now. My wife." The words send a shiver of excitement down my spine as Nikolai pulls up in front of the Four Seasons.

"Don't do anything I wouldn't do," Nikolai calls as we both climb from the backseat.

The minute we step inside the hotel, suit-clad concierge rushes from behind the counter. "Your key, Mr. King. I trust the room will be to your satisfaction."

The moment we are alone in the elevator, his hands and mouth are everywhere. He hoists me into his arms, and my legs wrap around him as he pins me to the icy elevator wall. The elevator dings, and he carries me down the hall toward our room, his lips not once leaving mine as he fumbles with the lock on the door.

We barrel inside when it opens, my back slamming against the wall as he claims my lips with a hunger I didn't know existed.

"You're beautiful, my wife," he murmurs, his lips trailing down my neck. "And you're all fucking mine." I lean into him, trembling beneath the certainty in his voice. This isn't just about the marriage. It's about *us*. About surviving this uncertainty and being whole together.

Pinned against the wall by his hips, his hands slide under my shirt, and he roughly palms my breast as he licks and sucks at my neck. He presses me more firmly against the wall, the cool stone biting into my skin. "Say it," he demands, roughly tweaking my nipple. "Say you're mine. Say you're my wife."

The pain shoots straight to my pussy, and I gasp against his lips. "I'm yours. Your wife."

His hands roam lower, tracing the curve of my hips before sliding beneath my sweatpants. He firmly palms my ass cheek, his fingertips dusting against the heat between my legs. Gripping the hem of my T-shirt, he lowers me to the floor and pulls it over my head.

"You belong to me now, firecracker," he growls, dropping to his knees like a sinner preparing to worship at the altar of my body. "And I'm going to show you exactly what that means."

His eyes never leave mine—dark and gleaming with hunger— as he slowly slides my sweatpants down, baring me, inch by inch. When he presses his lips to the inside of my thigh, he doesn't look away, his warm breath skating over my skin.

"My wife," he murmurs, his voice thick with possessive pride. "This pussy belongs to me now. Every inch of you does."

A shiver courses through me as he lifts one leg over his shoulder, then the other, bracing me against the hotel room wall and spreading me wide. The wall is cool and rough against my back, but his mouth is full of heat and devotion as he presses a slow, open-mouthed kiss to the lips of my pussy. I cry out, the sound torn from my throat as his tongue slides through me, slow at first, teasing. He groans, like the taste of me is everything he's ever wanted.

"You're already dripping for me," he rasps between licks. "God, I love how you soak my mouth. My filthy little wife."

My hips buck forward, hands scrambling to hold onto his hair, needing more of him, needing *everything*. But he keeps me pinned, locked in place, balanced on his shoulders as he licks me deeper, flicking his tongue over my clit in punishing short strokes that leave me whimpering.

"That's it. Ride Daddy's face," he growls, voice muffled against me. "Let me hear how good it feels to belong to me."

"Cillian—oh *God*—" I moan, my thighs quaking. "Daddy, please..."

"That's it. Scream for Daddy while I ruin this sweet little cunt." He chuckles darkly, the vibration of it sending another wave of pleasure through me. "*My* cunt. My wife's perfect pussy."

He sucks my clit into his mouth, and I nearly fall apart. It's too much. All of it, his mouth, his words, and the rough possessiveness of how he holds me like he'll never let me go again. He feasts on me like he's determined to drag every last orgasm out of me until I forget who I ever was before this. Before *him*.

"Daddy, I'm gonna—" My voice cuts off in a broken sob as pleasure rushes through me. I grind helplessly against his mouth, crying out his name as the orgasm crashes over me, my thighs squeezing around his face.

I beg for mercy, but he doesn't relent. He licks me slowly through the aftershocks with soft, gentle strokes of his tongue, savoring me until I'm a trembling mess. Finally content, he carefully lowers each of my legs, both shaking so badly I struggle to keep my footing.

He kisses his way up my body, his beard damp and eyes on fire. "That's the first of many tonight, Mrs. King," he growls, gripping my chin and pulling me into a bruising kiss, letting me taste myself on his tongue. "You don't get to sleep until you've screamed that pretty little throat raw for Daddy."

"Yes, Daddy," I whisper, lips parted, breath raspy. His thumb drags firmly over my bottom lip.

His eyes burn, and a dark smile spreads across his face. "That's my good girl."

Scooping me into his arms, he carries me to the bed and tosses me on the soft linen. He stands before me, stripping from his clothes with his eyes hungrily raking over every inch of my body.

He sheds his pants—his thick, veiny cock springing free—and I part my thighs, inviting him to take what he wants from me. What *I* need from him, his rough and demanding hands, making me feel wanted. *Like his.* I want him to use me as he kisses his devotion across my skin, vowing to love me.

As my husband.

I stare down at Madison.

My wife.

Legs still quivering, lips swollen from our bruising kiss, and pupils blown wide, she watches me shed the last of my clothes.

She's sprawled across the center of the king-size hotel bed, her dark hair a messy halo against the white sheets, and the glint of her delicious wetness still glistening between her parted thighs. And God help me, I've never seen anything so perfect.

"I'm going to spend the night claiming my wife," I growl, climbing on top of her and pulling her perfect body against mine. "And she's going to be a good girl and let me use every one of her perfect little holes, marking each of them as mine."

I don't deserve her, but fuck if I'm not going to spend my life worshipping her anyway.

I settle between her thighs and tenderly tuck her hair behind her ear. "My wife is fucking beautiful," I whisper, unable to pull my gaze from her.

The word sends a fresh spike of need through me.

Wife.

I slide my hand along her thigh, dusting my fingertips along her soft, bronzed skin. Her breath catches when I dip my fingers into her slick pussy, stroking between her lips with deliberate care, so slowly and gently that it's almost cruel. Her hips rise, silently pleading for more.

"Are you still aching for Daddy?" I teasingly ask.

She nods, wide-eyed. "Yes."

"Always such a needy little girl."

I press my cock against her entrance and still, teasing her with the weight of me. Cupping her cheek, I brush my thumb across her bottom lip. "Are you ready for me to make you mine all over again?" I ask with a soft whisper. "Ready for Daddy to show you how he's going to treat his pussy for the rest of your life?"

"Yes, Daddy," she breathes, so sweet and desperate. "Please."

I slide into her in one long, slow stroke, groaning at the way her pussy clenches around me—wet, hot, and welcoming. Her back arches, and she moans as fingers fist the sheets.

"Fuuuuck, firecracker," I grit. "So tight for me. And so perfect."

I set a slow pace, rolling my hips against her, letting her feel every thick inch stretching her open. Taking my time and repeatedly filling her with languid strokes, I savor it. Savor *her*. Because tonight isn't just about claiming her, it's about worshipping her.

Her hands slide up my back and cling to my shoulders, her nails digging into my skin like she's afraid I'll vanish if she lets go. I lean down and kiss her. Our tongues tangle as I claim her mouth in the same slow, deliberate way I'm taking her pussy.

"My sweet wife..." I growl against her lips. "I'm going to make sure you feel me for days."

"Do it," she gasps. "Show me."

I snap my hips harder, dragging a strangled cry from her throat. Her legs wrap around my waist, anchoring me to her as I bury myself in her cunt over and over. The slap of skin on skin fills the room as her moans grow louder with every stroke.

"You love being fucked by your husband, don't you?"

"Yes—*yes*—I love it—"

I reach between us, rubbing slow circles over her clit, my thrusts growing sharper as her cries pitch higher. Her body tenses under me, she's so fucking close to falling apart for me.

"Be my good girl and come for me," I softly demand. "Come on my cock like a good fucking *wife should*."

She shatters, her whole body convulsing, crying out my name like a vow and a curse. Her walls clamp down on me, and I fight desperately not to lose it and spill inside her.

I spend the hours pleasing her with my mouth, fingers, and cock, using her pussy and throat until she's a sweaty, whimpering mess. "Just a little bit more," I encourage, grabbing a small container of lube that the hotel so generously provided at my request.

After slathering it over my cock and carefully rubbing some into her asshole, I claim the last inch of my wife. I ease into her tight hole and pull her back to my chest, spooning her. I take her slowly, rubbing my fingers over her overstimulated clit, making sure she enjoys every stroke of my cock.

A gorgeous, garbled groan rattles from her lungs when she comes for me again. "Does my dirty girl like Daddy deep in her ass?"

"Yes, Daddy."

"Do you think you can handle more, firecracker? Because Daddy wants to fuck your ass. Hard."

She hesitates for a second before answering, "Yes."

Staying deep inside her, I roll us until she's on her stomach. I pull her hips into the air and increase the pace of my thrusts. She takes them with ease, like every inch of her was made to be used by me. I fuck her hard. My hips slam against her toned ass until she's fisting the sheets, her thighs are trembling, and she's screaming her release into the pillow.

I drive into her one last time, spilling inside her with a groan torn from the depths of my chest. My head drops to the back of her shoulder, our bodies locked together in the most primal, perfect way.

After a long moment, I pull out of her slowly, careful not to hurt her. She winces, her entire body sore from overstimulation.

"You did so good for me," I whisper against the sweaty nape of her neck with a kiss. "So fucking good."

I quickly clean her, wiping the salty sweat and cum from her skin before climbing back into bed with her. Rolling onto my side, I gather her against my chest. With a deep sigh, she melts into me, her skin flushed and her heart still racing.

I press soft kisses to her temple, down to her cheek, then to the corner of her lips. She turns her head slightly, nuzzling closer.

"Cillian..."

"I know, firecracker..." I stroke her back, my fingers tracing along her spine. "I'd burn the world for you. I don't give a fuck how we got here. All that matters is that you're still in my arms and that no one will ever take that from me. From *us*."

She nods, pressing her lips to my chest like she's making a vow of her own.

I stay awake long after her breaths become slow and even, my hand resting on the small of her back. Even then, I don't let her go.

Because I'll never let my wife go.

ABOUT A WEEK LATER

As I'm sitting on the sidewalk patio of the small coffee shop down the street from the apartment, the sun warms my back.

I cradle my coffee between my hands, the ceramic mug warm against my palms, and try to soak in the rare moment of peace. Across from me, Eavan lifts her sunglasses onto the top of her head and grins over the rim of her iced latte—a much better choice of beverage in this heat.

"I have to admit," she teases with a smirk. "I didn't think your first couple of weeks as a King would include a courthouse wedding, a federal arrest, and full-blown war crimes worth of sex bruises."

I laugh at the absurdity that is my new life. "Neither did I. But I guess I should've expected nothing less, right?"

"You really shouldn't have." She winks. Her expression softens, and she reaches across the table and lightly squeezes my hand. "But you're one of us now. For real. And no matter what happens next, that means something. To all of us."

Emotion tightens my throat for a second. Eavan doesn't owe me this kind of welcome, especially not with how things started. But she's looked at me like a sister from the moment Cillian moved me in with him. *Into our home.* There's no judgment in her eyes. Just quiet solidarity.

"Thank you." I return her squeeze. "For not hating me. For... giving me a chance."

"Please. If we started kicking people out of this family for being a little morally flexible, the penthouse would be a damn ghost town."

If that isn't the fucking truth.

"So... Um..." She takes a breath, her gaze flicking to the street and back to me. "There's actually something I want to tell you."

I blink, leaning forward. "What is it?"

She presses a hand to her stomach, and a small smile blooms across her face. "I'm pregnant."

My eyes widen. "*Eavan!* Are you serious?"

She nods, biting her lip, and her eyes quickly fill with tears—happy ones.

"We found out for sure two days ago. Haven't told anyone else yet, but... I wanted you to know first. You're family now."

I push my chair back and round the table, throwing my arms around her. "Oh my God. Congratulations!"

She hugs me tight, laughing into my hair. "I'm scared shitless. But I'm also so damn happy. Enzo's already talking about making this one a brother or a sister."

"That sounds about right." I laugh.

Finishing my coffee, I swear I hear someone calling my name. I glance around, but don't see any familiar faces. "Roark!" The deep voice slices through the air behind me, and my heart drops into my stomach. I turn slowly, dreading who I am going to find. Standing a few feet away on the sidewalk, dressed in a sharp navy suit and aviators, is the FBI agent who interrogated me when I was in custody. He pulls off his sunglasses and slowly eyes me suspiciously.

"Agent Warner. Or is it just Gary, since I'm no longer in custody?"

His jaw tightens. "Funny." *I thought so.*

Eavan sits back in her seat, eyes narrowing and hands slipping beneath the table.

"Can I help you with something?" I ask, keeping my tone neutral.

He steps closer, completely ignoring Eavan. "Just wanted to tell you in person that we aren't done with you."

"You came all the way down here for that? Must be a slow day at the Bureau."

His faux smile doesn't quite reach his eyes. "You think you got out clean, but traitors don't walk away without consequences."

I stiffen, rising to my feet slowly. "Are you threatening me?"

He leans in, voice cold. "No. I'm *promising*. You might've ducked out of custody with some legal loophole, but this isn't over. When we build the case on the organized crime charges and bring them to court, you'll be subpoenaed. You'll have no choice. You'll bury yourself with your own testimony when the Attorney General starts asking you about your involvement with Cillian King."

I stare at him in silence, then slowly raise my hand between us. The four-carat diamond ring on my finger sparkles in the sunlight. Warner stares at it as I wiggle my fingers. "Spousal privilege," I purr, letting a bold smile bloom across my face. "You can't compel me to testify about or against my husband."

His face sours at the realization he's lost any upper hand he had on me or the Kings and he sneers, "Your father would be fucking ashamed of you."

"You should probably leave now," Eavan snips before letting out a low whistle.

On the other side of the street, Enzo, Cillian, and Nikolai step off the sidewalk and cut through traffic like they own the ground beneath their feet. The three of them angrily stare at Warner as they step onto the curb.

Warner takes a long look at me, his face taut and lips pressed into a thin line. His eyes flick to the three murderous men walking toward him and wisely decides this conversation is, in fact, over. He turns without another word and stalks off down the street, jaw tight and shoulders stiff with swallowed rage.

Cillian is at my side in seconds, crouching beside me. His

hands cradle my face, thumbs brushing over my cheeks, anchoring me.

I suck in a breath as the last of the tension drains from my spine.

He presses a kiss to my forehead, warm and grounding. "You okay?"

"Yeah," I manage. My voice is hoarse, but steady.

Eavan grins. "She handled that like a fucking King."

His soft hazel eyes not leaving mine, he smiles proudly. "That's because she is one."

CHAPTER 48
cillian

ONE MONTH LATER

"Jesus, Cian," Madison says, casting a teasing glance my way. "You look like you're about to vomit."

I grip the steering wheel tighter, trying—and failing—not to let the nerves show. My knuckles are white against the leather, and sure enough, my palm is damp on her thigh.

She lifts her brows, amused. "You're seriously nervous." She grins. "*You.*"

I glare at the road ahead. "I'm not nervous. I'm... aware of the stakes."

"Your hands are sweating," she points out with a triumphant smirk.

"This is a big deal," I huff, adjusting my grip and wiping my hand down the side of my jeans. "Your mom already thinks I'm some kind of blood-soaked criminal, and she's not exactly wrong."

"Are you serious?" Madison snorts. "You walked me into your penthouse with two of your brothers ready to put a bullet in my head, and I had to confess all my sins to men who've actually *killed* people."

"And?" I glance over at her.

"This is *dinner*." She pokes my arm. "With my *mother*. I can guarantee she doesn't have a Glock tucked in the back of her jeans."

"You don't *know* that," I mutter.

She laughs—a real one, full and bright—and it melts some of the dread coiling low in my stomach.

We've been married for a month. A chaotic, beautiful, exhausting month. And this is the last loose thread in the life we're trying to build. Even if I don't deserve it, getting her mother's blessing is important to me.

The house appears around a bend. It's a small, single-story brick ranch. White shutters. A perfectly mowed front lawn with pristine flowerbeds. Two rocking chairs on the porch. It's simple. Normal.

It's nothing like the world I dragged Madison into, and maybe that's why it feels like the hardest battle I've ever fought.

She reaches for my hand as I park my Aston Martin on the long gravel driveway. "Hey," she says softly, her thumb brushing mine. "She already agreed to dinner, and that means something."

"Yeah... It means she doesn't want to piss you off," I mutter. "Or she's planning to murder me with a cast-iron skillet."

"Maybe. But if she tries, I'll take her out." Madison's lips curve, and I can't help but chuckle. "Let's go, Mr. King."

I nod once and open my car door. The air on the other side smells like grass and pine. A wind chime sings quietly from the porch. Everything is peaceful and serene, and I feel like I've stepped into a world I have no business stomping in on.

Madison's fingers thread through mine as I help her from the car, and she gives them a reassuring squeeze as we make our way onto the porch. She knocks twice, and a moment later the door creaks open.

"Hi, Mommy."

Her mother is tall and thin, with silver streaks in her dark hair. She has the same deep brown eyes as her daughter, just with a little crinkle in the corners. "Maddie," she gushes, pulling her in for a tight hug. "You look so good, sweetheart."

"Mom..." Madison pulls back from their embrace and turns toward me. "This is Cillian."

"Cillian," she greets flatly with a slight nod.

I extend my hand. "Ma'am." She studies my hand for a moment before taking it, her grip warm but measured. There's a gentleness to her, but her eyes search mine with a quiet scrutiny.

"Well. Come on in. Supper's almost ready."

I glance at Madison, who gives me a *see?* look and pulls me inside.

The house smells like fresh bread and something savory. I glance briefly at the family photos as Madison leads me toward the dining room. Dinner is set out on a heavy wooden table: roast chicken, mashed potatoes, green beans, biscuits. We sit, and Madison pours iced tea for everyone.

Two fingers of whiskey would be better. Maybe three.

Her mother watches me with sharp eyes over the rim of her glass. "So," she begins. "What do you do for a living, Cillian?"

Madison nearly chokes on her drink. I cough once, hard.

"I'm in... high-stakes logistics," I answer slowly.

Her mom raises a knowing eyebrow.

"He kills people and launders money," Madison chirps, shoving a biscuit into her mouth with a smirk. "But in a *very organized* way."

I shoot her a warning look, and she brattily winks at me.

"We get the news out here, too. I know exactly who you are. I've read everything they leaked after Maddie's arrest..." She pauses to reach for the butter. "I also know she hasn't smiled like this in years. She's glowing."

Madison lightly nudges my elbow, and I turn to find her smiling.

"I don't like the idea of my daughter living in danger," she continues, slicing her biscuit. "But I also know Madison never makes decisions lightly. She's always been a smart girl. Stubborn as hell and defiant, but smart."

If that isn't the truth...

Staring at me with renewed intensity, she asks, "You love her?"

More than anything.

"I'd go to war for her," I reply honestly. "And I'd die before I ever let anything happen to her."

The tiniest of smiles pulls at the corners of her mouth. "I can live with that."

Madison's hand reaches under the table, lacing her fingers through mine again as she gives it a loving squeeze.

Her mother asks questions as we eat dinner—what my family is like, what our apartment is like, what kind of future we're building. She doesn't pretend to understand our world, but she listens. She laughs at Madison's bratty sarcasm and smiles about her car karaoke. By the time dessert comes out—a warm blackberry cobbler with vanilla ice cream—I feel dangerously close to *belonging.*

After dinner, Madison offers to do the dishes. Her mom quickly waves her off.

"I'll get 'em later. Go walk around the yard or something. You used to sit on the porch after dinner every night."

We step outside into the warm Virginia dusk. The sun is sinking low, painting the sky in pink and gold. Crickets hum in the grass as we sit on the porch swing, the old wood groaning beneath us.

"See?" Madison bumps her shoulder against me. "I told you she wouldn't shoot you."

"She *still* might," I tease. "You're her baby."

Madison laughs, leaning against me. "She likes you."

"She likes *you*, and I make you smile," I correct.

She shrugs.

"Same thing." She curls into my side, head on my shoulder, fingers drawing slow circles over my thigh. "You did good, Daddy."

I press a kiss to her forehead. "I'd do anything for you, firecracker."

She goes quiet for a moment, then murmurs, "I know."

This place is a world away from the one I built on blood. And yet... sitting here with her, surrounded by the soft homeliness of where Madison came from, I can't help but think maybe we can have this, too.

Not a perfect life. *And definitely not out here in the country...* But *ours*.

CHAPTER 48
madison

The bass thumps low and slow through the floor of the club, a rhythm that pulses through the soles of my heels and up my spine. Crimson, violet, and gold lights shift in waves, and the scent of expensive cologne fills the air.

Standing at the end of the bar, I scribble down a few notes about the girl currently dancing on the stage. A pair of strong arms snake around my waist, pulling me against a wall of muscle and power I know better than my reflection. His lips hover near my ear, breath hot.

"Sir," I admonish, not looking up from my notes, "this club has a strict no touching rule."

Cillian chuckles darkly, dipping his fingers beneath the

waistband of my pencil skirt and grazing the waistband of my lace panties.

"I'm serious, Cillian," I hiss, even as my body responds to his touch. "I'm working."

His grin is audible. "That's my line, firecracker."

I twist in his arms just enough to shoot him a look over my shoulder. "You're going to get me fired."

"You're the house manager." He smirks. "You'd have to fire yourself."

"You're still my boss."

After a couple of weeks in the penthouse, pacing like a caged animal and bored out of my mind, I practically begged Cillian to let me do something—*anything*. I had no intention of coming back to dance at the club. It just so happened that Chloe, the former house manager, had announced she was moving to California to be closer to her sister. Right time. Right opportunity. And a job that doesn't require parading around in my underwear as drunk middle-aged men slip twenty-dollar bills into them.

I slid into the role like I was born for it; balancing schedules, keeping the dancers happy, resolving disputes with drunk customers before they turn into brawls. I've quickly earned the girls' trust and staff's approval.

"Fine." He sighs, letting his hands fall away from my body but staying close. "As much as I hate the idea of sharing you... I do miss watching that perfect ass of yours up on stage."

I grin and nudge him away with my hip. "You'll live."

He wanders off toward one of the back rooms where Enzo and Nikolai are holding a meeting with some smug, coked-out assholes from Colombia. I don't ask questions. I just keep the drinks flowing and entertainment on their laps.

The night passes in a blur of glitter, fishnets, and G-strings. We're close to closing, and the last wave of regulars is starting to trickle out. I make the rounds one last time, checking on the girls, talking to security, confirming tomorrow's supply order.

Finished with my work, I slip into the dressing room. I look through the new lingerie delivery and grab a set of black thigh-highs and a strappy wine-red number from the shelf. *He's going to love this one.* With it all tucked under my arm, I head upstairs to the VIP suites and make my way to the one at the end of the hall.

I send a quick text to security.

Kill the feed to VIP6.

Inside, I double-check the tiny red light on the camera to ensure it's off.

I strip quickly, sliding into the barely-there lingerie and rolling up the stockings slowly, savoring the ritual. I pour two fingers of whiskey into a crystal glass and set it on the low table.

Grabbing my phone, I set the timer and snap a handful of selfies. I swipe through them and settle on the best three: thigh-highs, the sheer bra not quite covering my tits, and a playful bite of my lower lip. I text them to Cillian.

Is this what Daddy wants?

The response comes fast.

CILLIAN

Fuck, firecracker. Don't tease me.

VIP6.

Within a matter of minutes, he barrels through the door, slamming it shut as quickly as it opened. His eyes are fire, raking over my body and already undressing me in his mind.

"You summoned me?" he drawls, accepting the glass of whiskey from my outstretched hand.

Smiling sweetly, I lead him to the couch and gently push him onto it. I climb onto his lap and straddle him. My hands pressed to his chest, I teasingly slide my ass up and down his thighs. Leaning close and brushing my tits across his chest, I whisper, "It's a private show for my favorite client."

"Your *only* client," he grits his correction. I grind firmly against his hips and slip from his lap, listening to his disappointed groan as I saunter to the pole in the center of the room. Listening to the sultry beat humming from the speakers, I wrap my fingers around it and lean into the curve of my spine. My hips circle in a deep, lazy roll as I stare at him across the room.

Pressing my back to the cool metal, my fingers trace up the inside of my thighs. They glide over lace and skin teasingly slow, just enough to leave him aching. Spinning quickly, I let the motion carry my hair over one shoulder, my body twisting as I grab the pole again. I slide down it with a slow grind until I'm crouched low, my legs wide, ass lifted, back arched. The music pulses, and I rise with it, chest out, hands skating over my sides to palm my breasts through the sheer red lace cups. Gripping the clasp, I undo it and let the lacy fabric fall to the floor.

I drag my tongue and teeth across my bottom lip as my eyes find his. His gaze is molten. Tracking every shift of my weight, every deliberate bounce of my breasts, every inch of bare skin I reveal like it's a gift meant only for him.

I turn and press my palms to the floor, grinding against it., Lifting my ass and pushing back onto my knees, I draw attention to the curve of my hips and the deep curve of my spine. I rise slowly, one leg wrapping around the pole, climbing it until I'm perched high. After flipping upside down, I spin to the floor in a slow, sinuous descent. My back presses to the floor just as the song is coming to an end.

It's not just a dance. It's a striptease for one man—designed to absolutely ruin him.

Cillian curls a finger, beckoning me forward.

I go over to him on my hands and knees, crawling from the pole to the couch. My hands slide from his knees to his chest as I sensuously slip onto his lap. I grind against him, giving him a lap dance that leaves his jaw clenched and his hands white-knuckled on the back of the couch.

"You're going to kill me," he grits, his hands sliding up the bare skin of my back and pulling me even tighter to him. "I'm ready to explode at the thought of sinking inside you."

Rolling my hips against his hard cock beneath his slacks, I smirk. "Sorry. Club and personal rule: I don't fuck clients."

He tucks a strand of hair behind my ear, eyes glinting. "Then I guess I'll just have to take you home," he whispers gravelly against my throat, "so my *wife* can fuck me."

"Deal." I grin. And God help me, I've never wanted him more.

By the time I get Madison home, I'm strung tight with need.

She knew exactly what she was doing in that private room. Every sway of her hips. Every glance over her shoulder. That wicked little smile on her lips when she crawled across the room and into my lap.

The second the penthouse door clicks shut, I pin her against it. Her back hits the cold steel with a thud, and I cage her in with my body, one palm flat beside her head.

"Still feeling like a tease?" I ask, brushing my nose along her jaw. "Or are you ready to behave for Daddy?"

Her smile is slow and sweet, but the heat in her eyes gives her away. Staring up at me through her lashes, she playfully chews

Wrong answer, firecracker.

I grab her wrist and pull her from the door, guiding her across the apartment and toward the spiral staircase with deliberate steps. Her breath stutters when I lead her straight into the bedroom and to the edge of the bed without saying a single word. I reach for my belt and slip it free from the loops with a snap. Taking a seat, I pat my lap.

She swallows hard. "Really?"

"Oh, we're past 'really.'" I fold the belt in my hand, making a big loop. "Skirt off and over my lap. Now."

Hesitating for a second, she undoes the zipper at the back of her skirt and lets it fall to the floor around her heels. She crawls across my lap, hair spilling over one shoulder, and her heart hammering hard enough for me to feel it where her chest presses into my thigh.

"You don't get to wind me up all night and walk away untouched," I grouse, running my hand over the curve of her backside. "You know Daddy has rules about being a bratty little tease."

She gasps when I bring my palm down. The swat isn't too hard, just enough to sting, enough to warm her ass up. I strike her again, smiling at the gasp she tries to hide.

"Do you think it's cute teasing me in my own club?"

"No, Dadd—" Her voice cracks mid-answer as my hand lands across her soft ass, followed a second later with another.

"Or sending me photos like that while I'm in a business meeting?"

"No..." she blurts breathlessly, her ass starting to burn a beautiful shade of scarlet.

"No?" I scoff, spanking her again. "Try again."

Her voice wavers. "No, Daddy."

I swing again, letting my hand rest where it lands, her beautiful red ass warm against my palm.

"Naughty girls get what they deserve." I lift my belt from the bed. "And you are a *very* naughty girl, aren't you?"

"Yes, Daddy."

Snapping my wrist, the belt thwacks against her skin, and a garbled moan-y yelp spills over her lips. Fisting the hair at the back of her head, I steer her gaze toward me and ask, "Do you need another?"

She timidly nods and answers at barely above a whisper, "Yes, Daddy." I swing the belt again, a yelp shrieking from her as it leaves a welt across her ass cheek. "Thank you, Daddy."

That's more like it.

I ease her off my lap and onto the bed. She sinks into the mattress as I quickly rid myself of my clothes. After kissing up the back of her thighs, I press my lips to the reddest of marks on her cheeks. I roll her over to find her face nearly as flushed as her ass, and her pupils blown wide. I settle my body over hers, and she lets out the softest whimper. Her body shifts restlessly beneath mine, and I press my hips down to still her.

"Look at me," I demand. Her eyes meet mine, heavy-lidded and waiting. "Daddy loves you, and I just want you to be a good girl for me."

"I know," she whispers.

I crash my mouth down on hers. No gentleness or hesitation. Just raw, filthy need. My tongue pushes past her lips like I own her, and I do. She moans into our kiss, her body arching beneath mine, her soft curves molding perfectly to my hardness. I pin her wrists to the mattress, grinding against her with deliberate force. My hips rut forward, and the friction between us pulls breathy, broken whimpers from her.

I pull back just enough to growl against her lips, "What do you want, firecracker?"

Panting, her voice a pained whisper, she pleads, "You. All of you, Daddy. Please…"

Fuck.

My restraint snaps like the panties I tear from her body.

Roughly, I drag my hand down her side and shove her thighs wider, spreading her open with no gentleness at all. I mold myself against her and press my cock to her dripping cunt. The high and desperate sound that blows from her shreds what's left of my self-control.

I push inside her in one demanding thrust, and she cries out beneath me. Her pussy is tight and wet, gripping my cock like it needs to be inside of her. "You're mine," I growl against her throat, my hand tangling in her hair as I slam into her again. "Say it."

"I'm yours, Daddy," she exhales, her voice ragged with need. "Only yours."

Every thrust is brutal and claiming. Her cries grow louder with every drive of my hips, her body jerking beneath mine as I fuck her like I'm trying to imprint myself on her soul. Her heels dig into the backs of my thighs, silently begging me to go deeper and harder. pulling me deeper, tighter, harder.

"Look at you," I rasp, watching her fall apart beneath me. "So fucking needy for Daddy's cock. Are you gonna be my good girl and come for me?"

Her lips part, but she doesn't answer me. Instead, I'm met with a string of mewls as she approaches the edge. "Is that a yes?" I pant between savage thrusts, her hips rising to meet each one. "Let go for me, firecracker. Come for me."

She shatters beneath me, crying out my name with her whole body seizing as she clenches around me. I keep thrusting through it, drawing it out until she's trembling and whimpering under my weight.

The second she breaks, I fall after her. Groaning against her neck, I spill inside her, every muscle taut and every nerve ending on fire. I grind into her until there's nothing left, and I collapse on top of her. Her chest rises and falls against mine as she struggles to catch her breath.

I don't give her the chance. Leaning in, I kiss her again—slow this time, lazy and deep. My hand strokes along her side, fingertips ghosting over her still-sensitive skin.

"You're going to be the fucking death of me," I mutter against her lips.

"But what a way to go, Daddy." She hums, smiling with a bratty, blissed-out little smirk that makes me want to spank her all over again.

CHAPTER 51
madison

The room feels like it's floating... Or *I'm* floating...

Tucked against him, my cheek rests on his chest, still warm and slick with sweat. His heartbeat is a deep, steady thump beneath my ear, grounding me in the aftermath. My limbs are jelly, my body boneless, and my is ass on fire. Cillian claimed me like he was making up for every second I made him wait. He's a demanding Daddy, both with punishments and sex. Yet, even with his demanding hands and the savage way he fucks, I feel loved, worshipped, and adored through every sting on my ass and thrust of his cock.

I might be the death of him, but my husband has absolutely

He brushes my hair off my face, trailing a soft line from my temple to my jaw. His touch is so gentle—a stark contrast to his roughness—as he slowly trails his hand down my back.

"Are you okay, firecracker?" he murmurs against the top of my head. His voice is low, hoarse, and full of genuine concern.

I nod, too lazy and floaty to find my words immediately. "Yeah. More than okay."

He lets out a breath, and his lips pull into a smile against the crown of my head. "Good. You were perfect."

I hum, nuzzling closer into the dip where his shoulder meets his chest.

"You were perfect, too," I whisper.

"You say that like I don't always know what my girl needs." His arm tightens around my waist. "Or how she likes to be fucked."

I roll my eyes and laugh lightly. "Cocky much?"

"No. I just know how to take care of my wife."

He reaches behind him, tugging the blanket over us, then wraps both arms around me like he can't stand the thought of not touching me for a second.

"I love you." My voice cracks a little, suddenly overwhelmed when I think about the fragility of our relationship.

He pulls me closer and kisses my temple again. "Talk to me."

"I just..." I breathe in slowly, filling my lungs with the scent of him; warm skin, sweat, a hint of his cologne. My fingers nervously trace lazy patterns across his chest—scar tissue, the hard ridges of muscle—as I turn my thoughts to words.

"Sometimes it scares me how much I need you. If this all went away, I wouldn't know how to breathe."

Cillian's hold doesn't loosen. If anything, he wraps himself around me tighter, one leg tangling with mine, his nose brushing my hairline. "I'm not going away."

"You can't know that."

"I do," he states firmly. "There is nothing that could keep me from you. I would burn cities to the ground and wage wars to bring you home if anyone dared take you from me."

"And if they took you from me?" I ask the thing I fear most about his line of work, knowing that every meeting could end with a prison sentence or a funeral.

"I would crawl back to you from the depths of hell to spend the rest of *your* life with you. And when your time finally came, I would fight my way through the pearly gates to have the rest of eternity with you. Because this one short lifetime isn't enough to show you how much I love you."

He shifts beneath me, and I barely have time to blink before he rolls us. His strong arms guide my weight with ease until I'm flat on my back, cradled by the mattress. Cillian rises over me, braced on his forearms, the golden hazel of his eyes molten with ravenous heat again.

I feel him—hard and growing harder—pressing against my thigh.

My breath catches. "Again?" I gasp, a breathless laugh tumbling out with the word.

His lips brush against mine in a kiss that's soft and slow. "Always." His voice is thick with emotion. "But this time, I'm going to fuck you like I have an eternity with you... because I will. I'll make sure of it."

The head of his cock nudges against me, and I gasp as he eases inside—inch by inch—steadily filling me and stretching me wide all over again. I feel *everything*. Every throb. Every breath he takes. Every tremble of his restraint as he buries himself in me fully.

Braced above me, our eyes lock, and he rocks his hips slowly, grinding deep until my toes curl. My fingers grip his arms and back, feeling every flex and quiver of the muscles caging me in. His eyes never leave mine. Not even for a second.

This isn't frantic, punishing, or desperate. There are no rough hands on my body or filthy degradation spilling over his lips. Just the man I love staring down at me like I'm the most fragile thing in his world.

"I love you," he vows. "In this life and the next. And in every one after that. I'll find you. And I'll love you all over again. And one day, maybe I'll deserve you."

Tears prick my eyes as he makes love to me, devotion written into every languid thrust and tender kiss. His hand finds mine, and he lifts it to his chest so I can feel his heart, wild and real. *And mine.*

"I might never deserve you," he breathes, his forehead pressed to mine. "But you... You make me believe I could still be good. For you."

My tears spill over, and I wrap my legs around his waist, pulling him deeper. My hips rise to meet each slow roll of his. "You are good. You protect people. You protect *me*."

He chokes on a groan, the emotion winding tight in his jaw,

and I see the moment it breaks him. How my words break him.

"I didn't know I was alive until I found you," he whispers into the side of my neck. "I was breathing and existing. But I wasn't living until you."

I hold his face in my hands and kiss him, tasting the salt of my tears and his unconditional love all at once.

Our bodies move in a quiet rhythm. No urgency. Just slow, aching pressure and the unbearable sweetness of being so deeply understood and still wanted. He grinds his hips as if trying to memorize the shape of me from the inside out. "You were made for me," he growls against my mouth. "And I was made to love you."

We fall apart together, quietly, trembling and clinging to each other. I cry out his name in a breathy whisper, and he presses his face to my neck, panting as I feel him pulsing inside me. Our bodies molded together, and his cock still buried deep, he kisses my collarbone, my cheeks, and my lips.

He pulls out with a low grunt and collapses beside me, dragging me into his arms. My back to his chest, his hand slides under the blanket to rest on my stomach, keeping me tethered to him like he's afraid I might vanish if he's not touching me.

"I meant what I said," he whispers. "About eternity. You're mine. Always."

I smile softly and link my fingers with his. "Forever."

His breathing evens out before mine does, warm and slow against the back of my neck. "Go to sleep." He kisses against the crook of my neck. "I've got you."

I drift off to sleep wrapped in the arms of a man who would destroy the world for me... Knowing that if it does all end tomorrow, he'd find me again. And love me harder next time.

There are worse ways to spend a lazy evening.

The sun has dipped behind the city skyline, casting shadows through the penthouse windows. The radio on, shuffling through playlists in the background, just enough noise to fill the room without being a distraction.

Madison is draped over me like a sleepy cat, one of her legs thrown over my thighs, her cheek nestled against my bare chest. She's tracing slow, absent-minded circles over my ribs, like she's lulling herself to sleep. And if I'm being honest, I'm not far behind her.

Peace like this is rare. Fragile. And every second of it feels like something stolen.

I let my head rest against the arm of the couch, my fingers dragging along the soft skin of Madison's bare thigh. Her breathing is steady and warm, blowing over my skin. She shifts a little, curling tighter into me with a sleepy hum.

I'm about to suggest we spend the rest of the night in bed—just let the world disappear—when the front door slides open. "Ugh..." Nik grumbles at the sight of us snuggled together, tossing his keys onto the counter. "God, I need to get my own place."

"What? We aren't even naked," I jest. An hour ago might've been a different story, but knowing Nik would be coming home, we both redressed in my clothes—Madison in my boxer briefs and T-shirt, and me commando in my sweats.

"Yeah, *this time.*"

I smirk, not bothering to lift my head. "I hear the other apartment on Enzo's floor is going on the market tomorrow."

"Great," he mutters. "Who wouldn't want to share a wall with that fuck-fest again?"

Madison snorts into my chest, trying and failing miserably to suppress a laugh.

Nik doesn't ease up. "What the hell am I saying? It's all of you. It's like tiptoeing around a porn set day in and day out."

Madison props her chin on my chest and flashes him a grin. "We could always find a nice girl for you at the club. Jasmine is sweet. Or maybe a not-so-nice girl, if that's more your style."

"Hard pass," Nik mutters, grabbing a bottle of water from the fridge and his keys from the counter. "I'm going out."

I arch a brow. "Now?"

"Yeah. Bar down the street. I'll find my own girl, thanks. Preferably one with her own apartment so I can fuck her in private."

"You worried we'll all hear you only lasting three minutes?" Cillian teases.

"Fuck you."

"I love you, too, Nik." I glance down at Madison and raise a brow. "A not-so-nice girl at the club?"

She smiles innocently. "What? He's not upset. He's lonely."

She's probably not wrong... She usually isn't.

My phone buzzes on the coffee table. I lift it and swipe the screen.

UNKNOWN

I know what you did.

The cryptic words catch my attention, and my pulse kicks up a beat.

I sit up straighter, gently easing Madison onto the cushions. She blinks, surprised. "What?"

"Nothing, firecracker. Just gimme a second." I stand, tightening my grip on the phone. She watches me with those sharp, too-perceptive eyes, pulling her legs up and tucking the blanket around herself.

I type a reply.

Who is this?

The response is almost immediate.

You'll find out soon enough.

You have a debt that needs to be paid.

A cold thread winds its way down my spine.

"Nik!" I bark as he's walking out the door, the edge in my voice sharp enough to make Madison sit upright.

Footsteps thunder from the foyer, and Nik reappears. "What?"

"Read it." I hold the phone out.

His eyes scan the screen. "What the hell…?"

I nod toward the dining area. "We need to call Enzo. And Eavan. *Now*."

Less than thirty minutes later, the five of us are sitting around the kitchen island, the overhead lights casting stark shadows across the granite from the Chinese takeout containers Enzo and Eavan grabbed when we interrupted their late dinner.

I set the phone down between us all. "Messages came from an unlisted number. It's probably a burner. Could be the FBI fucking with us…" I trail off.

Enzo finishes for me. "No. It feels personal."

"Debt. That's deliberate wording." Madison's gaze hasn't left the screen. "It's not the FBI."

"It's a threat," Eavan says flatly. "But vague."

Nik crosses his arms. "And vague threats are rarely empty ones. If they wanted to rattle you, they did a decent job."

I meet his eyes and snip, "They didn't rattle me."

He lifts a brow and grandly gestures at the small buffet of

takeout and the five of us. "They rattled you enough to call a meeting."

He's not wrong.

Madison leans forward. "So... who have we pissed off lately?"

"Define 'lately,'" Enzo mutters.

"And who haven't we pissed off?" Nik adds.

"Could be a former client," Nik muses. "Or someone from before we took over. Hell, even someone from the club—"

"No," Nik cuts me off. "If it were someone local, they wouldn't be this quiet. *We* wouldn't be."

Madison glances at me with nervous eyes, and I know immediately what she's thinking.

Whoever sent that message knows where to aim. They didn't say *your crew.* They said *you.* And there are only two things in this world that could still be used as leverage against me. And one of them is sitting six inches to my left.

"What's the play?" Enzo leans on the counter, arms folded. "Do we bang on some doors and see who rattles?"

I shake my head. "Not yet. We keep this quiet until we know what we're dealing with."

Nik scoffs. "So... do nothing."

"No," I correct. "I'll send this to Hawk and see what he can come up. And we'll go from there."

Nik drops into the barstool at the end of the island and sighs, grabbing a spring roll. "As they said... we'll find out soon enough."

With a makeshift plan in place, Enzo and Eavan disappeared to their apartment and against everyone else's better judgment, Nik went to the bar down the street to find the love of his life. *Or of tonight.*

Madison and I have found ourselves back on the couch. Only now, she's curled against me in silence, her knees pulled up between us, her face pressed to my collarbone.

"You okay?" I ask, brushing my fingers through her hair.

She nods slowly. "Yeah. Just thinking."

"About?"

Her voice is muffled. "About how fast things can change."

I press a kiss to her forehead. "Whatever this is... You're safe. I promise you that."

She tilts her head up. "Cillian..."

"No," I insist firmly. "You're mine, Madison. And whatever comes, whoever's behind this... If it's you they want, they'll have to go through me."

She exhales slowly, resting her head back against me. "How can you sound so sure?"

"Because I am."

The water in the tub has gone lukewarm. Not cold, not hot, just that weird in-between temperature where I don't know whether I should relax a little longer or get out. My legs stretch along the tub, coated in soft bubbles, my arms resting on either side. The air is scented faintly with the lavender oil I dumped in a little too aggressively to help calm me. *It hasn't helped.*

Cillian is finally home, and I can hear him pacing in our bedroom. His voice cuts low and rough through the air, taut with frustration. It doesn't take me long to realize he's on the phone again with Hawk, trying to get answers that still aren't coming.

"—You said you had a lead. And now suddenly you don't?"

His footsteps echo back and forth across the hardwood floor.

It's been three days since that text. Three days since someone decided to poke the hornets' nest with a cryptic message, leaving us all antsy with no clue what they want.

The door creaks open, and he walks in mid-call. His eyes scan the room, landing on me, submerged in the tub. I roll my head along the edge, watching him as he argues with the poor, sweet man on the other end.

"Don't tell me you hit a dead-end," he gruffs, staring at me and undoing the first few buttons of his shirt. He undresses purposefully, each button revealing the tight muscles hidden beneath his shirt. The buckle of his belt clinks when it hits the floor, and by the time he steps out of his pants, I've forgotten that Hawk is still on the other end of the phone.

"—No. Don't bother calling back until you have something useful," he bites out, hanging up. He tosses the phone onto the vanity and finally turns toward me.

"Does every phone call with Hawk get you this excited?" I tease, my eyes dropping to his semi-hard cock.

"No, my little brat," he playfully snarls. Stalking toward the tub, his weighty cock swings with every step. "Knowing what's waiting under those bubbles does."

My breath stutters.

The water sloshes gently when he climbs into the tub behind me. His legs slide to either side of mine, and I feel the heat of his body press to my back as he settles me between his thighs.

He leans forward, and his lips brush my shoulder. "I've been thinking about you all day."

"Shouldn't you be thinking about criminal things when you're in meetings?" I arch into him slightly. "Or at least paying attention to Hawk when you're on the phone."

His hand comes up to stroke along my jaw, tipping my face up.

"My wife is naked in a tub full of bubbles," he says, voice low, commanding, "and you think I have any idea what the fuck Hawk was talking about."

The answer is obvious. I feel it against my lower back, thick and hard, pressing up beneath me.

"No," I whisper. "Guess not."

He smirks and slides his hand down my chest until it's beneath the water's surface, cupping my breast. His thumb brushes my nipple, slow and teasing, until I can no longer stifle my moan.

"That's right, firecracker," he praises. "You know better than to doubt where Daddy's attention is."

I moan softly when his other hand dips between my thighs, parting them under the water. His fingers circle my clit with agonizing slowness, and I squirm in his lap, grinding into his hand. The feel of him—strong and unrelenting behind me—sets me on fire.

"Such a needy little thing, huh?" His breath skims over my neck.

"Daddy—" The word leaves me on a shaky breath.

"I've got you," he growls, his voice deep and possessive. "Daddy's gonna take care of you and make your little pussy feel so good."

"Fuck... It already feels so good," I pant.

"Daddy knows exactly how you like it." *He does.* He knows every sound I make. Every shift in my body. Every tiny tremble that says I'm close. His teeth scrape gently against my neck, his rhythm picking up as he plays me like an instrument he's been proficient in for years.

"Come for me." His fingers bring me right to the edge. Rolling my clit firmly between his fingers, he demands, "Tell me who you belong to when you come."

"I'm yours," I breathlessly scream. "Only yours, Daddy."

Cillian's pleased groan vibrates against my neck. His strong hands grip my waist, and he lifts me slightly. "Such a good girl." He guides me forward, and I feel the thick head of his cock nudging against me. "Relax," he whispers. "Let Daddy's big cock into your little pussy."

"Yes, Daddy." I sink down onto him slowly, inch by inch, and we both groan as I stretch around him. Once I've taken all of him, I still, clutching at his thighs.

"Ride me," he whispers, his lips brushing my ear. "Show me what a needy little slut you are."

Using my grip on his thighs for leverage, I roll my hips slowly. The drag of him against my walls is pure heaven—his girthy length rubbing every sensitive spot. The water ripples with every swirl of my hips as heat coils low in my belly.

His hands guide my hips, helping me find the pace he wants until I'm taking him faster.

"Look at you," he breathes. "Bouncing on Daddy's cock, like you were made for this." His words go straight to my core, tingling my pussy and fueling my need. "You are, aren't you?" he growls. "Made to take me. Made to *please* me."

"Yes! Daddy!" I cry out, as pleasure crashes through me.

His hands dig into my hips, and he works me roughly over his length, water sloshing over the tub with every push and pull. Moans and whimpers spew from me uncontrollably as he fucks me so good.

"Are you going to come again?" he whispers. "Be a good girl and come so hard that I spill inside you."

Another wave of euphoria overtakes me, loud and unstoppable. My body trembles as I quiver around him. He holds me tight, his hips jerking for a few more deep thrusts before he groans against my neck and comes inside me with a deep, raw sound.

Then his arms wrap around me, pulling me to his chest as he leans against the back of the tub. "You okay?" he asks, still buried inside me.

I nod and exhale, "More than okay, Daddy."

CHAPTER 54
cillian

TWO WEEKS LATER

The smell of burned espresso and cheap aftershave clings to the air. The café is just off a narrow alleyway in Williamsburg, not too upscale, not too grimy, exactly the kind of middle-ground place where you can talk about illegal weapons while pretending to argue over the merits of fair-trade and tariffs.

Nik sits across from me, looking bored and inattentive as usual, tapping a sugar packet against the edge of the table. I'm keeping my eye on the café while Enzo finalizes the terms for this deal with the men sitting at the table to our left. South American cartel. Smug, sun-leathered bastards with loud designer shirts and dead eyes. The older one—Luis, I think— chuckles at something the younger one says.

But I'm not listening. This is the last leg of the deal. It's quiet, clean, and almost quite boring.

And it's all Madison.

She's the one who convinced us to start splitting the brokering process.

Her pitch was sharp, logical, calculated, and just dangerous enough to be genius. Handle the business away from the club. Keep records analog. No more piles of cash passed under glowing pink lights or guns stashed behind the bar. Let the clients show up to *King's Temptation* like they're just another group of high-rollers. Let them get drunk. Loud. Flash their money and show off. Let them request private cars to drive them home, and then those cars just happen to contain a discreet package of guns or product in the trunk.

Under the radar. No paper trail. The club's security footage will show drunk assholes stumbling out with bottle girls and barely any memory of the night. And if the Feds get curious? All they'll see is a booming nightlife business and the King brothers staying the hell off the floor and far away from anything illegal. It was brilliant, and exactly what I'd expect from my firecracker.

The cartel men sign-off on the final detail of the shipment—eight crates, three calibers, no serials. We all nod like it's a brunch reservation. Nik finishes his cappuccino in one last bitter gulp and mutters, "Let's get the fuck out of this hipster café before I start looking for an apartment in Bushwick. I'm already growing an affection for avocado toast."

We're standing from our seats when my phone vibrates in my jacket pocket. I pull it out and swipe my thumb over the screen.

UNKNOWN

Tomorrow. King's penthouse. 7pm. Don't be
late.

My stomach tightens, and I lock the screen without
responding.

"Everything all right?" Enzo asks beside me. His voice is low
and casual, but his eyes say he saw something change in mine.

I shake my head with a practiced eye roll and sigh. "Women."

Nik barks a laugh and plays into my lie. "Ugh, sounds like Her
Highness is in one of her moods again."

I force a dry laugh. "Tell me about it."

Our South American friends buy it. Or at least pretend to.

We go our separate ways, us out the front, and our cartel
friends exit through the side alley. The pickups will happen at
the club later tonight when everyone is at home with alibis.
They'll act drunk. Tip the girls big. And stumble out like they
just had the time of their lives. Clean. Just like Madison said.

We slide into Nik's Range Rover, and the silence stretches for
about two blocks before I finally speak. "I got another
message."

Nik's knuckles tighten slightly on the wheel. "Same number?"

I nod. "Same tone."

Enzo twists in the passenger seat to face me. "What did it say?"

"Meeting," I answer. "Tomorrow. Our place. Seven."

Enzo stiffens. "*Our* place?"

"Yeah."

Nik mutters something in Russian and swerves around a cab.

"Whoever it is," Enzo says slowly, "they know where we live."

"It's not a bluff," I lament. "They've got something. Access, intel. Or someone watching us."

"Could still be bluffing," Nik offers. "Could be trying to smoke you out."

I shake my head. "Not with this kind of precision."

Enzo exhales through his nose. "The girls are there."

"I know."

"And now they're coming to the damn *apartment*—"

"*I know*," I snap, louder than I mean to. I pinch the bridge of my nose. "Sorry."

Nik grunts. "Don't apologize. You know what we would sacrifice to keep Madison and Eavan safe."

Everything... because they're family.

Enzo leans forward, elbows on the center console. "You really think it's someone inside?"

"Honestly, I have no fucking idea."

We ride the rest of the way in silence.

By the time the elevator hums to a stop at the floor beneath the penthouse, the whole air inside the car is wired with tension. The doors slide open. Enzo steps out, and Nik follows. I plant my hand against the doors to hold them open and call after Nik. "Hey. You know I was only giving you shit about getting your own place, right?"

Nik raises an eyebrow, and a smug smile pulls across his face. "Do you think I swooped in and bought this unit because you hurt my feelings?"

I hesitate. "No... but you wasted no time getting out."

"Do you know how many times you can walk in on your best friend's balls swinging as he drills his wife from behind?" Nik scoffs before grandly raising his finger in the air. "It's one. *One* was more than enough."

Enzo snickers as he steps into his apartment. "One would've been enough for me, too."

"You don't get to talk," Nik snips at him. "A few more nights of listening to you railing his sister and I would've been checking into the Plaza."

Upstairs, the penthouse is quiet. Madison's curled up on the couch, hair still damp from her bath, reading yet another book with a jacked, shirtless man holding an axe on the cover. She doesn't look up when I come in, clearly engrossed in her lumberjack smut.

"You got it done?" she asks softly.

"Smooth as butter," I say, leaning over to kiss the top of her head. She smells like oranges and cinnamon. *Like home.*

She looks up then, eyes sharp despite the softness of her tone. "You okay?"

"Yeah."

I take the seat beside her, wrapping an arm around her shoulder.

She leans into me, tucking her face against my chest. "You're lying," she murmurs.

"Only a little."

"Did something happen?"

I hesitate for a second. "We've got company tomorrow."

She stiffens slightly but doesn't pull away. "Another message?"

"Yeah. Seven o'clock."

She exhales and is quiet for a moment, her fingers curling into the hem of my shirt. "Then we'll be ready."

CHAPTER 55
cillian

There's a loaded stillness in the apartment.

Nik leans against the counter, chewing on a toothpick. Enzo is seated at the island with his fingers drumming on the granite. I can't sit still and have been pacing for the past thirty minutes. My hand keeps drifting to the Glock tucked in my waistband at the small of my back, my body humming like a live wire. Our surprise guest is expected in less than five minutes.

After hours of back-and-forth, we made the call to keep the girls here. Safer to have them in our line of sight than out in the open with someone watching from a distance. If this was about leverage, we weren't going to let whoever was coming get the upper hand.

Or either of them.

Eavan and Madison are sitting on the couch, as far from the kitchen as we can get them. The two of them look like they're oblivious to the meeting, but I know better. My sister is a nervous wreck, her pregnancy upping what she has to lose. *What we all do.* Madison is hyper-aware of every movement and hanging on every word. *Just like me.*

Before I left her side, I slipped her Glock into the couch cushion by her thigh. She nodded once, understanding immediately. If things go sideways, she won't hesitate. None of us will.

The buzzer breaks the silence in the room, the tension suddenly palpable.

Nik moves first, pressing the intercom. "Yeah?"

"Guests for the Kings," the doorman replies. "Three men. Are they cleared for the penthouse?"

We share a look, and I nod.

"Send them up," Nik calls back through the intercom. Madison shoots me a quick look, a subtle message in her eyes. She's ready.

I move to the front door, one hand on the pistol tucked into the back of my pants, as I open it. The elevator dings, and when the doors slide open, I get the first glimpse at our guests.

Two older men in dark suits step forward first. Pure muscle. Both are in their early forties. Clean-cut. Cold eyes. Military or private security. But it's the third man who first catches my attention. He looks barely old enough to buy himself a drink. He's dressed in baggy joggers, designer sneakers, and has a gold chain swinging over a too-tight shirt.

It takes a second. Then it clicks. *Alek Sargsyan.* The man Eavan was *supposed* to marry.

My grip tightens on the gun at my back, and my entire body coils like a spring. "What the fuck are you doing here?" I growl, already moving as Alek strolls into our penthouse like he owns it.

"Relax." He holds his hands up in mock surrender. "All of you. I'm not here for *my wife.*"

The way he spits the words makes my blood run hot.

Enzo is out of his seat before I can so much as blink. "**My** wife," he snarls.

I throw an arm out, blocking his path without taking my eyes off Alek. "Then why *are* you here?" I ask.

Alek shrugs, looking around the place like he's touring a fucking rental listing. "Trust me, I don't want your sister. I'm here to give you mine."

"What!?" Nik exclaims, brows furrowing.

Alek nods to one of his security guys, who steps forward and hands me a thick folder.

He grins like he's just handed me a gift basket. "I'm done. With all of it. That business of the selling girls... That was my father's kingdom, not mine. And frankly?" He gestures at the windows, the skyline, our empire. "You run things better, cleaner... And I want a piece of it."

I open the folder and start flipping through the contents, tossing them on the island for my brothers to see. Photos. Ledger copies. Internal memos. Meeting notes. Surveillance stills.

Fuck. It's proof. Proof of our involvement in all of our father's deaths.

And his uncle's and father's, too.

Nik swears under his breath.

Enzo's jaw locks. "You've been *holding* this?"

"I only came into most of it recently," Alek says smoothly. "Turns out my old man was more paranoid than I gave him credit for. Bastard kept receipts on everyone."

"Why bring it here?" I ask.

"Because you have something I want. And *I* have something I don't."

I narrow my eyes. "What do you want?"

Alek smiles like a shark. "Simple. I have two conditions, and all of that disappears forever."

"Let's hear them," Enzo pushes.

"First, I join your empire. I've got more connections than you can count in the little gun game you've got going. And my connections have a lot of fucking money."

I glance at Nik and Enzo, both giving a subtle nod. "And," I huff after a bit of hesitation. "What else?"

"Second..." He smiles wider and looks at Nik. "You marry my sister."

"I'm sorry, what?" Nik chokes, standing straighter.

"My sister," Alek repeats, as if we didn't hear him the first time. "That bratty bitch needs to be someone else's problem. So, that means she's your responsibility now."

Nik blinks blindly in disbelief. "Wait. You're fucking serious?"

Alek shrugs. "She's pretty. She's not *completely* insufferable. But she needs someone who can keep her in check. Someone who won't be intimidated by her tantrums and sharp mouth. And from what I hear..." He smirks. "You like the ones who bite."

Nik grumbles, pinching the bridge of his nose. "I'm not marrying some... some mafia handoff just because *you* don't want to babysit her anymore."

Alek raises a brow. "Then I guess I'll take this little folder to a few old friends at the FBI. Or the press. Whoever answers my call first."

"Hold up—" Enzo growls, stepping forward again.

"I'm offering you a deal," Alek interrupts coolly. "One that lets you keep your kingdom and makes mine one I actually want to deal with. It's good business."

I glance at Nik. He's pale. His mouth opens, then closes. His eyes flick to me, to Enzo, then back to Alek. "This is a *fucking joke.*"

Alek tilts his head. "She's arriving later tonight. I'll text you the location in the morning."

"You already brought her?" Nik exclaims.

"Would've been a waste of time if you'd said no." He shrugs, flipping his phone in his hand. "But you won't. You *can't*. Not if you want to keep what you've built or stay out of prison."

He starts walking backward toward the elevator, the front door still open behind him.

"We can all finalize terms over breakfast." Alek and his men step back into the elevator. His gaze flits to a very nauseous looking Nik. "I'll let her know you're excited to meet her," he adds with a grin and a wink.

The doors close with a soft ding, and the three of us are left standing in stunned, heavy silence, the girls staring at us from the living room.

Enzo and I barely breathe, waiting for Nik's reaction.

He finally runs a hand down his face. "You've gotta be fucking kidding me."

Enzo leans back against the counter, jaw tight. "This isn't good."

"He's not wrong," I mutter. "He's got us by the balls."

Nik glares at me. "Don't you dare tell me marrying her is a *good idea.*"

"I'm not saying it's a good idea. I'm just saying it might be the *only* idea."

Eavan steps cautiously toward the kitchen, eyes flicking between all of us. "What the hell just happened?"

Nik mutters, "Apparently, I'm getting married."

"Congratulations!" Madison stifles a snort, returning his sentiment to our surprise wedding.

"That's not funny." Nik drags a hand through his hair. "We are so fucked."

Thank you to my husband—the cock bag, who somehow thinks that because he gave me the piano wire idea that he deserves credit for this whole book. I love him anyway. 😉

To Katie—who I am running out of ways to thank—for putting up my codependency and giving me the encouragement I needed throughout this story.

To my entire team for alpha reading, sharing your love of everything I write, and lifting me up with your excitement on the days I need it most. I could not do this without all of you.

And to my readers for loving the voices in my head.

DARK DADDIES OF NEW YORK

- Claimed by Daddy
- Kneeling for Daddy (Coming October 2025)

THE MEN OF CLUB TRISKELION SERIES

- Owned
- Bound
- Primal
- Master
- Shared
- Daddy

THE SAVAGELY DEPRAVED SERIES

- Dark Devils
- Family Ties
- Wicked Love
- Brutal Bond

THE BOTTICELLI BROTHERHOOD SERIES

- Sold to the Syndicate
- Capo Dei Capi's Daughter
- Indebted to the Enemy
- Falling for the Mafia Dom

THE MARCANO MOGULS SERIES

- Tryst
- Crave
- Intern
- Savage

Join my Facebook group, J.L. Quick's Good Little Readers, to get first glimpses at covers, works in progress, chapter teasers of new releases, and more!

Want to follow me on Instagram or TikTok? Check out my online store for swag and signed books? Or maybe just join my newsletter?

The QR code above has links to all of those and more too!